THE RUMOR

JUN — – 2019

D0405124

ESTES VALLEY
LIBRARY

THE

A NOVEL

THE RUMOR

LESLEY KARA

Ballantine Books

NEW YORK

The Rumor is a work of fiction. Names, characters, places, and incidents are the products of the author's imagination or are used fictitiously. Any resemblance to actual events, locales, or persons, living or dead, is entirely coincidental.

A Ballantine Books Trade Paperback Original

Copyright © 2018 by Lesley Kara

All rights reserved.

Published in the United States by Ballantine Books, an imprint of Random House, a division of Penguin Random House LLC, New York.

BALLANTINE and the HOUSE colophon are registered trademarks of Penguin Random House LLC.

Originally published in hardcover in the United Kingdom by Bantam Press, an imprint of Transworld Publishers, a division of Penguin Random House LLC, in 2018.

LIBRARY OF CONGRESS CATALOGING-IN-PUBLICATION DATA
Names: Kara, Lesley, author.
Title: The rumor : a novel / Lesley Kara.
Description: Ballantine Books Trade Paperback Edition. |
New York Ballantine Books, 2019.
Identifiers: LCCN 2019007585 | ISBN 9781984819345 (paperback) |
ISBN 9781984819352 (ebook)
Subjects: | BISAC: FICTION / Suspense. | FICTION /
Contemporary Women. | GSAFD: Suspense fiction.
Classification: LCC PR6111.A73 R86 2019 | DDC 823/.92—dc23
LC record available at https://lccn.loc.gov/2019007585

Printed in the United States of America on acid-free paper

randomhousebooks.com

2 4 6 8 9 7 5 3 1

Book design by Debbie Glasserman

To my parents, Harry and Doreen, with love

He who fights with monsters should be careful lest he thereby become a monster. And if thou gaze long into an abyss, the abyss will also gaze into thee.

—FRIEDRICH NIETZSCHE

THE RUMOR

THE RUMOR

It's happening again. Don't ask me how I know. I just do. I see it in the roll of the waves, the way they're bearing in at a slant. Fast. Relentless. I feel it in the nip of the air on my skin, smell it in the rotting leaves and damp earth, hear it in the silence of the watching crows. You're coming for me again and there's nothing I can do to stop you.

This is how it happens. One night I go to bed and everything's fine. Everything's under control. The story has ceased to be a story. It's real. Solid. Unbreakable. Then I wake up and it's changed. Cracks have appeared overnight and I realize that I've been fooling myself all this time, that I've only ever been the most fragile of constructions.

I'm the hunted. I'll always be the hunted.

1

IT STARTS WITH A RUMOR. WHISPERS AT THE SCHOOL GATE.

I'm not really listening at first. I promised Dave I'd pick up the keys to the Maple Drive property and meet a client there. I don't have time to stand around in a gossipy huddle with this group.

But then I catch sight of Debbie Barton's face—the way her jaw's just dropped—and my curiosity gets the better of me.

"Say that again," she says. "I don't believe it."

I edge closer, as does little Ketifa's mother, Fatima. Jake's mother—is it Cathy?—looks from side to side before she speaks, milking her moment in the spotlight for all it's worth.

"There's a strong possibility that a famous child killer is living right here in Flinstead," she says, pausing to let her words take effect. "Under a new identity, of course. She murdered a little boy when she was ten, back in the sixties. Stabbed him with a kitchen knife, right through his heart."

There is a collective gasp. Fatima brings her hand to her chest.

"Sally McGowan," Cathy says. "Google it when you get home."

Sally McGowan. The name rings a bell. Probably from one of those Netflix documentaries I sometimes watch when I've nothing better to do. *Kids Who Kill* or *Serial Killers I Have Known*.

"Who told you this?" I ask.

Cathy takes a deep breath. "Let's just say it's someone who knows someone whose ex-husband used to be a cop. Well, this cop's buddy heard him talk about her one time. She was released when she was a young woman, has been moving around since then by all accounts, trying to keep a low profile. Now she's ended up here. It might not be true, but you know what they say, there's no smoke without fire. And what better place to hide out than somewhere like Flinstead?"

Debbie sucks her teeth. "I think it's disgusting that people like her get to start all over again. Where's the justice in that?"

"You'd rather they were kept in prison their whole life?" I ask. "For a crime they committed when they were children?"

Debbie stares at me. "Adult crime, adult time, isn't that what they say? And if they *are* released, don't we have the right to know where they are?"

"What, so they can be mobbed by vigilantes?"

Now all three women are staring at me. I wish I'd kept my mouth shut, but sometimes I can't help myself. I don't even know why I'm listening to all this crap. I should know better.

Cathy sniffs. "It's not fair that someone like that gets a second chance. What about the parents of the little boy who was murdered? They don't get the luxury of starting a new life, do they?"

"Well, it probably isn't true anyway," Fatima says. "And if it is, there's nothing we can do about it. It was years ago. I doubt she's still dangerous."

Lovely, sensible Fatima. I must suggest she drop by for coffee and a chat soon. Get to know her a little better. But not today. I'll be late if I don't get a move on.

"THANKS, JO. I REALLY APPRECIATE YOU DOING THIS ON YOUR day off."

Dave hands me the keys and the freshly printed property listing for 24 Maple Drive, the new Pegton's logo emblazoned at the top.

"It's no problem," I say. And it isn't. There aren't many employers as flexible as Dave Pegton. It's been a godsend finding a job that fits in around Alfie's school times, and so close to home as well.

Home. I've got Dave to thank for that, too. The tiny two-bedroom cottage he generously described as "in need of some TLC." You've got to love the jargon. What it actually needs is intensive care, but seeing as it was the only place I could afford, I ended up putting in an offer on it. New house. New job. And all because I walked into the right realtor's office at the right time. Serendipity, isn't that what it's called?

Dave walks back to his desk. "Good luck with Mrs. Marchant, by the way," he says over his shoulder.

"Why? What's up with her?"

Dave smirks. "You'll find out soon enough," and before I can quiz him further, the phone rings and he's talking to a client.

———

MAPLE DRIVE IS A MIXTURE OF 1920S AND 1930S HOUSES.
Some of them are single-family, but most are two-family
townhouses. It's not the most expensive street in Flinstead—
the area known as the Groves is where the seriously mon-
eyed live—but it's popular, especially the water end of it,
which is where number 24 is situated. Dave has described it
on the listing as having an "ocean view," and it probably does
if you open one of the bedroom windows, lean out, and crane
your neck to the left. An ocean *glimpse* might be a better de-
scription, but it's a nice-looking house. Well maintained. Es-
tablished front garden. And even a *glimpse* of the water adds
dollars to the value.

Susan Marchant opens the door before I've even rung the
bell. A curt nod is all I get in response to my cheery good
morning. I'm expecting her to step back and usher me in, but
she just stands there as if I'm one of the "cold callers" listed
on the sign above the bell. The ones who aren't welcome.

"I was hoping to have a quick scoot around on my own
first," I say. "Just so I'm familiar with the layout."

I always find it helps if you're prepared for what you're
about to show someone. Not everyone tidies and cleans their
house prior to showings. I've come across all kinds of strange
and unsavory things before. Dirty underwear tossed all over
the floor. A large brown turd coiled in a toilet bowl like a
sleeping snake. Although from what I can see beyond Susan
Marchant's shoulder, that won't be the case here. It's clean to
the point of being clinical, the rooms half empty. Looks like
she's moved most of her stuff into storage already.

"Why?" she says, her brows knitted together. "Don't you
have the floor plan on your listing?" There's a coldness in
her eyes and voice that throws me.

"Well, yes, but . . ."

"Too late anyway," she says, squinting out at the street. "That must be Anne Wilson."

I turn to see a blue BMW pull up. A woman in a pale-green raincoat and with two-tone hair—dark blond with coppery ends—climbs out of the passenger seat, raises her hand at me, and smiles. Thank God for smiley people. Now the driver has joined her. He's tall and distinguished-looking. Silver-gray hair. I get the feeling he'd like to have opened the door for her if only she'd given him the chance. They're walking up the driveway toward us holding hands, so either they're one of those rare couples still very much in love after years of marriage, or this is a new relationship. I'd put money on the latter.

It's one of the things I love about this job—meeting new people all the time. Trying to guess from the snippets they reveal about themselves what they're really like. And viewing clients' properties is absolutely the best part of what I do. Tash, who's one of my oldest friends, says it's because I'm a nosy parker. But that's okay, because she's exactly the same.

Once, when she and her boyfriend were on vacation, they pretended to be interested in buying an expensive penthouse apartment, just so they could have a look inside. I suppress a smile. They had to park their dilapidated old Volvo a couple of streets away so the realtor didn't see them get out of it. I often think of that story when I'm meeting prospective buyers. You never really know if people are genuine.

"Hi, I'm Joanna Critchley from Pegton's. Nice to meet you." We shake hands. Anne Wilson is an attractive woman but she's definitely had work done on her face. Her skin has that shiny, taut look, and her lips and cheeks are plumped out with filler. I look away in case she thinks I'm staring. "And this is Susan Marchant, the owner."

But Susan Marchant is already walking away from us toward the stairs, her heels clicking on the parquet flooring. What a rude woman. No wonder Dave was so eager for me to handle this one. And who wears high heels in their own house?

I take a deep breath. "Let's start in the living room, shall we?"

It's not the best of starts. Buying a new house is stressful enough as it is. A frosty homeowner can be enough to put some people off. Although maybe that's what Susan Marchant *wants* to do. Maybe she's being forced to sell the house by a philandering ex-husband desperate to get his hands on his share of the assets and is determined to put off as many buyers as she can. I can't honestly say I wouldn't do the same myself.

WHEN I GET HOME LATER THAT MORNING, I CAN'T HELP COM-paring my cramped little cottage and its dated décor with the lovely, spacious house I've just been looking at, and before long I'm scrolling through paint colors online. I promised myself I'd make a start on the decorating once Alfie was settled at school; it's now October and I haven't done a thing.

Then I remember what Cathy said about Sally McGowan. It's bound to be a load of nonsense, something she's cooked up to create a little drama, but I might as well have a quick look. Anything to distract me from thoughts of decorating.

I type the name in the search bar and up pop 109 million results, plus a grainy black-and-white photo of a child's face. Unsmiling, defiant, but strikingly beautiful nonetheless. I've seen it before. I remember it now. The iconic mug shot.

According to Wikipedia, Sally McGowan was born in

Dearborn, Michigan. In 1969, age ten, she stabbed five-year-old Robbie Harris to death. It was a sensational case that divided the nation. Was she a cold-blooded psychopath, or the victim of abusive parents and a long history of neglect? She insisted it was a game that went wrong, but no one believed her. Well, the public certainly didn't. People were furious when her conviction was for manslaughter, not murder.

I check out more websites. She was released in 1981 and disappeared off the radar. Six years later, reporters tracked her down. By then she was working as a seamstress in Iowa and had a child of her own. I scroll through more images. A seventeen-year-old Sally playing pool in a juvenile detention center. There's something provocative about the way she's draped herself over the table, or maybe it's just the camera angle, the composition of the shot.

Now I'm looking at a young, svelte woman in her twenties shielding her face from the cameras. I skim a few more sites. Apart from the odd piece in the tabloids about alleged sightings and the ongoing anguish of Robbie Harris's family, nothing more has been heard of her.

I take a sip of coffee. What if she really is living in Flinstead? I mean, she's got to be somewhere, so why not here? That ghastly client suddenly enters my head. Susan Marchant. It has to be a coincidence that her initials are the same, but even so, I can't help superimposing Sally McGowan's ten-year-old face on hers. The features merge.

I toss my iPad to the other end of the sofa. This is ridiculous. Listening to stupid gossip at the playground and letting my imagination run away with me. Just because Susan Marchant is a miserable bitch, it doesn't make her a killer.

2

"I STILL REMEMBER THE BLOOD,"
SAYS CHILD KILLER SALLY MCGOWAN'S FORMER
FRIEND AND NEIGHBOR MARGARET COLE

By Geoff Binns

TUESDAY, AUGUST 3, 1999
DAILY NEWS

Thirty years ago today, Sally McGowan became notorious for stabbing five-year-old Robbie Harris to death in a derelict house in Dearborn, Michigan. She was ten years old.

Yesterday, her former school friend and neighbor Margaret Cole shared her memories of that time.

"It was so different back then," said Margaret. "Another world. All of us kids played outdoors. Our mothers didn't know where we were half the time. Whole blocks of houses were derelict. It must have been hell for our parents, but us kids, we loved it. It was one great big playground."

Many abandoned houses were demolished in the 1960s to make way for concrete housing projects. Chronic poverty, deprivation, and unemployment—this was the world Sally McGowan grew up in.

"But that was just the way things were," said Margaret. "We didn't know we were poor. We were just kids. Out playing.

"Then, one day, everything changed. I still remember the blood. The way it seeped out of him and turned his shirt red. The way it bubbled up around the knife. And his eyes. His little blue eyes. I knew he was dead just from looking at them."

Asked about her reaction to the fact that McGowan is reported to have been released in the early eighties and has been living as a free woman ever since, Margaret said: "It's not right, is it, after what she did? I mean, I know she had a hard time at home, but plenty of kids suffered just as bad and they didn't do what she did. My heart goes out to Robbie's family. This anniversary must be raking it all up again."

I glance at the clock. Shit. It's almost two thirty. Time to get Alfie.

I grab my bag, stuff my feet into my sneakers without undoing the laces, and open the front door. I can't believe I've wasted all this time messing around on the internet, and now I haven't made any notes for this evening's book club.

ALFIE IS FIRST OUT OF THE CLASSROOM, HIS FRIZZY HAIR damp with sweat.

"Why are you so hot?"

"Gym," he says. "I got to the very top of the climbing wall."

I'm not sure how I feel about him scaling one of those things. When I was a little girl, I was bullied by some over-zealous first-grade teacher into climbing higher than I was comfortable with and ended up falling onto the mats on my back and having the wind knocked out of me. I thought I was going to die. But I don't want to discourage Alfie. He's clearly not as awkward and uncoordinated as I was—as I still *am*. Alfie actually *likes* gym.

"Wow!" I say. "That was brave."

"Liam and Jake said I was a show-off and Jake told Miss Williams I pushed him, but I didn't."

Oh no. This is supposed to be a fresh start. New school. New friends. I couldn't stand it if he was bullied again. It's one of the reasons I came back here in the first place. That and feeling guilty about working such long hours and having to rely on a babysitter.

Alfie kicks at a stone. "Jake's always saying mean things."

Jake Hunter, Cathy's son. That figures. I squeeze Alfie's hot little hand. "He's probably just jealous that you're a better climber than he is."

Alfie tugs at my arm. "Is Grandma still coming tonight?"

"Of course. And she's bringing cupcakes."

He grins and punches the air. My shoulders relax. This spat with Jake Hunter can't be that bad, not if he's forgotten it already. It helps having Mom around the corner, of course. Not to mention the beach. It was definitely the right decision to leave the city and move here. Even if I did have to say good-bye to my lovely little apartment and my well-paid job and my friends (thank God for Facebook) and . . . well, my whole *life* basically. Having a child changes everything. And when your child is unhappy, you do whatever you can to make them smile again.

Before Alfie came along, I hadn't been in a relationship for years and having a baby was the last thing on my mind. I'd worked my way up to becoming the listings manager for a large real estate firm, overseeing their entire rental-property portfolio. I drove a silver Audi A3, I lived in a small but fashionable second-floor apartment that was all sharp lines and minimalism, and my cooking skills didn't extend to much more than popping a Trader Joe's meal into the microwave.

Then I hooked up with Michael Lewis, an old friend of mine from college. It was only ever going to be a casual fling. Michael's an investigative journalist, which isn't exactly a career that lends itself to a stable family life, and to be honest I was enjoying my independence, too. We became—what's the expression?—"friends with benefits." What we didn't realize was that one of those "benefits" would turn out to be Alfie.

I'll never forget Mom's face when I told her. I don't know what was the bigger shock: me being pregnant or Michael being black.

Michael was fabulous. Still is. He didn't freak out or immediately offer to pay for an abortion. He sat me down and told me he'd support me in whatever it was I decided to do. He said that if I went ahead with the pregnancy, he'd play as big or as little a role as I wanted him to. He even offered to marry me.

I can't pretend I wasn't tempted, but I knew he was only offering because of Alfie. Besides, if we'd gotten married and it hadn't worked out—and let's face it, how many relationships *do* these days—we might have ended up hating each other's guts like my parents did, and that wouldn't have been good for Alfie.

This way, we're still the best of friends and Alfie gets a

proper relationship with his dad, which is more than I ever had.

Alfie waves at someone on the other side of the street. It's the woman from the ranch house opposite the school. She straightens up from where she's been bending over her rosebushes and waves back at him, pruning shears in hand. A few weeks ago, just after Alfie started school, he fell over and scraped his knee on the sidewalk and she was kind enough to come out with a Band-Aid. Made a real fuss over him.

An unwelcome thought pops into my mind. What if *she's* Sally McGowan, with an unencumbered view into the school playground? I'm being paranoid, I know I am. There's no reason it should be her any more than this woman walking toward us now with her shopping bag on wheels.

The demographic in Flinstead is older than the national average. People retire here. From the city, mostly, drawn to the sea and the slower pace of life. Except for the beach and one main street of stores, that's it. For anything more exciting, you have to drive for half an hour, or jump on a bus if you don't mind waiting forever. It's why I was so desperate to get away and live in the city the minute I turned eighteen, but it's different now. I've got Alfie to think about.

Back home, in my little galley kitchen that will be utterly transformed when I get around to painting the cabinets, I make Alfie his after-school snack and listen to the familiar strains of the *Star Wars* soundtrack blaring out of the living room. I can't imagine life without Alfie. Nothing could have prepared me for the joy of having a child. Or the terror. I take his sandwich in and try not to think about the nightmare that poor Robbie Harris's mother had to endure, all those years ago. But try as I might, I can't stop the images spooling out in my mind, imagining that it's Alfie's limp, bloodstained body I'm cradling in my arms.

I always do this. Conjure up the worst possible thing that could happen to him. Maybe every parent does. Maybe this morbid imagination is what we need to keep our children safe.

I snuggle up to him on the sofa and kiss the top of his head. What kind of child could stab a five-year-old boy through the heart?

3

"I'LL BE BACK BY TEN," I TELL MOM. "DON'T LET HIM HAVE ANY more cupcakes."

Mom ruffles Alfie's freshly washed hair and laughs. "It's a good thing you're always running around, young man, or you'd look like one of those big fat sumo wrestlers."

Alfie throws back his head and roars with exaggerated laughter.

Outside, I pull my jacket on and set off toward Liz Blackthorne's house for book club, head bowed against the sudden gust of wind. The nights are getting colder and darker now. The smell of damp earth and wet leaves hangs in the air. I push my hands into my pockets and walk faster.

Liz lives right on the waterfront. The wind is even stronger here, barreling in off the ocean. As usual, I evaluate each house I pass. Michael often jokes that, like journalists, real estate agents are never off the clock. While he's always on the lookout for newsworthy stories, I'm sizing up properties. Writing sales copy in my head. Guessing the market value.

When I pass the empty house with the boarded-up windows and the overgrown garden, I can't help wondering who it belongs to and why they've never done anything with it. It could be stunning if it was renovated. Maybe the owner died without a will or didn't have any heirs. Or maybe they just don't want it anymore. Imagine that. Imagine letting an investment rot away. Although you'd have to spend a bundle to bring it up to code. It's like a lot of old houses around here—they might look great on the outside, but inside they're falling apart.

Liz's house is one of those Dutch-style affairs with a gambrel roof. It reminds me of a face—the sharply pitched roof slopes like straightened hair and the two semicircular upstairs windows look like hooded eyes, peeping out across the water. I love it.

"Come in," Liz says, and we give each other the customary peck on each cheek.

With her three-quarter-length harlequin jacket and her long white hair, which this evening she's wearing in a thick braid coiled around her neck and over the front of her shoulder, she looks even more stylish than usual. If I look half as good as Liz Blackthorne when I'm her age, I'll be thrilled.

I follow her into her dining room, where the other four are already sitting around the polished mahogany table, tucking into olives and Kettle chips and drinking wine. This is just the kind of room I'd like. Floor-to-ceiling bookshelves in the alcoves on either side of the chimney, original artwork on the walls—most of it painted by Liz—and, under the window, a Turkish ottoman draped in vintage fabric and heaped with cushions. Liz has a gift for dressing a room that makes it look like a bohemian salon. A hodgepodge of patterns and colors that miraculously complement one another. It must be the artist in her. If I tried something similar, it'd look a complete mess. Maybe I should ask her to advise me on what to do with my place.

"You've just missed a very interesting conversation about flashers," Liz says.

She gives me a pointed look and I smile. I feel a real connection with Liz. I've always been drawn to friendships with older women. Women comfortable in their own skin. Women who aren't afraid to be unapologetically themselves.

One thing's for sure: Mom was right about me joining a book club. It's just what I need. Most of my old school friends have long since left the area and, though I occasionally see one or two familiar faces, we've little in common now. I still meet up with Tash, of course, and one or two of the others from my old life, but not as often as I'd like. It might only be four months since I washed back up in Pleasantville, as Tash somewhat disparagingly calls this town, but in many respects it feels like a lifetime.

Laughter ripples around the table and glasses are refilled. Liz slides an empty glass toward me and nods at the array of bottles on the sideboard.

"I started it, I'm afraid," Barbara says, her deep, plummy voice loud in my ear. If she drinks any more, she'll lapse into her native Georgia accent.

Barbara is a member of the town council. A large woman with an even larger personality whose wardrobe seems to consist mostly of smart black trousers and sensible shirts. She reminds me of one of my old colleagues: loud and opinionated, but very funny, too.

"Now, why does that not surprise me?" I say. More giggles. I've definitely got some catching up to do in the wine department. Even Maddie, who usually sticks to tea, is knocking it back tonight.

"Okay, then." Liz's voice is only fractionally louder than everyone else's, but something in its tone brings us all to attention. "I suppose we'd better start," she says.

This month's read—Alain de Botton's *Consolations of Philosophy*—was entirely Liz's choice and is a departure from our normal fare of contemporary fiction with the occasional classic thrown in. It's Barbara's turn next month and, judging by what I've just spotted poking out of her handbag, she's chosen Mary Shelley's *Frankenstein*. I was hoping for something a little lighter, to be honest. Something feel-good for a change.

As usual, Barbara isn't backward in coming forward. This is my fourth meeting and I don't think she's liked a single book yet. She tells us she doesn't care for this populist reading of great minds and, as someone who's virtually given up all hope of meeting a suitable partner, she isn't comforted by Schopenhauer's views on love being merely a vehicle for the propagation of genes.

"I mean, what does that say about me? That my genes aren't worthy of being passed on? Not that I could pass them on now," she mutters into her wineglass. "Not without divine intervention."

We all chuckle.

"Well, if you won't be consoled by Schopenhauer, what about Nietzsche?" Liz says, fixing Barbara with her large, serious eyes. "I love his idea that we're nourished by all the shitty things that happen to us in life, that we become better people as a result."

Barbara snorts. "I've had so much shit thrown at me over the years, I'm surprised I'm not a paragon of virtue by now."

I tell them how much I enjoy following de Botton's

School of Life posts on Twitter and Facebook. Barbara makes a face. "Thank God I've never gotten involved with social media," she says, as if I've just admitted to a shameful vice.

Inevitably, as the evening wears on, the focus of our conversation moves away from Socrates and Seneca and the rest, and turns to one another and our respective news. Tonight, it's poor Jenny under the spotlight. Jenny is our youngest member. A newly licensed nurse, slim, shy, and intelligent, with dark-blond hair in a ponytail and a taste for short dresses and opaque black tights. Karen is quizzing her on her love life and Jenny looks distinctly uncomfortable.

I know what it's like to be on the receiving end of one of Karen's inquisitions. She tried it on me once, and I hated it. I wasn't in the mood to explain my unusual relationship with Alfie's dad. I didn't see why I should and I don't like being put on the spot like that. Neither does Jenny, by the look of things.

I'm not sure I could tolerate Karen's company more than once a month, which is a shame because, on the face of it, we're quite similar. Both in our mid-thirties with a school-aged child. Both avid readers. And, like me, she moved here from the city, although she's been here a few years now. She and her husband run a computer-graphics company, and she's heavily involved with the PTA at Alfie's school. At my first book-club meeting, she started giving me the lowdown on life in Flinstead as if she were the old hand and I the newcomer. When I told her I went to school here and that there isn't a square inch of Flinstead I don't know about, she looked almost annoyed, as if I was trying to show off. Maybe I was.

I help myself to more wine. "Can I top up anyone's

glass?" I say, hoping to divert the attention from Jenny. But only Barbara takes me up on my offer.

"So how long have you been seeing him?" Karen says. She leans in toward Jenny, eyes wide behind her geeky glasses, the blunt ends of her straight dark hair swinging out over the table. "Is it serious?"

Jenny blushes. The poor woman's neck has turned all red and patchy and I feel a sudden need to protect her from Karen's persistent questioning. Aren't people allowed to have a love life without the whole town knowing about it?

"Just out of curiosity," I say, "has anyone heard of Sally McGowan?" It's the first thing that pops into my head.

Karen looks at me, astonished. Oh dear, why on earth did I say that? Typical me, engaging my mouth before my brain. Liz shoots me a quizzical frown. At least I *think* it's quizzical. I get the impression she'd rather steer the conversation back to books. Which is exactly what I should have done.

Karen stares at me from behind her glasses and blinks like an owl. "The only Sally McGowan I know of is that child killer from the sixties. I remember my mom telling me about it."

"God, yeah," Maddie says. "You're not thinking of making us read a book about her, are you, Jo? Because I honestly don't think I'd want to read anything like that." She shudders. "I'd find it too distressing."

I don't know what to make of Maddie yet. She reminds me of a little bird. Bright, beady eyes always darting from one face to another. High-pitched voice that warbles when she gets excited. Her daughter works in finance. Something high-powered downtown. I get the feeling she takes advantage of Maddie. It must be a lot cheaper and more convenient than a nanny. I know Mom helps me out a lot with Alfie, but I'd never expect her to do it full-time.

"No, nothing like that. I heard her mentioned earlier today, that's all."

"So what was it?" Liz asks, casually reaching for an olive. "Something on the news?"

"No. Just something I overheard when I was dropping Alfie off at school. A silly piece of gossip. You know what Perrydale Elementary's like. It's a hotbed of salacious tidbits."

Maddie laughs. "You're right about that. Every time I pick up my granddaughter, I hear something I wish I hadn't."

"Come on, then, Jo," Liz says. Her eyes are wide. Inquisitive. "Don't keep us on tenterhooks."

I clear my throat. It's too late to wriggle out of it now. Everyone's waiting for my answer.

"I'm sure it's a load of garbage, but someone mentioned they'd heard something about her living in Flinstead, under a new identity."

"Jeez," Jenny says.

Barbara puts her glass down on the table and stares at me, openmouthed. Her cheeks are flushed from the wine. "My parents used to say you could tell she was evil just from looking at her eyes."

Liz snorts with derision.

"Actually, it wouldn't surprise me at all," Karen says. "Flinstead would be the perfect place to hide out. I mean, who'd ever think to look for her *here*?"

The question hangs in the air, unanswered. Is it my imagination or has the rumor changed the mood of our gentle, bookish gathering?

4

MICHAEL ARRIVES AT TEN PAST EIGHT ON SATURDAY MORN-
ing, straight from the airport. I open the front door, and for
a few seconds I can't speak. Whenever I see him after some
time away, I'm struck by his physical presence. The way he
occupies space. The way he *owns* it. He's not bodybuilder-
big, but there's this aura of strength about him. Strength and
gentleness—a very sexy combination—and this morning,
combined as it is with a couple of days' stubble and the fact
that his crumpled white shirt looks *so* good against his black
trousers and black skin, he looks even sexier than usual,
which is infuriating when I know how tired he must be.

He's been visiting his cousin in Las Vegas and ended
up reporting on the concert shooting and staying on to do
follow-up pieces. It must have been horrendous, although I
know there's a small part of him that's glad he was there
when it happened.

He crouches on the doorstep and opens his arms wide.
Alfie hurls himself at his dad's chest and flings his arms
around his neck.

"I've missed you, little man," Michael says, rubbing his stubbly cheek against Alfie's face.

Alfie shrieks in delight.

"Thanks, kiddo, that's doing my headache a whole lot of good." He looks up at me and grins. "Any chance of coffee? I feel like shit."

Alfie gasps. "You said a bad word, Daddy."

"Yes, he did. I don't want *you* saying that word, Alfie."

Michael gives me a sheepish look from under his eyebrows and smacks his own hand. Now it's my turn to be hugged. "Sorry, Mommy," he whispers in my ear. He looks down at Alfie. "Seeing him makes it all worth it, though. I didn't want to let him down."

I nod, gratefully. Normally, he takes Alfie to his sister's place in Woodbridge or back to his apartment sixty miles away. Now, I don't know whether it's because I feel sorry for him having to get back in the car again when he's so obviously beat, or whether I'm worried that he'll fall asleep at the wheel with Alfie in the back—it's probably that, to be honest—but all of a sudden I find myself suggesting he chill out here instead, stay over maybe. I've got to go to work this morning, but I'll be back around two.

The relief on his face is instant. It's as if I've waved a magic wand and his tiredness has evaporated. He holds my cheeks in his hands and presses his forehead against mine. I close my eyes. Who am I kidding? I know exactly why I've made the offer.

While Michael's drinking coffee and trying to rebuild Luke Skywalker's Lego landspeeder, I watch the two of them, father and son, absorbed in their task, and guilt settles over me. Michael didn't want me to leave the city. It was so much easier for him to see Alfie when we lived nearby.

But he wasn't always free when I needed him—dashing off somewhere for work or writing through the night, meeting deadlines—and it wasn't Michael who had to witness Alfie's meltdowns every time I got him up for school in the morning. Having my mom just a few blocks away has been wonderful. I never have to worry about babysitters, and it's lovely for her, too, having us so close. Although I must be careful not to rely on her too much. I don't want to be like Maddie's daughter and start taking her for granted.

Luke's landspeeder is taking shape before my eyes. I had a try at it yesterday, but I've never been great with my hands. My dad was a carpenter and he was always making things, but I never got to learn from him because he ran off with another woman when I was only four and started a new family.

Couldn't keep it in his pants is one of Mom's favorite expressions. One of the more pithy ones, anyway. He never paid Mom a cent for child support. He sent letters for a while, and made promises about coming to visit, about taking me on vacation, but they never came to anything.

"You did it!" Alfie yells, clapping his hands together, eyes shining with pleasure.

I smile. He might not see his dad as often as either of them would like, but at least he still *has* a dad. Even when Michael's off God knows where chasing the next big story, he always tries to call Alfie as often as he can, and sends him funny postcards and presents. It might not be the perfect arrangement, but so far it's worked. For Alfie, at least.

WHEN I GET HOME FROM WORK, ALFIE'S NAPPING. MICHAEL'S worn him out on purpose. By the time we reach the bedroom we've both stripped down to our underwear. Now that, too, is discarded on the floor. With a six-year-old who could wake up at any second, there's no time for foreplay.

It isn't until my legs are wrapped around Michael's lean, muscled back, my ankles pressing into him, urging him deeper and faster, that I remember the resolution I made the last time this happened. That it wouldn't happen again, no matter how much my body craved it. Alfie's growing up fast. He notices things he never used to.

Sometimes I wonder whether I should have married Michael when he asked me. Maybe I let what happened with Mom and Dad influence me too much. For all I know, we might have been one of those lucky couples who get to live happily ever after. Not that we're *unhappy* now. Far from it. What does Tash say? All the thrills of an affair with none of the fights or the laundry. And, I might add, none of the fear of him leaving me for good. But still, I can't stop myself from imagining what things might have been like if we'd been together all this time.

Michael sprawls out on his back when we've finished, hands clasped behind his head. I lie on my side and drape my leg across his thigh, my flesh the color of milk against his skin. We talk. About Alfie and his new school. About Michael's last assignment. The one thing we *don't* talk about is our relationship. It's as if neither of us dares bring it up. And yet lately, ever since I moved here, it feels like another conversation is always lurking beneath the one we're having, just waiting to break through.

Michael looks pointedly at the patch of wall in the corner where I've peeled off a small section of the hideous old wallpaper.

"Is that as far as you've gotten?"

I sigh. "You try juggling a job at Pegton's with looking after Alfie."

Before I moved in I had all these plans about how I was going to strip the walls and paint everything white till I'd decided on color schemes. But now that I'm actually living here, the reality of redecorating seems overwhelming. Michael would probably help—maybe he's just waiting for me to ask—but there's a part of me that wants to do it all by myself, to prove that I can. My stubborn streak, Tash calls it.

Michael laughs. "Maybe your subconscious is telling you not to put down roots here. Flinstead isn't exactly stimulating."

"What do *you* know?" I say. "There are secrets in this little town you could never imagine."

Michael snorts. "Let me guess: Mrs. Beige from the Bungalow Blandlands has confessed to having the undertaker's love child in 1973?"

I slap the top of his thigh. "Idiot!" He's always teasing me about small-town life.

"Or the Flinstead-in-Bloom brigade have finally admitted to guerrilla pruning tactics on their nearest competitors' rosebushes?"

"Okay, how about this one, then?" I'm determined to prick his balloon. "Sally McGowan, the notorious child murderess, is living in Flinstead."

Michael twists around to face me. "Where did you hear that?"

"From some of the mothers at school. Why? You don't seriously believe it?"

"Of course not. But it's still a story, isn't it?"

He reaches for his phone and I tug at one of the curly black hairs on his chest. He's like a terrier with a rat when it comes to things like this. It's all those years of writing for the tabloids.

"Don't go digging, Michael. Please! I live here, remember?"

"I won't," he says, already scrolling away. "I'm just intrigued, that's all."

5

MONDAY MORNINGS ARE ALWAYS TOUGH. IT'S TAKEN ALFIE
ages to accept the fact that the long summer vacation and all
those days on the beach are now over and that, yes, he really
does have to go to school, even if it's a different school now.
Without the bullies from before. But Monday mornings after
a weekend with his dad are doubly hard.

"My tummy really hurts," he says, clutching his stomach
and faking an expression of such agony I have to suck my
cheeks in to stop myself laughing.

"Hmm. Maybe I should phone Grandma and cancel our
dinner this evening. What a shame. I think she's made brown-
ies."

Alfie's forehead puckers. I think I see the exact moment
he starts to feel better.

MADDIE WAVES AT US AS WE HURRY ONTO THE PLAYGROUND,
against the tide of parents. She's wearing a fur-collared jacket
and brown hat pulled down tight over her forehead like a
character from an Agatha Christie novel, and she's clutching

a pack of photographs to her chest. Her granddaughter's face beams at me through the cellophane. Damn. I've left my order form at home again. I hope I'm not too late. Class photos are ridiculously expensive, but I can't *not* buy one. It's come as a bit of a shock how little I'm earning now.

"You're late this morning," she says, all shiny-eyed and smiling.

"Yes, well." I slide my eyes toward Alfie. "Someone needed a bit of persuasion."

"Do you mind if I wait for you at the gates?" Maddie says. "I need to talk to you about something."

MOST OF THE OTHER PARENTS AND NANNIES HAVE DISPERSED by the time I catch up with her.

"What's up?"

She sighs and looks over her shoulder. "What you said at book club, about that rumor you heard . . ."

My heart sinks.

"It's just a silly piece of gossip, Maddie. I wouldn't give it another thought."

"Well, that's just it," she says, her voice now lowered to an urgent whisper. "I don't think it *is* just a silly piece of gossip. I think there's something in it."

"What makes you say that?"

She leans in a little closer. "I was talking to an English friend of mine from Pilates. She used to be a probation officer in the UK and she knows all sorts of things."

I stifle a groan.

"She said that in England, people like Sally McGowan are given witness protection when they're released. And although that doesn't happen over here, she bets that McGowan would have been given help to relocate. She also said that it's more than likely she kept her first name, or at least the same initials. It stops them from getting confused."

I look at my watch as discreetly as I can. Maddie's lovely, she really is, but I'm due at work in ten minutes.

"Go on," I say.

"She said that people who take on a new identity are likely to set up their own business. It's easier for them to stay below the radar if they're self-employed." There's a gleam in Maddie's eye. She's enjoying this—the excitement of it, the guessing game.

"I'm sure all this is true," I say, "but it still doesn't mean Sally McGowan is living in Flinstead. America is full of small towns like this. She could be anywhere. She might even be abroad."

Maddie shakes her head. "She isn't. I've been on the internet all weekend. Did I tell you my daughter signed me up for one of those Silver Surfer courses?"

"No, you didn't."

"Well, I've learned so much about different search engines." She leans in again. "Sally McGowan is in a small seaside town and she works in a store."

It's as much as I can do not to laugh out loud. She said it with such conviction as well. I thought Maddie was too sensible to believe everything she reads.

She waits till a middle-aged couple has passed by before continuing. "Have you ever been into Stones and Crones on Flinstead Road?"

"The New Age store? Yeah, I buy the occasional thing in there. Why?"

Maddie takes a deep breath. "I feel bad about saying this because I know Liz is friends with the owner—Liz loves all that hippie-dippie stuff, doesn't she?" She pauses. "The thing is, my sister-in-law Louise works in the boutique next door and, apparently, *Sonia Martins* has turned down all her invitations to join the Flinstead Business Group and refuses to get involved in any of the street fairs."

She looks at me as if this is incontrovertible evidence.

"And according to Louise, Sonia once told her she used to live in Dearborn, and then, when Louise brought it up some time later, Sonia said that Louise must be mistaken and that she used to live in *Deer Creek*, Arizona."

Maddie's voice is getting higher and faster as she speaks. She's trilling like a warbler.

"But Louise insists there's no way she misheard her. Sonia definitely said Dearborn because Louise remembers having a conversation with her about Bob Seger coming from Dearborn. So when you add it all up, this is what we know: Sonia Martins looks like Sally McGowan. She's a shop-keeper in a small seaside town who keeps herself to herself and she has an inconsistent backstory."

Now I really can't help but laugh. "*Inconsistent backstory?* You sound like you're discussing a crime novel at book club."

Maddie blushes. "I know, and you're probably right. But it makes you wonder, doesn't it?"

6

A BELL TINKLES AS I PUSH THE DOOR OPEN AND STEP INTO the fragrant interior of Stones and Crones. I need another scented candle. Well, no one *needs* scented candles but the smell does help me unwind and relax, especially after a stressful day in the office. I also need to pick up some batteries for the smoke alarm, and this place is right next door to the hardware store. It's got nothing to do with Maddie's ludicrous theory. Nothing at all.

As soon as the door closes behind me, I know it's a mistake. I feel awkward, ill at ease. My heart thuds so loudly the noise fills my ears, fills the entire shop. Heat flushes into my neck and face. I might just as well have a sign stuck to my forehead saying, I'VE COME TO GET A CLOSER LOOK AT YOU, TO SEE IF YOU'RE SALLY MCGOWAN, CHILD KILLER. Who do I think I am? Miss Marple? I should be ashamed of myself.

Sonia Martins is sitting behind the counter. Poised and perfectly still, the merest hint of a smile on her heavily lipsticked mouth. Her skin is very pale.

"Morning," she says.

"Morning." My voice is high and tinny, not at all like it normally sounds.

There is, I suppose, a certain likeness in the eyes. She has the same color hair, too, only hers is threaded with gray. But really, there must be tons of women with hair and eyes like that. Susan Marchant, for instance. And surely, if you didn't want to be recognized, your hair color would be the very first thing you'd change. What on earth was Maddie thinking?

I wander over to the CD stand and start rotating it slowly, letting my eyes roam over the soothing titles. *Zen Mystique Music for a Calm Mind. Angelic Reiki. Music for Crystal Healing.*

I sense her watching me, in that subtle way small-business owners do. The discreet glance in my direction, just to make sure I'm not pocketing anything, then eyes down again. I slide a CD from the rack—*Journey to the Temple*—and turn it over to read the back: "Featuring seven chakra tracks blended together with natural sounds of water and birdsong." My heartbeat slows. I really should find a yoga class. I used to go once a week in the city.

The candles are on the display table right in front of the counter. Right in front of the woman called Sonia Martins. The woman who refuses to join the Flinstead Business Group and doesn't participate in the annual street fairs. The woman who in all probability has nothing whatsoever to do with Sally McGowan, who no doubt spent a peaceful childhood in Dearborn, or possibly Deer Creek, playing with her dolls and reading Dick and Jane, and grew up to be a kind, gentle soul.

I check the price on the candles, but even the smallest is $9.99.

Sonia looks over at me. "They smell beautiful, those candles," she says.

I smile in response and wrestle with the dilemma of whether to buy an overpriced candle I don't need or to leave empty-handed. That's the trouble with these little stores: Once I'm inside, I always feel compelled to buy something, as if it's my moral obligation to support a stranger's business.

I replace the candle and grab a packet of incense sticks instead, smiling broadly, as if these were what I was really looking for, the reason I came here in the first place.

"That'll be two dollars and fifty cents, please," Sonia says. Do I detect a subtle tone of disappointment?

I fumble in my purse. Her voice is quiet, reasonably educated. A bit like mine, I suppose.

Although of course, accents can be picked up. Learned. Discarded, too. I think of Barbara's mid-Atlantic voice and her occasional drunken lapses into a southern drawl.

Sonia Martins slips the incense into a brown-paper gift bag. Our eyes meet when she hands it over. I'm being neurotic, I know I am, but I swear those eyes can see right through me. I smile and turn to leave, aware of her gaze on the back of my neck. The weight of it.

It isn't till I'm outside on the street again that I realize I've been holding my breath. What am I doing? I must stop this nonsense right now. Put it out of my mind once and for all.

DAVE WAVES A POST-IT NOTE AT ME AS SOON AS I GET BACK to the office.

"Anne Wilson wants a second showing of the Maple

Drive property," he says. "I thought, seeing as you've already met her, you might like to—"

"Enjoy the warmth of Mrs. Marchant's smile one more time?"

Dave grins. "Something like that. I'd do it myself, but I've got two appraisals to do this afternoon and I'm behind as it is."

That's one of the things I like about Dave Pegton. I'm just a part-time employee now, trying to gain experience in residential sales, and he's my boss and the owner of the business, but he always makes it seem like we're equals.

"I'll call Mom and see if she can pick Alfie up today. Then I can catch up on that pile of paperwork when I come back."

Dave sticks his thumb in the air.

I PARK AT THE TOP OF MAPLE DRIVE, FACING THE WATER. Today, it is a deep violet-blue and there's a hazy shimmer that makes the horizon seem barely visible. I never tire of looking at the ocean. It's part of my soul; it's etched on my DNA. All those long summer afternoons I used to spend sprawled on the sand with my nose in a book, the sound of the surf rasping on the shore. Then later, as a teenager, huddled around an illicit fire as dusk gave way to night, smoking and swigging beers or, if we got lucky, necking with the boys who worked at the carnival on Mistden Pier. I always knew I'd come back one day.

This time, I wait for Anne Wilson to arrive *before* getting out of my car. The less time I have to spend in Susan Marchant's company, the better. I switch the radio on and open the window, watch the leaves on the sidewalk shift and separate in the breeze. With winter only a couple of months away, golden days like this have to be savored. The last breath of summer.

Most of the tourists have left now that the school year has started up again. Flinstead is being returned to its inhabitants. It's as if the town can finally breathe. If the tourists stopped coming, this place would surely die. But oh how glorious it is when they pack up their deck chairs and sunscreen and trundle back to their cars and don't come back, when the boardwalk isn't cluttered with their beach toys and their giant inflatables and their sunburnt legs.

There's still the odd day-tripper or dog-walker parked up on the esplanade, of course. A man and two children are flying a kite. A traditional diamond kite—bright yellow with a long red tail. It dips and soars in the sky, its tail streaming after it. Maybe I should buy Alfie a kite. He'd like that. In fact, I'd much rather buy him a good-quality kite than those overpriced school photographs. Which reminds me, I must find that order form when I get home.

I check my rearview mirror for Anne Wilson's blue BMW, but she hasn't arrived yet. The time of the appointment comes and goes and, since there's no message from her, I keep waiting. It's no hardship to be sitting here, with the afternoon sun warming me through the windows, the sound of seagulls squawking overhead. Even so, a small kernel of unease has lodged itself in the pit of my stomach. The dead leaves rattle across the sidewalk. Maybe it's the thought of dealing with Susan Marchant again. Or maybe it's my recent encounter with Sonia Martins, how weird she made me feel.

Susan Marchant. Sonia Martins. Am I going to start suspecting everyone with the initials *S. M.* from now on?

My eyes slide to the brown-paper bag on the passenger seat, the one that contains my incense sticks. I must have been in that store several times since moving to Flinstead, enticed by the gorgeous scents and chill vibes. If I were someone trying to hide my real identity from the world, someone with demons to suppress, what better place could I choose to spend my days than a peaceful, calming environment like Stones and Crones?

It must be so difficult having to keep all those lies in perpetual motion, like plates spinning on sticks. How could anyone live like that without going nuts? I pull my shoulder blades back toward each other and squeeze them tight to release the tension. So much for vowing to put Sally McGowan out of my mind. She's taken up residence there like an unwelcome guest.

While I'm waiting, I scroll through Facebook. Tash has posted a picture of her ankle, which is massively swollen and badly bruised. She's written *Great excuse to stay at home and watch Netflix*. I press LIKE and tap out a comment: *Too much vodka last night???*

She responds within seconds. *Running to catch bus, tripped on curb. We need to catch up. Come and stay SOON.*

Will do, I reply. *Miss you.*

Shouldn't have moved then! followed by a winking emoji is her speedy response.

I just have time to send her one with a tongue sticking out before I see Anne Wilson's BMW pull up on the other side of the road. She gets out, grimacing and mouthing *Sorry*. The highlights in her hair gleam in the sun as she hurries toward me. There's no silver-haired man with her today.

"I was going to call to say I'd be late," she says. Her voice has an apologetic, breathy quality. "But that would have wasted even more time. I thought it best to just keep going."

Her skin looks even tighter and shinier than before. It's impossible to gauge how old she is, but she isn't young.

"It's fine," I say. "Honestly."

Like last time, the front door of number 24 opens before I've even rung the bell. Susan Marchant's eyes flick from me to Anne and back to me again. For a minute I have the impression she's going to tell us off for being late, but then she gestures for us to come in. An imperious wave of her arm.

"I'll be in the backyard," she says, and disappears down the long hallway.

Anne Wilson shakes her head in disbelief. As much as Pegton's needs this sale to go through—things have been a bit slow lately; Dave calls it the Trump Effect—I can't help hoping she decides not to make an offer, and that nobody else does, either, so that Susan Marchant is forced to drop the price. It would serve her right for being such a cold fish.

7

MOM'S TOWNHOUSE AND THE ONE NEXT TO IT MAKE ME THINK
of those before-and-after photos. Both halves are covered in
the same sandy-brown shingles, but the windows of the townhouse on the left where her elderly neighbor lives are dirty,
with sagging curtains, whereas Mom's are sparkling and
have neat vertical blinds. Likewise, each half of the shared
concrete driveway tells its own story, although I notice that,
recently, Mom's taken to pulling next door's weeds up out of
the cracks as well as her own. I'm surprised she hasn't offered to wash the windows, too.

She opens the door, a dish towel slung over her shoulder
and her cheeks all pink from the heat of the kitchen. Sol
barges past her legs to greet me. He's a ten-year-old yellow
Labrador and he's another reason why Alfie is so pleased to
be living here. Alfie is dog-crazy, and now that he gets to see
Sol almost whenever he likes, he's stopped pestering me for
one of his own.

Looking after retired guide dogs is something Mom's
been doing ever since I was a little girl. Granddad was blind
so she grew up around working dogs. I can still remember all

their names: Lulu, Nero, Pepper, and the biggest rascal of all, Quenton, who once ate an entire birthday cake when no one was looking. *My* birthday cake, as it happens, but I couldn't be mad at him for long. Especially when he started shaking with sugar overload and we had to rush him to the vet's.

When her last dog, Oona, a gorgeous German shepherd, died of cancer, I thought she was going to hang up her leashes for good. All her dogs have been special and, as she often says, you can't afford to get too attached to them because they're already old when they come to you, but Oona was a particular favorite.

In the end, though, she relented. The house didn't seem the same without a dog in it.

Alfie comes running out of the living room for a hug. His hands are covered in green felt-tip and there's Play-Doh stuck under his fingernails, but oh, he smells so gorgeous I never want to let him go.

Mom smiles. "Alfie, do you want to finish your coloring book while Mommy and I set the table?"

"Look at my alien spacecraft first," he says, thrusting his handiwork under my nose for inspection. "It's got a special rocket blastoff. Look, Mommy. Look!"

"That's gorgeous, Alfie. And what's this little creature here?"

Alfie and Mom exchange a look as if to say, *Imagine not knowing that.* "It's a space robot. That's his antenna and those are his special claws."

"Oh yes, of course. Silly me. Aren't you a clever boy?"

Alfie marches mechanically into the living room, chanting, "Affirmative, affirmative."

"He loves that book," Mom says, laughing. "The one *you* didn't want me to buy."

"It's the title that annoyed me. *The Boys' Coloring Book,* as if girls don't want to color spaceships and airplanes. No wonder there are so few female engineers."

Mom rolls her eyes and waves me into the kitchen. She shuts the door behind us. "Can we have a quick word?"

I dump my bag on the floor and perch on one of the stools at the breakfast bar.

"What's he done now? He hasn't been saying 'shit' again, has he? I've told Michael not to say it in front of him, but you know what he's like."

Mom makes a face that says, yes, she knows exactly what Michael's like. "No, he's been good as gold. It's just that . . ." She pauses. "I'm worried about him, Jo. Especially after what he went through before." My heart constricts. "Has he told you about lunchtimes?"

I stare at her, puzzled. "Lunchtimes?"

"How no one wants to sit next to him?"

The backs of my eyeballs burn as I remember the tummyache excuse this morning. "He hasn't said anything about that to me."

Mom takes three placemats out of the drawer. "This is the second time he's mentioned it. I didn't think much of it at first because, well, you know what kids are like at this age—they're so fickle when it comes to friendships." She hands me the mats. "But he's clearly upset about it. And he says Jake and Liam are always being nasty to him."

I go through to the sunporch and set the mats on the table. I'm glad he feels able to confide in her, of course I am. I just wish it was me he'd told first. Maybe if I'd asked a few more questions about Jake and Liam the other day, he'd have told me what was going on. I can't let this happen again.

"He did say something about those two, but I had no

idea about the lunch thing. I'll have a word with Miss Williams tomorrow."

Poor Alfie. I can't bear to think of him sitting all on his own.

Mom frowns. "And that's not all I'm worried about."

Oh God. What else have I missed about my own son?

"He told me that Michael stayed over last weekend."

Hmm. I should have guessed Alfie would say something about that.

"I've never interfered in your life, Joanna, and I'm not about to start now," she says. "But if I don't say this, it's just going to play on my mind."

"Go on, then. Say it."

"Alfie could so easily get the wrong idea about things. You've said yourself how he sometimes wonders why his daddy can't live in the same house. If Michael starts staying over, it's bound to confuse him."

Mom presses her lips together. She's never really understood about Michael and me. She's very old-fashioned in that respect. Probably feels a bit awkward explaining our "situation," as she calls it, to her friends, although I know deep down she has only my best interests at heart. She told me once that she thinks I've settled for second best, but I don't need to justify my relationship with Michael—it's *my* life, not hers.

Even so, I find myself explaining. "He was exhausted after his flight. It felt mean sending him off again as soon as he'd arrived."

"So he slept on the sofa, then?"

I open my mouth to respond, but there's nothing to say.

Mom does one of those laughing sighs. "He might only be six, Jo, but children are much savvier than we think."

She turns the gas off under the peas and takes a colander from the cupboard. "I hope he uses protection."

"Mo-om! For God's sake! Of *course* he does. *We* do."

Apart from the one, notable exception that led to Alfie, of course, but we don't need to go over that again.

"Because he's probably sleeping with other women besides you," she says. "You do realize that, don't you?"

I breathe in through my nose and count to five. "We've never been exclusive, Mom, I've told you that. But one thing I *do* know about Michael is that he's honest."

Too honest, sometimes. On the rare occasions he *has* gone out with someone else, he's always made a point of telling me, almost as if he needs my approval. And I know I could, too, if I wanted to. Except I don't. I haven't. Not since Alfie.

"He hasn't been seeing anyone else for a long while now," I say. "And if he does meet someone he wants to be with, he'll tell me. I know he will."

Mom sighs. "I'm sorry, darling. I can't help worrying about you. It's all part of being a mother, you know, worrying about your children. It never stops, even when they're all grown up. I just want you to be happy and not have to go through what I went through with your *father*."

She puts the usual sour emphasis on the word. Poor Mom. It's hardly surprising she has such a dim view of men.

She squeezes my shoulder. "Do you remember when you were little and you had that imaginary friend? I was *so* anxious when you started school. I thought the other children would tease you about it."

"Oh yeah, Lucy Locket." I smile at the memory.

Mom laughs. "I can't tell you how relieved I was when you stopped chattering away to yourself in your bedroom."

"Actually, it's perfectly normal for young children to have imaginary friends. I looked it up once. It's a natural part of their development."

"I *know*. I'm only teasing." Mom passes me the salt and pepper to put on the table. "It sounds like Alfie just needs a bit of help settling in. Maybe it would help if you made friends with some of the other mothers, invited their children over for playdates or something. I got talking to Hayley's mom when I picked him up today. Karen, is it? Her mother was there, too—nice lady, way too thin. She's just moved in with Karen, I think she said. They both seemed really lovely."

"Karen goes to my book club," I say. "I think she's also the secretary of the PTA. I find her a little intense, to be honest. And anyway, Alfie's not too crazy about girls."

Mom laughs. "You wait till he's a teenager." She takes three plates from the cupboard and puts them in the bottom of the oven to warm.

Alfie's head appears around the door. "I'm starving!"

Mom rests her hands on her hips. "Well, it's a good thing supper's ready, then, isn't it?"

She's right. Of course she is. I'll have to try harder with the other mothers. For Alfie's sake. Get myself invited to their coffee-morning circuit if I have to. What did Tash say when I told her I was moving out here and going part-time? That it wouldn't be long before I became one of those mothers who take over a whole coffee shop and talk endlessly about their offspring. I told her, "No way."

But still, if it makes Alfie's life a little easier . . .

8

LATER THAT NIGHT, ABOUT FIVE MINUTES AFTER ALFIE'S GONE
to sleep, the phone rings. I grab it before it wakes him up.

"I think I might be on to something about Sally
McGowan," Michael says. We've barely said hello.

"You're kidding."

"I'm not. I bumped into an old pal of mine who cut
his teeth on the first big exposé. You know, when she was
hounded out of Iowa."

When Michael uses the phrase *old pal,* it could mean absolutely anything. An old hack he crossed paths with once.
An ex-criminal-turned-informant. An innocent bystander
delighted to embellish a story for five minutes of fame and
the gratitude of a good-looking journalist with kind eyes.
What it rarely means is a "pal."

Bumped into is also not how it sounds. It's not like me
bumping into Maddie at the school playground this morning. *Bumped into* in Michael's world means "tracked down by
any means possible."

"He heard that some guy who used to work in the Witness Security Program helped set her up somewhere else," he says. "Unofficially, of course. Gave her a new name. A new legend."

A *legend*? He's really enjoying this. I can tell from his tone of voice, the way he's spinning it out, like some CIA operative in a spy movie.

"It sometimes takes months before people with new identities are ready to go it alone. My source says Sally McGowan was a quick learner. She had to be. She didn't have the cushion of WITSEC behind her."

"Your source or your pal?" I say.

"Ha ha. Now here's the thing. One of *his* sources—and he swears this guy was legit—got smashed one night and let it slip that she was safely stashed away in one of those seaside towns you go to die in."

"Hmm. So you automatically thought of Flinstead."

"Well, if the shoe fits . . . No. I haven't finished yet. The last thing this guy said, before he became too inebriated to speak, was that, if it was him, he'd rather take his chances with an angry mob than wind up in a town with no bars."

He waits for this to sink in. Flinstead used to be famous for being a "dry" town. It was big news when it finally got a bar.

"Who *was* this source?" I say. "I mean, if it was someone on the inside, someone privy to Sally's new identity, he wouldn't be stupid enough to go drinking with a reporter, would he?"

Michael laughs. "There wasn't much my pal could do with it, anyway. No decent editor would touch it with a barge pole. Some outlets have strict policies on that kind of thing. And I certainly wouldn't want to go out on a limb and expose her. I just thought you'd be interested."

Am I interested? This is the question I ask myself when

we've said goodbye and I'm getting ready to go upstairs, checking the stove burners are all turned off, even though I know full well they are—we didn't even eat here tonight. It was all such a long time ago. If it's true and Sally McGowan really is living in Flinstead, what difference does it make to my life, or anyone else's for that matter?

She was a child then, an abused, damaged child. From what I've read, the police found lots of cuts and bruises on her body. Old wounds, some of them. Her father, a drunken bully of a man by all accounts, swore she was a devious child who'd inflicted the damage herself so that people would think it was him. The mother went along with this story. What's so terrifying is that people actually believed them.

I can't get Sally McGowan's ten-year-old face out of my mind. Those startlingly defiant eyes. If anyone should have been sent to prison it was Kenny McGowan and, arguably, the mother, Jean. Although it's pretty clear now, from a twenty-first-century perspective, that she was also being abused. We've come a long way since the 1960s, thank God.

Or have we? I've been trawling through Twitter and the comments sections of various online articles lately, looking at the sort of things people are still saying about Sally and other, more recent child killers. The hatred and venom are staggering. The lust for revenge like something out of the Middle Ages. And all from people who aren't even the victims' families, who don't even know them.

What was it Cathy said? That she'd prefer it if someone like that was mobbed by vigilantes rather than protected. Is that what would happen in Flinstead if this rumor got any traction and someone tracked Sally down? Would Cathy and Debbie and the rest of them be standing on the sidewalk outside her house, hurling abuse, or worse? Would our quiet little town be forever known as the place where Sally McGowan was discovered? And how would I feel if that happened, knowing I was instrumental in passing it on?

I take one last peek at Alfie before turning in. He looks so adorable, I can't resist planting the softest of kisses on his cheek. It's shocking to think that when Sally McGowan killed that boy, she was barely four years older than Alfie is now. I tiptoe out of his room, taking care to leave the door ajar the way he likes, so that he can see the landing light if he wakes up.

As I snuggle down in my own bed I remember the batteries I bought earlier, still sitting in that paper bag along with the incense sticks. I took the dead ones out of the alarm this morning and there's no way I'll get any sleep if I don't put the new ones in.

Halfway downstairs, I realize I've forgotten something else, too. I didn't tell Michael what Alfie said to Mom, about no one sitting next to him at lunchtime. Tears fill my eyes as I picture him at an empty table, swinging his little legs under his chair and pretending he doesn't care. The sooner I make friends with the other mothers, the better.

9

WHATEVER MOM SAID TO ALFIE YESTERDAY, SHE MUST HAVE reassured him, because there's no sign of a tummyache this morning. He does seem quieter than usual, though.

"Shall we go to the beach after school and get ice cream?" I say. His little face lights up. "Maybe some of your friends at school could come with us."

Alfie looks doubtful. "Maybe," he says.

I widen my eyes to stop them from filling with tears. If only I could make his troubles disappear. Kiss it all better like a scrape on the knee. I sweep him into my arms and hug him tight, blow raspberries on his neck to make him giggle.

"Come on, finish your cornflakes and let's get going. We don't want to be late."

It's the first time we've left the house this early, but I want to have a quick word with Miss Williams. Normally, we set off at exactly seven minutes to eight. That gives us just enough time to get to the school and join the line outside the classroom before the bell rings.

I've been selfish, I realize that now. Timing it so that there's less time standing around with the other mothers. If

I'd thought about it earlier, I could have gone to one of their coffee mornings and maybe Alfie would have a few more friends by now.

Cathy and Debbie barely glance at me as I arrive. It's hardly surprising. They tried extending the hand of friendship a few weeks ago and I turned it down. After my comment about vigilantism the other day, they're hardly likely to try again. Nobody ever warns you about this sort of thing before you have children. Nobody tells you it pays to make friends with the other mothers, even if you have nothing in common. I'm going to have to swallow my pride and appeal to their better natures. Tell them Alfie's having trouble settling in and that I'd appreciate their help.

When I've spoken to Miss Williams and she's reassured me that she'll keep an eye on the friendship situation, and I've said goodbye to Alfie and watched him file in with the others, I go over to where Cathy and Debbie are standing. They're still talking about the Sally McGowan rumor.

"Hi there."

Debbie gives me a quick, tight smile. Cathy starts tapping away on her phone.

"I was wondering whether Jake and Liam would like to come to the beach with me and Alfie after school today. Maybe get some ice cream while the weather's still warm enough?"

Cathy glances up from her phone. "Today? Sorry. Jake's got a judo lesson."

"And Liam's going to Harry's house to play," Debbie says. "Maybe another day, okay?"

I nod. She said it in that offhand way that basically means no. This is excruciating. It makes me feel like I'm back at school, humiliated by bitchy girls. Back then, I just slunk away, hurt and resentful. But not now. Because this isn't about me, it's about Alfie.

"By the way," I say, already turning to leave the playground. "I think you may have been right about Sally McGowan living in Flinstead."

"What makes you say that?" Cathy asks.

I turn to face her. Suddenly, I'm a whole lot more interesting than her phone.

"Oh, just something I heard. It's probably nothing . . ."

The two women move closer. Sharks circling their prey. And yet their faces are softer than they were a minute ago, more open and friendly. Is this all it takes to penetrate their firewall?

My brain races. Which bit of what Michael told me last night should I share with them? None of it, of course, but this is working so well. They're all ears. Debbie's even offering me a stick of chewing gum, which I don't want but take anyway. Besides, it's not as if Michael's going to write an article about McGowan. At least, I hope not.

I lower my voice. "Someone I know, someone who knows about these things, heard that she was relocated to a dry town."

The two women stare at me, eyebrows knitted. "A *what*?" Cathy says.

"A dry town. You know, one with no bars."

Cathy narrows her eyes. "When did the Flinstead Arms open?"

"The late nineties, I think," Debbie says. "Don't you remember, Cath? There was a big thing about it in the papers? We were still in middle school."

It doesn't sit right with me, all this. I've already passed

the rumor on to book club. Now I'm stoking the fire all over again. What's happening to me?

But then I remember Alfie's little face this morning when I mentioned the word *friends,* and I know that if this is what it takes to help him make some, I'll do it.

"Hm," Cathy says, a thoughtful look on her face. "That's very interesting. Hey, Joanna, I don't suppose you want to join our babysitting circle, do you? We're meeting tomorrow. Nine thirty. My house. Fourteen Flinstead Road. The house with the blue garage?"

"Oh right. Yes. I think I know the one you mean. Thanks, I'd love to—that's if I can arrange to go into work a little later than usual."

I'm not sure I really need to belong to a babysitting circle, not with Mom living around the corner. Still, there's bound to be a time when I have to go out and Mom *can't* come over. It'll be like a safety net. And it's the perfect way to get to know them all a bit better.

One casual remark. One whispered secret. That's all it takes to set the wheels in motion and change the course of a life. Once, some poor woman they thought was me was driven out of her home. She lost her job, her reputation, her peace of mind. Ended up throwing herself in front of a high-speed train.

I often think about that woman, that stranger, how our lives are now inextricably bound. And I ask myself, who is to blame for her death? The rumormongers for spreading the lies? Or me, for being the monster in the first place?

The monster. That's what they called me.

I stare at my reflection in the mirror. No extra heads. No horns. Just an ordinary woman. Not bad-looking, despite the crow's-feet and the crêpey neck. Despite the lipstick radiating into the fine vertical creases on my top lip. But if I look long enough, really stare into the mirror without blinking, someone else takes my place.

The girl they locked up. The one I've spent my whole life trying to erase.

It's her that's brought them out again. Circling like vultures. Her that draws them ever closer. She makes bad things happen. She disturbs the air.

10

"SHE MIGHT JUST AS WELL HAVE STUCK A KNIFE IN MY HEART, TOO," SAYS SYLVIA HARRIS, MOTHER OF ROBBIE HARRIS, TRAGIC VICTIM OF CHILD KILLER SALLY MCGOWAN

By Alex O'Connor

SUNDAY, AUGUST 3, 1975
The Times

Today, six years after the murder of her five-year-old son, Robbie, Sylvia Harris sits in her living room chain-smoking, a shadow of the woman she once was.

Flanked by her teenage daughter, Marie, Sylvia stares at her hands.

"It wasn't only my little boy Sally killed that day," Sylvia says. "She might just as well have stuck a knife in my heart, too."

Sylvia is now 35 and battling an addiction to alcohol; her marriage to Derek Harris is over. Marie lives with her father a few blocks away but visits Sylvia every day after school. With news of McGowan's temporary transfer to a new juvenile detention center, this week has been particularly hard.

"Maybe if we never heard about her again, we'd be able to get on with our lives," says Sylvia. "What's left of them."

But one senses that this is a family that time will *never* heal.

Sylvia picks up a framed black-and-white photograph that shows blond-haired Robbie playing on a beach with his bucket and spade.

She squeezes her daughter's hand. "However long they keep her locked up won't be long enough. I hope she rots in hell."

I close my iPad and rub my eyes. The typeface on this scanned image of the original front page is small and blurry. I've been doing too much of this lately. Endlessly scrolling through Google for interesting articles about the McGowan case. It's become a bit of an obsession.

AS I REACH THE END OF THE STREET, I SPOT LIZ BLACKTHORNE coming out of the co-op. She's looking straight at me, so I give her a wave and am about to cross the street for a quick word when she turns on her heels and hurries off in the other direction, the tip of her white braid poking out of the bottom of her jacket like a tail. That's odd. I could have sworn she saw me. Oh well, she must have her mind on other things this morning. I'm the same when I'm busy. Charging around like a horse with blinders, oblivious to everyone and everything around me. Besides, I'm late as it is.

Cathy lives in one of the new houses at the top of Flinstead Road, the opposite end from the ocean. Inside, it's light and spacious and could have come straight out of the Ikea catalog. There are six of us here, including Karen from book club—I didn't realize she was chummy with this crowd—and three toddlers. I'm pleased to see Fatima's friendly face, too. Cathy has just finished making everyone tea and coffee and is now leafing through a fat accordion file.

"I hate it when people don't fill the chart in properly," she says.

Debbie makes a mock-worried face. "That'll be me. Sorry. I thought I'd done it."

Cathy gives me a pointed look. "This is what happens, Joanna. And then they all start complaining their points aren't up to date."

I smile, as if I know what she's talking about. Charts? Points? What on earth have I gotten myself into? I can just imagine what Tash will say when I call and tell her about it.

Fatima leans in toward me. "Every time you babysit for someone, you get points. The more points you have, the more sits you can request. We take turns to keep track of the file and host the meetings."

"That's right," Cathy says. "I was just going to explain all that. It's basically a quid pro quo arrangement. You get a point for every half hour you sit. So two points per hour and a point for every quarter of an hour after midnight."

I nod, as if I'm following all this.

"After-midnight sits have to be negotiated in advance," Karen says. "And if you've got zero points, you can't request a sitter."

"Well, you *can*," says a tall woman with red hair whose name I've already forgotten. "If someone volunteers to help you out and if nobody else has priority over you."

Karen's jaw tightens. "But then you'd be minus points," she says. "And we agreed we'd try not to keep doing that because it all gets out of hand and it's unfair."

I have a sudden urge to giggle.

The doorbell rings at just the right moment. "That must be Kay," Fatima says. "She said she'd be late."

The woman Cathy shows into the room a minute later looks vaguely familiar. Judi Dench hair and kind, crinkly eyes.

"Kay's one of my neighbors and honorary mother," Fatima tells me, patting the seat next to her for Kay to sit down.

Of course. I've seen the two of them chatting on their doorsteps—they live up the block from me. Fatima did tell me a while back that her own parents disowned her when she refused an arranged marriage. It's hard to believe what some people have to endure.

"She's also Ketifa's honorary grandmother."

Kay smiles. "My daughter and grandchildren live in Australia, you see. Melbourne. No matter how many times we Skype each other, it's not the same as having them close. That's why I'm so happy to be part of all this."

"All right, then," Cathy says. "Down to business, ladies."

Later, after Cathy has made a note of everyone who needs a sitter in the next month and checked that all the points are up to date, I hear myself offering to babysit for the woman with red hair, whose name turns out to be Teri Monkton. I'll have to square it with Mom, of course.

"Thanks so much," Teri says. "Ruby and Hamish are very well behaved. Although they will try to keep you upstairs reading endless bedtime stories."

When the business side of things is concluded and we're

making moves to leave, Teri says: "I don't suppose any of you have heard this rumor that's going around? The one about Sally McGowan?"

Debbie laughs. "You're a little late to the party, aren't you?"

"I'm always the last to hear about these things," Teri says. "Is there anything in it, do you think?"

"I doubt it," Fatima says. "Think about it. If you wanted to keep out of sight you'd settle in a city, surely. It's more anonymous."

Kay nods. "You're right."

Cathy shoots me a look. There's a gleam in her eyes, just like Maddie's the other day. "Joanna, tell them what you heard."

I don't want to say it again. I especially don't want Cathy *commanding* me to say it.

Karen is staring at me from across the room. "Has there been an update, then? Since what you told us at book club?"

Damn. Now I look like the biggest blabbermouth in town. But I'm not going to do it again. It's bad enough that I repeated it in the first place.

"It was probably nothing. Just one of those silly stories doing the rounds."

Cathy frowns. "That's not the impression you gave yesterday," she says, and proceeds to repeat the story about the dry town.

Teri grimaces. "I hate the thought that I might be walking past her house when I take Ruby and Hamish to school, or that she could be watching them play in the park or on the beach. Have you seen that photo of her staring at the camera? It gives me the creeps."

"These kinds of rumors always surface from time to

time," I say. "I mean, I'm not saying it isn't possible. It's just not that likely."

Teri makes a face. "I hope you're right about that."

I WALK HOME WITH FATIMA AND KAY. IT FEELS LIKE WE'RE escaping from something, but none of us wants to admit it. The cold wind scours my face and dispels some of the awkwardness I felt earlier. There's a feeling of rain in the air.

"So, Joanna," Kay says. "Your name is on Cathy's sacred chart now. I hope you know what you've gotten yourself into."

Fatima nudges her in the ribs. "Come on now, Kay. Don't scare her off before she's even started."

"I'm just wondering how everyone's going to fit in my living room when it's my turn to host the meeting. There's barely room for me and Alfie."

"Don't worry about that," Kay says. "We don't all have immaculate big houses like Cathy. You could fit my entire ground floor in her living room."

"I *love* your house," Fatima says. "It reminds me of the house I grew up in."

Kay laughs. "That's her way of saying it's old-fashioned."

We've reached my cottage now so we say our goodbyes. As I close my front door, I stand for a moment in the hall, letting the silence wrap itself around me. If it hadn't been for Mom's suggestion the other day, there's no way I'd have joined a babysitting circle. She was right, though. Debbie's already given me an invitation for Alfie to go to Liam's birthday party in a couple of weeks.

I open the little envelope to check the date and make a note of it on the kitchen calendar. As soon as I see that it's for October 31 and spot the pumpkin border, I realize she's made it a Halloween-themed party, which means all the children will be in costume.

I'm not a great fan of Halloween. It's just another big retail event designed to drag money out of hard-pressed parents. Money I simply don't have. Not anymore. Still, I can probably order something inexpensive online, or cut a hole in a sheet and send him as a ghost.

The important thing is, Alfie will be thrilled when I tell him.

11

"YOU'LL NEVER GUESS WHAT," DAVE SAYS BY WAY OF GREET-ing. "Mrs. Marchant's accepted an offer from Anne Wilson and Jeremy Sanders."

I raise my eyebrows. "Really? I thought she'd hold out for the full asking price."

"So did I," he says. "And it was a ballsy offer, in my opinion. Thirty K below." He sifts through a pile of papers on his desk. "They're cash buyers. Did I tell you?"

"No. It doesn't surprise me, though. They don't exactly look hard up."

Dave grins. "I reckon she's had a bit of Botox, don't you?"

I laugh. "And the rest."

"I did suggest to Mrs. Marchant that it was probably just an opening bid and that they might very well up the offer if she didn't bite." He sighs. "She didn't even need to turn them down, she could have just waited and they'd have come back with something else, but she wasn't interested. Obviously wants a quick sale, and that's that."

The morning passes in a blur. After three quiet weeks

we're suddenly inundated with inquiries: people popping in off the street and asking about something they've seen on Zillow, five people registering with us as potential buyers, and three appraisal requests. Not to mention the usual phone calls from frustrated clients fretting about exchanging contracts and closing dates.

And in between all this I've been trying to update the Pegton's Twitter account—a job Dave is more than happy for me to manage. I can't resist having a quick scroll through my own Twitter feed while I'm at it, so I don't notice Kay at first. People are always standing outside peering at the photos in the window. I tend to ignore them unless they actually come in, and in my experience most people who scrutinize real estate agents' windows have no intention of coming inside. They're either visitors curious to check out house prices in the area, or nosy neighbors trying to see what the house at the end of their block is going for and speculating on what their own might be worth.

Then I see something move out of the corner of my eye and realize it's her, waving at me through the glass. I wave back and she comes in.

"Hello, dear," she says. "I didn't realize you worked in here." She flops down on the chair opposite my desk and gives me a sheepish look. "To be honest, I was about to pop in and see if you wanted anyone part-time. I'm looking for a little job, you see. I can type forty words a minute and answer the phone, and I'm terrific with people." She leans forward. "I also watch every episode of *Property Brothers* and *Love It or List It* and anything else that's remotely related to buying and selling houses. I'm completely addicted."

Dave's mouthing *no* at me over her shoulder. I don't

know whether Kay's just noticed my eyes flick toward him or whether she'd have done this anyway, but she turns around in her chair to face him. "I make delicious coffee as well," she says. She's got some nerve, I'll say that for her.

Dave does his awkward laugh. He hates it when this sort of thing happens, and it quite often does. I did it myself, although I was a bit more subtle about it. Let it slip when he was showing me around a property that I'd worked in real estate and was about to start job hunting.

"I'm really sorry," he says. "But we don't have any openings right now."

"You can leave us your contact information, though," I quickly suggest. Dave nods vigorously. He always forgets to say that. "And if ever we *do* need some extra help, we'll be in touch."

Kay nods and gets to her feet. She looks tired all of a sudden, and a bit embarrassed. I glance at my watch and catch Dave's eye. "It's almost time for my lunch break. I'll go now, if you don't mind, Dave. Then I can have a chat with Kay."

Kay brightens at this.

"Tell you what," I say. "Why don't we go for a quick coffee? My treat."

Five minutes later, we're sitting in the Shrieking Kettle, each nursing a giant cup of cappuccino.

"I've tried everywhere," Kay says. "I've even asked in here and at the Fisherman's Shack, but no one's hiring."

I blow on my coffee and distort the chocolate-powder shape on top of the foam. "I'm sure you'll find something soon."

"I know," she says. "And if I don't, I can always go back to cleaning." She grimaces. "Look, I'm just feeling a bit sorry for myself at the moment. It's always the same at this time of year. You know, the months running up to Christmas. I miss Gillian and the babies so much."

"How often do you get to see them?"

She opens a second packet of sugar and stirs it into her coffee. "I haven't. Not since they left. It's the expense." She stares into the middle distance. "That's why I need to get another job, so I can save up for the fare."

"*Another* job?"

"Yes," she says. "I do a few alterations for the dry cleaner. It's not very well paid, but I can do it from home. That's why I like it."

"How often does your daughter come back to visit?"

Kay screws her nose up. "They *try* and make it back every eighteen months or so, but . . ." She dabs at her eyes with a paper napkin. "It's such a long while to wait, and the kids change so much in that time."

"What made them move?"

Kay hesitates, then shrugs. "The usual, I suppose. Better standard of living. Better weather. Barbies on the beach," she says, in the worst Australian accent I've ever heard.

A couple of people look our way and we fold over our coffees in laughter. When we've recovered, Kay wrestles her complimentary cookie from its packet and shakes the now broken pieces into her hand.

"So what brought you to Flinstead, then, Joanna?" she says. I look out of the window. While we've been sitting here, the sun has vanished and it's started to drizzle. "Not the weather, that's for sure."

"It was mainly for Alfie," I say. "I felt like I was never fully *there* for him. Do you know what I mean?"

Kay nods. "I do, hon. They're only young once."

"I wanted Alfie to grow up in a safe place, and to be by

the water. I loved living here when I was a child. And I wanted to be near Mom. Alfie gets to see her all the time now. She's on her own, too, so it's been lovely for all of us."

Kay shifts in her seat. Oh God. After everything she's just been saying about missing her grandchildren. How insensitive can I be? But before I have a chance to apologize, she's speaking again.

"You're a single mother, then?"

"Yes, well, kind of."

"Sorry, tell me to mind my own business."

"No, it's fine. It's just that . . . most people find it a little odd that Alfie's dad and I are so close but not actually together." I take a sip of coffee. "Like Simone de Beauvoir and Jean-Paul Sartre," I say, observing her reaction over the top of my cup.

Kay gives me a blank look. I thought she would. Liz Blackthorne would get the reference immediately. Which reminds me, I must give her a call and see if she's all right. I hope she doesn't think less of me for passing on the rumor about Sally McGowan. What if she was deliberately ignoring me when I saw her this morning?

"Okay. Try Helena Bonham Carter and Tim Burton? Except, no, they've split up now, haven't they? And they lived next door to each other, whereas Michael lives in the city."

"I don't think it's strange at all, dear. Makes a lot of sense to me. You're never going to get fed up with each other if you have your own space. Maybe Larry and I should have tried that. Might not have ended up in divorce court."

"Has there been anyone else, since Larry?"

Kay looks horrified. "God, no."

I laugh. "You sound like my mom. The trouble is, it's

given her a skewed view of all men, including Michael. I keep telling her he's nothing like Dad, but . . ."

Kay pats my hand. "As long as you and Michael care about each other, and about Alfie, and as long as it's what you both want, then that's all that matters in the long run."

"Yes," I agree. "It is."

I eat the last fragment of my cookie. Mom said something similar once, when she'd finally wrapped her brain around the peculiar parameters of our relationship, except she made a point of putting the emphasis on the word *both*— "as long as it's what you *both* want"—which made me feel like I was the one making all the compromises. The injured party.

"I'd better get moving," Kay says, twisting around for her coat. "Tell you what, why don't you drop by sometime and I'll show you photos of my Gillian and the grandchildren? There's a long weekend next week, isn't there? Bring Alfie with you. I have a tropical-fish tank he'll enjoy looking at. Ketifa loves them. She's named them all after characters in *Finding Nemo*."

I smile. Kay's lonely. That much is obvious.

"Thank you. I will," I say. "Alfie loves *Finding Nemo*."

12

ON MY WAY BACK TO PEGTON'S, I NOTICE A SMALL GATHERING at the end of the block. Something unusual is happening outside the hardware store.

My first thought is that someone has fallen and hurt themselves. One of Flinstead's frail retirees has tripped over a wonky paving slab. Or a mobility scooter has toppled in the wind that shoots up the road from the beach. Once, I saw a helicopter land outside the Chinese takeout and a heart-attack victim was stretchered inside and flown away.

But as I get closer I realize they're standing outside Stones and Crones and nobody is lying on the sidewalk injured. People are pressing up against the plate-glass window, pointing and exclaiming. Snippets of conversation reach my ears:

"Looks just like her, you've got to admit."

"Some kind of sick joke."

"Who did this?"

"Maybe there's something in it."

Reluctantly, I move toward the window. I've got a horrible feeling about this. And there it is. Someone's stuck an enlarged photocopy of that photo of Sally McGowan, the famous one of her at ten years old, looking directly at the camera with those unnerving eyes, and right next to it is a picture of Sonia Martins, the shopkeeper. An old one that's been cut out of the *Flinstead Shopper*—a promotional feature from when the shop first opened.

The shop is empty and the CLOSED sign hangs at the door. She always closes on Wednesdays. She's one of the few shopkeepers around here who do. Most can't afford to lose out on a day's business. So whoever's stuck these pictures up has chosen the day on purpose, to get maximum exposure. Whether it's true or not, the damage will be done.

"Never liked this place much anyway," says a woman to my right. "My friend June says she sells a lot of that Wiccan stuff."

"That's witchcraft, isn't it?" says someone else, and an uneasy murmur ripples through the crowd of onlookers.

A horrible thought pops into my mind. What if Maddie did this? She wouldn't, surely. She's not that kind of person, and yet, when I think of how she cornered me that time at the playground, how convinced she was . . .

Oh God. If this is Maddie's doing, then I'm partly responsible. Maddie doesn't mix much with the other mothers. If it weren't for me blabbing about it at book club, she might never have heard the rumor. But surely she wouldn't have done something like this. It's a horrible, spiteful thing to do. And based on what kind of evidence? A weekend trawling the internet? No, I can't believe she'd stoop this low. And yet, how well do I really know her?

"I think we should take them down," I say. "It's someone's idea of a nasty joke."

"I wouldn't get involved, if I were you," a voice from the crowd warns. "It's her store, let her deal with it."

I turn and see a woman in a gray sweat suit with greasy hair swept off her face in a tight ponytail. "But she can't, can she? She's not here."

She gives me a sullen look. "What if it's true, though? Do you really want someone like that living and working here? Someone who murdered a little kid?"

As fast as people drift away, more gather on the sidewalk to take their place. Barbara from book club appears. She stands right next to me, screwing up her eyes to read the small print. She's so close I can smell her face powder.

"Joanna, isn't this what you were talking about at book club?" she says, in that annoyingly loud, high-class voice of hers.

Heat floods into my face. I give her a withering frown. Is she stupid or something? Doesn't she realize how that might sound?

"Sorry. I wasn't implying it had anything to do with you. I was just . . ." She flounders for something to say, something to salvage the situation, but there's nothing she *can* say. She's just making it worse. She makes a face and mouths *sorry* at me. I want to tell her what an idiot she is, but all I do is sigh and give a little shake of my head.

"I can't believe someone would do this," I say, in the loudest, most indignant tone I can muster. "It's not right to make accusations about someone, especially when they're not here to defend themselves."

The man from the hardware store comes out to see what's going on. He takes one look at the pictures then silently peels them off the glass and takes them into his store. It's what I should have done. It's what I *would* have done if I weren't so worried about Barbara and her big mouth. At least, that's what I tell myself as I hurry back to work.

ANNE WILSON IS SITTING AT MY DESK DRINKING A GLASS OF water when I get back.

"Ah, here she is now," Dave says. "I'm sure Jo will work it all out for you." He's wearing his usual professional mask, but there's a slight wariness in his eyes as he looks at me.

Anne puts her glass down and gets to her feet, extending one well-manicured hand toward me. "Joanna, how nice to see you again. I'm making a nuisance of myself, I'm afraid."

I smile and try to put the last few minutes out of my mind. For the moment, at least.

"How can I help you?"

Anne sits down again and crosses her legs. She's wearing a very short skirt with sheer black tights. "I want to have a third showing of the Maple Drive property."

I glance at Dave, who's trying not to look at her legs. "Oh, I thought you'd already made an offer."

"Yes, I have. But I'd like to bring a contractor in to have a look at a few things. It's all right," she says, leaning forward. "I'm not going to change my mind. The house is perfect. Well, it *will* be, when I've completely changed it." She laughs then. A high, tinkly noise that's as false as her eyelashes. "It's just that I'm rather impatient and I'd like to get someone lined up for the job right away. You know what contractors are like. All the good ones are booked up for months, and since we're cash buyers and Mrs. Marchant isn't looking to synchronize the sale with a new purchase, I'm sure we can sign the contract and close at virtually the same time."

Dave sucks his cheeks in and I have to look away.

"Well, that does *occasionally* happen," I say. "But you

never know how long these things are going to take, and we'd always recommend—"

"I've got a very good lawyer," Anne says, as if that's all it takes to cut through the bureaucracy of buying a house. I'm starting to dislike this woman. What I'd previously interpreted as confidence now has a whiff of arrogance about it. That sense of entitlement some people have. Especially those with money. First impressions aren't always to be trusted.

"The thing is . . ." she says. "I was rather hoping it could happen without . . ." She hesitates and glances at Dave. He already knows what's coming. That's why he said, *I'm sure Jo will work it all out for you*, and gave me that funny look when I came in. ". . . without the owner being present," she says, and lets the words settle in the air before continuing.

"The changes I have in mind are fairly—how shall I put it?—*radical*. And she's hardly the friendliest of people, is she? I'm afraid she might be offended and put the property back on the market." She gives me a conspiratorial glance. "She certainly looks the type."

I keep my face as still as possible. However rude or ill-mannered our clients, and Mrs. Marchant certainly isn't the friendliest, we never, ever, badmouth them to buyers. In a town this size, it would be professional suicide. A fleeting twitch of the mouth is the furthest I've ever gone to indicate my agreement with someone, and now that I've cast Susan Marchant in the role of aggrieved ex-wife, coerced into relinquishing her lovely house, I'm not even sure whether I *do* agree with Anne Wilson's damning character analysis. There must be a reason why Susan Marchant is so unsociable. Perhaps she's depressed.

"I can't promise anything," I say. "Mrs. Marchant has always wanted to be present during showings, so it may be a little awkward." I clear my throat. "I can't really ask her not to be there."

Something flickers over Anne Wilson's face, something akin to annoyance, but it's immediately replaced by one of her effusive smiles, which I see now are not warm and generous at all but manipulative and insincere.

"But you could suggest that she might prefer *not* to be," she says. She stands up then and, once again, holds out her hand. Reluctantly, I shake it.

"I'm sure you'll find a way," she says, her voice a curious blend of honey and steel.

As the door clicks shut behind her, Dave lets out a long sigh.

13

WHENEVER THERE'S A BRIEF LULL AT WORK THE NEXT DAY, my mind inevitably wanders to those pictures stuck on Sonia Martins's shop. I make a point of updating the Pegton's window promotions more often than I normally would, and each time I go outside to check what it looks like from the street I glance toward Stones and Crones. There's no crowd gathered outside today, although Karen from book club and a woman I don't recognize are peering through the window.

I go back to my desk. Sonia Martins must know what's happened by now. How could she not? Unless the man from the hardware store decided not to show her the pictures. But if she doesn't know yet, chances are she'll find out soon enough. Flinstead is a small town. Something like that will get out. There's only one strip of stores, after all.

I try to imagine what I would do in her position. I'd have opened up the shop and carried on as usual. The worst thing would be to stay closed and avoid people. They'd be more likely to think it was true if you did that. And it can't be, can it? I mean, if Sonia Martins is Sally McGowan, would she really have chosen to open a store? All those customers trooping in and out every day, getting a close look at her. It would be far too dangerous.

"Jo," Dave says. "Someone just waved at you from the window. You look like you're a million miles away."

I glance up to see Karen and the woman she's with turning away, arms linked. It must be her mother. Mom said something about meeting her on the playground the other day. I walk toward the door and, as I do, the older woman looks back at me over her shoulder. I smile and raise my hand in a wave, but she doesn't smile back. Maybe she can't see me through the glass. Mom was right. She does look way too thin. Maybe she's sick.

Just then, my phone vibrates in my pocket. It's probably Teri. I'm supposed to be babysitting for her and her husband, Mark, this evening. She said she'd call me in the morning to confirm times. But it isn't Teri, it's Michael, and he's using his serious voice.

"There's something I need to talk to you about."

My stomach tenses. Whenever he starts a sentence like that, I panic that he's going to tell me he's met someone else—maybe even *the one*. Much as I try to kid myself that I've got the best of both worlds, this continual worry that I might actually end up with nothing at all never goes away.

"Hold on a sec, the connection's terrible."

I take my phone out to the kitchenette at the back of the office, collecting Dave's empty mug as I go. My throat tightens. Last weekend seemed different somehow. More special. Was it because he's seeing someone else? Was it guilt that made him so loving?

"I'm thinking of doing a bit more research into the Sally McGowan case."

I let out a soft, slow exhalation.

"I know it's a long shot," he says, "and it'll probably come to nothing, but I've gotten a couple of really interesting leads from a new source, and I mean *really interesting*. If there's any way I can track her down, I'd like to try and write a book about her, see if I can gain her trust and get her cooperation. Her identity would be protected, of course. I wouldn't want to create a shitstorm by disclosing where she is, but if I could tell her story of what actually happened . . . I've sounded my agent out and he's practically wetting his pants with excitement.

"The thing is . . ." He pauses. "I don't want this rumor that's going around to screw things up."

I chew the inside of my lip. I haven't heard Michael this excited about something for ages. How can I tell him the rumor's just taken on a whole new dimension and that it's probably all my fault?

"If my latest source is right," he says, "and there's a good chance he is, then Sally McGowan really is living in Flinstead. So if there's any way you could put the word out that it's all a load of garbage, you'd be doing me an enormous favor. A book like this could generate publicity. It could make us a lot of money, Joey."

Us. There's never been an *us* in relation to money. There's only ever been his money and my money and what he pays toward Alfie's care.

"That's the other thing I wanted to ask you." He hesitates, hearing my silence on the other end. "I hate not seeing you and Alfie all the time. I miss him. I miss *you*. What do you say about me moving in with you while I'm researching this book?" He laughs, almost nervously. "We could see what it's like, living together like a real couple." I hear him take a breath. "A real family, I mean. For Alfie."

I open my mouth, but nothing comes out.

"Will you at least think it over?"

I try again to speak, but all I can manage is a small squeak.

"Look, I know you're probably at work and can't say much right now, Jo, but call me when you get home. Okay?"

How I manage to make two mugs of drinkable coffee and get through the rest of the day, I don't know. It's the first time he's ever referred to us as a *real couple*, even in a jokey way. My heart does a stupid little flutter.

"Everything all right?" Dave says.

"Yeah, fine."

"You just look a little off, if you don't mind me saying. Why don't you get yourself home? I'll finish updating those listings."

"Are you sure?"

"Positive. Go on."

"Thanks, Dave."

Outside, the leaves are swirling on the sidewalk and there's a misty vapor in the air that catches at the back of my throat. I know I should go straight home. Mom picked Alfie up from school today and she's gone back to my place so she can stay with him while I babysit for Teri this evening. But she's not expecting me for another half hour, and I need to get some air and clear my head. Think things through.

I walk toward Stones and Crones and the gray wall of sea at the bottom of the road. For a few seconds I allow myself to imagine this wall moving inexorably toward me, obliterating everything and everyone in its wake, like a scene from a disaster movie.

I blink to dispel the image and hurry on toward the shop. How's Michael going to react if this business with Sonia Martins gets out of hand? And what if the allegation is true? He seems so adamant that Sally McGowan is here, and there is, it has to be said, an uncanny resemblance between her and Sonia. But if it *is* true, then surely she'd have left by now. Maybe she already has.

The thing is, even if she moved someplace else, her safety would still be compromised, because people will know what she looks like. Some hate-filled headcase will post a photo of her on Twitter and the whole thing will go viral.

But it isn't her. I feel sure it isn't.

The closer I get to Stones and Crones, the more I realize I'm pinning all my hopes on it being open as normal, catching a waft of fragrance as I pass the open door, seeing Sonia Martins in her usual position behind the counter, serving a customer while another browses peacefully among the scented candles.

As I get closer to the store, I see that the door is shut. My jaw clenches.

But there she is, huddled in a big woolly sweater behind the counter, arms crossed against her chest. I exhale in relief. The door is shut to keep out the cold, that's all. And yet, as I pause in front of the window display, pretending to examine the artfully arranged statues and charms and books, I see the expression on her face. That blank, vacant stare into the void.

Someone has told her. She knows. She looks up, and our eyes meet. Now she's looking right at me, as if she knows

I've come to gawk. I hear Barbara's voice in my head from yesterday—*Joanna, isn't this what you were talking about at book club?*—and I feel sick. What if one of Sonia's friends was in that crowd? What if they told her what they heard, described me to her?

Is that why she's looking at me as if it's all my fault?

It won't stop with pictures on a store window. That much I know.

Rumors are like seeds, scattered on the wind. There's no telling where they'll land, but land they will. Settling in cracks and crevices, the roots take hold. The seeds sprout. It doesn't matter if they're true or false. The more times they're spoken, the faster and stronger they grow. Like weeds, waving in the air.

Maybe I should break my silence, once and for all. Give myself up to the baying crowd. That's what they want, the mob. It's what they've always wanted. My suffering writ large for all the world to see.

It's been happening more and more lately. A yearning for recognition. It's the strangest of feelings—a yearning mixed with dread. For what if someone did see me? What if they looked into my eyes and knew it was me? What in heaven's name would happen then?

What in hell's?

14

WHAT WITH EVERYTHING SPINNING AROUND IN MY BRAIN, I wanted to phone and cancel tonight's sit, but in the end I couldn't bring myself to let Teri down, and I don't want to screw up with the babysitting circle before I've even started. Maybe a change of scene will help me clarify my thoughts, help me work out how to respond to Michael's suggestion.

The Monktons live on what is arguably the nicest street in Flinstead—Waterfield Grove—and their house is a large villa that must be worth at least a million.

I thought Alfie's bedroom was untidy, but Ruby Monkton's is off the scale. Toys and clothes litter the floor like debris from a tide. I can barely see the carpet beneath. And yet the room itself has been exquisitely decorated, like something out of a fairy tale. One entire wall is a mural of unicorns cavorting in a magical garden, and she has a fancy daybed—swirling soft curves of white steel—with a lacy canopy over the top. It's the sort of bedroom I dreamed of having as a child.

Hamish, who's in Alfie's class, has the room next to Ruby's. It's smaller, but no less messy, and has a pirate theme. He even has a bed in the shape of a boat. A beautifully crafted wooden boat that must have cost a fortune. I think of Alfie's tiny little room with its tired off-white walls and old blue carpet, its cheap curtains from Walmart. I've tried to make it as nice as I can by hanging a few *Star Wars* posters on the wall and buying him a *Star Wars* comforter, and I've painted his pine chest of drawers white and let him cover it with stickers. But this . . . this is something else.

Michael's words come back to me: *A book like this could generate publicity. It could make us a lot of money.* He's always wanted to write a book, and he's right: If he could pull this off and get Sally McGowan's cooperation, the papers would be full of it. It could mean a whole new life for us all. We could sell his apartment and my cottage and buy a place together. A home for the three of us. It won't be as upmarket as this place. I doubt we'll ever be able to afford something like this, but even so, the more I think about us living together, the more appealing it becomes. And I can't pretend I haven't fantasized about it.

But is it really the right thing to do? What if the reason we're so good with each other is precisely because we *don't* live together? And how do I know for sure it's what he really wants? What if he has the scent of a story and suddenly it's more convenient for him to live here? If that's the case, then what's going to happen if his sources are wrong and McGowan isn't here after all?

And even if she *is* here, and he gets to write this book, how long will it be before he gets fed up with country life and moves back downtown? Flinstead is the very *last* place he'd want to live. He jeers at it at every opportunity. He's a city boy through and through. Always has been. Always will be.

And yet, if it was just about investigating the Sally McGowan case, he wouldn't have to move all the way to Flinstead to do it, would he? We're only an hour and change away from each other and he knows he's welcome to stay whenever he likes. It might have sounded like an afterthought, the way he tacked it onto the end of the conversation, but I *know* Michael. That's how he always broaches subjects he wants to talk about. As if he has to work his way up to it, approach it indirectly. Maybe this has been weighing on his mind for ages. Ever since I moved here. Maybe even before.

I've always loved him. Ever since that time at college, when some idiot set off a smoke bomb in the common room and I had a panic attack. I honestly think I might have died of a heart attack if he hadn't been there. His calm voice talking me through it, him staying by my side the whole time, telling me I was safe. He understood what I was going through.

I told him everything that night. About the fire when I was a little girl, only a couple of years younger than Alfie is now. The smoke in my nostrils. The terror until the firefighters arrived to rescue us. Some men might have taken advantage of my vulnerability, but not Michael. There'd been a party and I'd been drinking all night. Far more than I'd ever drunk before. It was my very first semester and I was trying to keep up with everyone else. How stupid was that? Michael stayed with me for ages, and he didn't try anything. Not once. He just rubbed my back and talked to me till I fell asleep.

When I woke up he'd gone, but there was a bucket by the side of my bed and a glass of water on my bedside table with a bottle of Advil next to it and a note.

Joanna the Brave and Beautiful. That's all it said.

———

"ARE YOU GOING TO PUT YOUR TOYS AWAY BEFORE GETTING into bed?" I ask Ruby and Hamish, before the three of us settle down on Ruby's bed to read some stories.

The two of them exchange a secretive look. "No," Ruby says. "They like being on the floor."

"Lisa's coming tomorrow," Hamish says. "She usually tidies our toys."

"Who's Lisa?" I ask.

"Our housekeeper."

"Oh."

Later, when Ruby's fallen asleep and Hamish is tucked up in his boat bed, listening to *James and the Giant Peach*, I tiptoe downstairs and put the kettle on in Teri's gleaming white kitchen. I open the obscenely huge side-by-side fridge and reach in for the milk. Before he got into bed, Hamish showed me the Dracula cloak and vest he's wearing to Liam's Halloween party. It looked like something you'd pay a lot of money for in one of those costume stores.

"Mommy made it for me," he said. "And Jake's mommy's making him a werewolf costume. What's Alfie going as?"

Good question, Hamish. Good question. I smiled. "You'll just have to wait and see."

Last night, I had a look at various costume sites online. Some of them seemed reasonable enough in the photos, but I know they'll look flimsy and cheap once they arrive and I open up the package.

It's all right for Teri and Cathy. They've both got big houses and plenty of money, husbands who work in finance. Above all, they don't have jobs, which means they've got time to do all those things good moms are supposed to do. Like baking cakes and organizing birthday parties and making fantastic outfits at the drop of a hat. Like choosing themes for their children's bedrooms.

It's not that I'm envious of their lives. I'm not. I'd hate it if Alfie refused to clean his bedroom because that's what the housekeeper does. And it's not about trying to compete. I couldn't even if I wanted to. I've always been a disaster when it comes to making things. But still, if all the other boys are going to turn up in amazing costumes, Alfie will be the odd one out.

I carry my tea into the dining room extension with its massive skylights and sit down at the table. Alfie's already having to contend with being the new boy and, apart from Ketifa, he's the only non-white face in his class. The last thing he needs is something else to make him feel like an outsider.

I take a sip of tea and gaze up at the night sky. It must be romantic sitting here of an evening, under the stars. My mind drifts into a daydream: Michael is sitting opposite me and we're drinking champagne, toasting the success of his book. This is our new house and Alfie is sleeping peacefully upstairs in his beautiful new bedroom.

I pull my phone out of my pocket and check it for messages. Michael's sent me two since our phone call and I haven't answered either of them yet. It's about time I did.

I tap out a response. *Okay. You're on. Let's give it a whirl! Xxxxx*

I press SEND before I mean to. Fuck! *Let's give it a whirl!* Why the hell did I say that? It sounds so silly. So glib.

He replies at once. *I love you, Joey. Lots to talk about. I'll come tomorrow. M xxxx*

I love you, Joey. He's actually said it, after all these years.

Well, texted it. I get up and pace around the room, read his message again. And again for good measure. I float around the house in a dream. All those niggling worries about that horrible business with Sonia Martins are starting to ease off. I didn't start that rumor, and lots of people have been talking about it, not just me. It'll die down soon enough.

People will recognize those pictures for what they are: a malicious prank. This is Flinstead, after all. It's a nice town. A real community. And people *like* Stones and Crones. It's popular with locals and tourists alike. Nobody's going to want to see another independent business close down.

But if it does all go south and Michael's search for Sally McGowan goes cold because of it, well, so be it. He'll have to find another book to write. Another story. Stories are everywhere. You just have to find them. Isn't that what he told me once?

I sink into the Monktons' gorgeous cream sofa. Teri's left a couple of DVD box sets out, but I doubt I'll be able to concentrate on much this evening and there's nothing on TV. I pull out my phone again and press the Twitter app. I'll see what's trending, maybe check out the latest nonsense Trump's been coming out with, or what people think of that new drama I watched the other night. Anything to while away the hours till Teri and Mark get back.

I've got six notifications. Most of them are just telling me who liked this and who retweeted that, but there are a couple of new followers, so I check out their profiles to see if they're worth following back. One is a well-endowed spambot that I immediately block. The other is . . .

A chill passes through me. The letters swim before my eyes. The other is somebody called Sally Mac (@rumormill7).

I try to swallow, but there's no saliva in my mouth. I click on the photo, which isn't a photo at all but a cartoon avatar of a woman holding a finger to her lips—the classic gesture to keep quiet. I force myself to read her one and only tweet:

Rumors can kill.

15

I STARE AT THE SCREEN IN SHOCK. ANOTHER TWEET HAS JUST popped up: *A lie can travel halfway around the world while the truth is putting on its shoes—Mark Twain.*

Okay. So there's no way this can be the *real* Sally McGowan. If she'd gotten wind of the rumor and was worried her cover was about to be blown, the last thing she'd do is draw more attention to herself by setting up a Twitter account in the name of Sally Mac. That would be crazy.

Perhaps it's Sonia Martins. The hairs on the back of my neck prickle as I think of how she looked at me earlier today. As if she blames me for what's happened. But she doesn't know my name. Oh God, maybe she does. Barbara said it out loud, didn't she? *Joanna, isn't this what you were talking about at book club?* Anyone could have heard that and passed it on to her. It wouldn't take too much detective work on her part to discover my last name and find me on Twitter.

But then, she'd hardly start tweeting as the person she's falsely accused of being. That wouldn't make any sense. Unless she's just trying to scare me.

Her face hovers behind my eyes. If someone did one of

those aging techniques on that infamous mug shot of McGowan as a child, I wouldn't be at all surprised if Sonia Martins's face was the result. Perhaps she really *is* McGowan and she's waiting to see what happens, getting ready to pack up and try her luck in another state.

Either that, or by some amazing coincidence I just happen to have a new Twitter follower called Sally Mac who's tweeting quotes about lies and rumors. I try to convince myself that this is possible. Lots of people share the same name. You've only got to google yourself to realize that. Perhaps this is simply one of those boring accounts that spews out stupid quotes and has an app that follows random people. Not personal at all.

I take a few deep breaths to calm myself down, to put things into perspective. There's another possibility, of course. It could be one of the mothers playing some kind of joke. In fact, the more I think about this, the more likely it seems.

Uneasy, but not quite as freaked out as I was a few minutes ago, I tuck my phone into my back pocket and stand up. I need to move around. I can't just sit here worrying.

Upstairs, Ruby is curled up in a little ball on her side, clutching her doll. Hamish is flat on his back, arms flung out like a starfish, his cheeks like rosy apples. I tiptoe along the corridor and pause outside Teri and Mark's room. The door is ajar and they've left their bedside lamps on. I can't resist having a quick peek. She must have wanted me to or she wouldn't have left the lamps on and the door open. It's as if it's been staged for a showing.

The room is spacious. Pale-gray walls and dark, solid-wood flooring. Those white wooden shutters at the window that everyone seems to have these days. It's a restful, warm-looking room with a master bath. I can just glimpse the chrome bars of a heated towel rack. So different from my own small bedroom with its squeaky floorboards and mismatched furniture.

I go downstairs again and turn on the TV. Only another half hour before Teri and Mark get back and I can go home. Mom'll probably be dozing on the sofa by now. It's well past her usual bedtime.

My phone buzzes. I brace myself for another tweet from Sally Mac, but then I remember. I haven't followed her back, so I won't get notified when she tweets again. I'll have to click on her account and check for myself. Which I won't. This must be something else, and it is. It's a text message from Michael.

See you tomorrow. I'll get to you about one. M xxx

I JUMP WHEN I HEAR THE KEY IN THE DOOR, EVEN THOUGH I'VE been expecting it for the last few minutes. Teri promised they'd be back by eleven thirty and here they are, right on time. Teri sways a little as she quizzes me about the children.

"They were fine," I tell her. "Very well behaved."

"I hope you helped yourself to some chocolates and wine," she says, slurring her words.

"No, just a cup of tea."

Mark offers to drive me home, and for a second or two I'm tempted. But his eyes have a slightly glazed look about them. For all I know, he's been drinking, too, and there's something in his voice that gives me the impression he'd rather not, that Teri's *made* him ask.

"It's okay, thanks. I'm only around the corner. It won't take me five minutes."

But as soon as the front door has closed behind me and I've walked to the end of their driveway, I wish I'd said yes. There's something eerie about walking along Waterfield Grove in the dark. The silence is so thick it's almost claustrophobic, and all I can think of is that someone called Sally Mac is following me on Twitter.

I look over my shoulder, scan the street for signs of life, but it's empty. Being followed on Twitter is not the same as being followed on the street. Of course it isn't. And Flinstead has one of the lowest crime rates in the state. The odd bit of antisocial behavior by bored teenagers or mindless beach-cabana vandalism is about as bad as it gets.

Even so, I quicken my pace and, when I reach the ocean-front and see how empty it is, feel the brooding presence of the sea to my right, I'm glad I don't have too much farther to go. As I pass the derelict house, I find myself breaking into a little run. I don't slow down till I've turned onto Warwick Road and see my cottage up ahead.

By the time I put my key in the front door, I've made up my mind. I'm going to come clean with Michael tomorrow. Tell him the rumor's escalated and I'm partly to blame. I'll show him Sally Mac's tweets and tell him to rethink this book idea. I mean, if by some miracle he tracks her down, and if she agrees to being interviewed—and those are two big ifs—it's bound to create trouble. A backlash from the victim's family. More sensationalist nonsense in the papers. Hateful comments online.

We're so much less forgiving than we were back then. Or maybe not. Maybe the hatred was just as strong when Sally was released, but because there wasn't any internet it wasn't in the public domain so people didn't get all riled up. The news caused a brief stir then faded away, got replaced by something else.

He won't be happy, but he'll get over it. And if he doesn't . . . if he blames me for screwing everything up and we end up splitting up over it, well, then, maybe us living together isn't such a good idea after all.

At least I'll know what's more important to him: resurrecting McGowan, or Alfie and me.

16

WHEN I GET HOME MOM'S ASLEEP ON THE SOFA, MY THROW draped over her like a blanket. The TV is gabbling away to itself and there's a full mug of tea on the coffee table. I touch it, expecting it to be lukewarm, but it's stone-cold.

I pat her gently on the arm. "Mom, I'm back."

She opens her eyes and blinks at me. Then she sits up and yawns. "Hello, darling. I must have dropped off for a couple of seconds."

She reaches for her tea, then frowns and puts it down again.

"Sorry," I say. "I shouldn't have dragged you out. Why don't you sleep here tonight? I can make up the spare bed."

She shakes her head. "Don't be silly. Anyway, you know I prefer my own bed."

I do know this. She's told me often enough. When I lived in the city and she used to come and stay, she always complained about the mattress: too lumpy. Or the pillows: too flat. She was never an easy guest, which is why living so close to her is ideal. We can drop in for friendly visits and not have to inflict ourselves on each other for long periods of time.

But tonight is different. I don't tell her that I *want* her to stay. That I need her to. Just this once. Because then she'll ask why, and I'll have to tell her. She can be infuriatingly obtuse about Twitter, in that way some people are. I've tried to explain it to her, just like I've tried to explain it to Dave, but she just can't see the point of it: "Why do you want to talk to a bunch of strangers about nonsense?"

And if I tell her about the rumor, she'll be even more scathing. I'll end up explaining about Michael and his book and him asking me if he can move in, and though I'll have to tell her soon, I really don't think I'm up for that conversation tonight. She'll only make some kind of barbed comment about what's going to happen when the book is finished, and the implication will be clear.

"Shall I make you another cup of tea before you go?" I ask her.

"No, I'd rather get back, if you don't mind."

She kisses me on the cheek and I give her a hug.

"Are you okay, darling?" she says as we separate, her hands still resting on my shoulders. "You look a bit worried about something."

She's always been able to tell when something's on my mind. But what can I say that won't freak her out? I'm worried I'm being followed on Twitter by some woman who murdered a five-year-old boy when she was ten. I'm worried that I'm complicit in the false accusation of Sonia Martins and responsible, at least in part, for ruining her reputation.

And I'm also worried that Michael has suddenly announced he wants to move in with me and Alfie and be a family. I'm worried that he's pinning all his hopes on tracking Sally McGowan down and she's going to get wind of this rumor and disappear before he has a chance to meet her. I'm worried that, if that happens, he'll change his mind about living here and we'll go back to how we were before. And I'm worried that if he *does* change his mind, we won't be *able* to go back to how we were before. That we will, in effect, be over.

"Not really," I say. "I'm just tired, that's all."

AT THREE FORTY-SEVEN A.M. SOMETHING INSIDE ME SNAPS and I give up the effort to get to sleep. I sit up and switch the lamp on. My worries have mutated and multiplied like rogue cells and, though I don't want to look at my phone, I find myself tapping it into life and swiping the screen till I see the Twitter icon. The little white bird, its beak open mid-tweet, its wings lifted in flight. Irrepressible.

I click on my followers. She's still there. Right at the top of the list. Sally Mac (@rumormill7). My thumb hovers over her name, then presses it before I can change my mind. Judging by the new tweets, the last of which was posted just fifty-seven seconds ago, she, too, is finding it hard to sleep. I read them all, from top to bottom:

Rumors voiced by women come to nothing—Aeschylus

Rumor grows as it goes—Virgil

What some invent, the rest enlarge—Jonathan Swift

A lie can travel halfway around the world while the truth is putting on its shoes—Mark Twain

And then there it is, the very first one:

Rumors can kill.

SO THEY'RE ALL LITERARY QUOTES, APART FROM "RUMORS can kill," which is a saying and impossible to attribute to anyone in particular, although of course someone, somewhere, must have said or written it down first. Should I read anything into that? That the very first tweet she sent is *not* a literary quote and that it's shorter and more obviously threatening than the others?

Because I do. Clearly I do.

I get out of bed and put on my robe, pull some socks on before padding downstairs, trying not to make the stairs squeak.

THREE HOURS LATER, I'M STANDING AT THE KITCHEN WINDOW, watching the sun rise. The bones in my face ache from lack of sleep, and the headache that's been hovering behind my eyes all night now flares out toward my temples and ebbs across the top of my skull. What would help, apart from the two Advil I've just swallowed, would be to walk on the beach. Let the sound of the surf lull my frayed nerves, the astringent smell of seawater scour my nostrils and clear my head.

It's a tempting thought. Alfie never wakes till after seven. I could be back before he even starts to stir. I miss my solitary early-morning walks. Before Alfie was born, I used to walk along the river, buy a coffee before heading back. And when I was a teenager, living here, I'd sometimes get up early before school and head down to the beach, walk along the shoreline if the tide was out. On a good day, I might get to see a barge sailing by, or find something unusual that the tide had washed up: a pleasingly smooth pebble or a pretty shell for my collection, an unusually shaped piece of driftwood to hang from the picture rail in my bedroom.

But I'd never leave Alfie alone in the house. Too many bad things could happen. He could wake up early and panic when he can't find me. Trip over something and hit his head. Fall down the stairs and land in a crumpled, broken heap at the bottom.

Or maybe he wouldn't panic at all. Maybe he'd just get up and help himself to breakfast. But even then he might shovel too many cornflakes in his mouth and start choking.

Then of course there's fire. My own worst nightmare. If a fire broke out, Alfie might not wake up at all. He'd be overcome by fumes as he slept in his bed. There are so many things that could go wrong. He could open the front door and go out on the street. Cross the street without looking and get run over. Or someone might see him, a beautiful little boy still in his *Star Wars* pajamas, and pluck him into their arms. Drive off with him. An opportunistic abduction. And all because his selfish mother craved an early-morning stroll on the beach.

No. There's no way I'd do that. I'll take the scenic route to work after I've dropped him off at school. Even five minutes on the beach is better than nothing.

I go into the living room and draw the curtains, settle down on the sofa with my iPad. Resisting the temptation to look at Twitter again, I find myself scrolling through more articles about Sally McGowan. Then I remember what Michael told me about her being helped by a former WITSEC officer, which sets me off on a whole new tangent. It isn't long before I stumble across a piece in the *Post*.

WITNESS PROTECTION: A LIFE SENTENCE
By Martin Knight

WEDNESDAY, MARCH 12, 2014
The Post

WITSEC (Witness Security Program) protects members of the public deemed to be at risk of serious harm— witnesses to organized crime who are often criminals themselves. Some states also have their own witness protection arrangements for crimes not covered by the federal program. Martin Knight, whose documentary *In Identity Limbo* will be aired on Friday, March 14, on PBS, explores the psychological impact of adopting a new identity.

The inner workings of witness protection have always been shrouded in secrecy, and rightly so. What little we *think* we know is largely the result of various myths and clichés that abound in popular culture. One of these myths is that people in witness protection are set up for life at the expense of the state, enjoying material trappings that many think they do not deserve. The tabloid press does little to prevent the proliferation of such views. In reality, protected persons are encouraged to become financially independent as soon as they are able.

Being in witness protection is nowhere near as glamorous as a Hollywood movie. It's been likened to a life sentence and often causes lasting psychological damage.

Imagine having to leave your old life behind at an instant's notice: your family and friends, your possessions, your home—everything that defines you. Imagine being taken somewhere new and strange and having to learn about someone else's life—their personal history, their family, the places they've lived—because that's what you must now become: an entirely *new* person. There may be only a handful of people who know who and where you are. It's hard to make friends because you can never be your true self with them, and the closer you get to someone, the harder it is to keep on lying.

"Mommy? Mommy? Where are you?"

I rub my eyes and yawn. "Down here, darling. Come and have your breakfast."

I heave myself off the couch. The documentary was aired almost four years ago, but it might still be available to watch. I'll have a look later. Maybe Michael and I can watch it together. That's if I manage to stay awake long enough.

17

THE SEA IS STILL, EERILY SO. A VAST GRAY MILLPOND AS FAR
as the eye can see. Despite the chill in the air, I have the urge
to strip off and swim naked. Slip below the glassy surface
and push into a long, gliding breaststroke. Feel the cold
water slip against my skin like a silk sheet. But though the
beach is empty except for me and the seagulls, I'm far too
timid to take my clothes off in broad daylight on an exposed
stretch of sand. Someone might come down the cliff path, a
jogger or dog-walker, or someone else like me, drawn to the
water's edge, as humans have been since time immemorial.
And anyway, I have to be at work in twenty minutes.

I follow the tide line and watch my sneakers leave im-
prints on the hard-packed wet sand. There's something
dreamlike about this in-between space that straddles sea and
land. Something magical. As I surrender to the two-beat
rhythm of my steps, the muscles in my neck and shoulders
unclench and the sensation of dread that's been hanging
over me since last night recedes like the tide. But it's still
there, lurking in the pit of my stomach. The tide always
rises.

I've almost reached one of the groynes that divide the beach into sections—horizontal boards bolted into wooden uprights—when I spot a lone figure up ahead. A tall woman standing still and facing the water. Something about her is familiar. Her height and posture, perhaps. Her hair.

As I draw closer, I see who it is and instinctively want to avoid her. But it's too late for that. She has turned her head to one side and registered my approach. If I turn back now or swerve inward, toward the seawall and the boardwalk, it will be obvious I'm avoiding her. Perhaps if she weren't a client, I wouldn't care so much, but then, if she weren't a client, I wouldn't know her in the first place.

"Good morning," I say, not knowing how she'll respond, or even if she will.

"Miss Critchley," she says, inclining her head toward me, almost smiling. Away from her house, she seems less hostile.

Her gaze returns to the horizon. "It looks different every day, doesn't it?" she says. "The ocean."

I can't believe she's actually initiated a conversation. I'm about to say that, yes, it does, when she speaks again.

"I want to apologize," she says.

"What for?" Of course, I know exactly what she wants to apologize for. Her coldness. Her distinct lack of courtesy. But professionalism dictates that I act surprised.

"It's that house," she says. "It holds so many bad memories." She clears her throat. "Sometimes I think he's still there." She laughs then. A dry, dismissive sound. "Even though I know for a fact he's dead and buried."

"Are you talking about Mr. Marchant?" I ask, revising my theory from philandering *ex*-husband to philandering *late* husband.

Her head whips around. "Did you know him? My father?"

"Your father? No. No, I didn't. Sorry, I assumed you were talking about your husband."

"The house belonged to my father," she says. "I inherited it when he died."

"Oh, I see."

We fall silent. I'm unsure whether the conversation has finished. I presume it has, and therefore I need to say goodbye and continue with my walk, but then I remember Anne Wilson's request about viewing the house again with her contractor. I've been dreading the phone call with Mrs. Marchant, but maybe I can bring it up here. It might be easier now.

"Anne Wilson wants to bring a contractor to look at the house," I say. How can I phrase this? "If it makes things any easier, you don't have to be there. You could drop the keys off and I'll accompany them."

"She's not going to change her mind, is she?" Her voice is sharp. Anxious.

"I don't think so. At least, that wasn't the impression she gave."

"What does she want to do, then?"

"Just a few changes to the layout, I think."

Susan Marchant tilts back her head and inhales deeply through her nose. "It wouldn't bother me if she gutted it and started again. I have no emotional connection to that house. None whatsoever. Well, that's not entirely true. I *do* have an emotional connection to it, but it's not a healthy one, if you know what I mean."

I don't know what she means, but I'm guessing she had a difficult relationship with her father. An unhappy childhood, perhaps. I think of Sally McGowan's early years. The awful things I've read.

"You've heard that poem by Philip Larkin, I suppose?" she says. "The one about your parents fucking you up?" She turns slightly, to gauge my reaction, to see if I'm one of those people who take offense at the F-word. Plenty of those around here, I should think.

I nod and wait for her to continue.

"My father abused me, sexually, for the best part of ten years. The *worst* part of ten years. And he *did* mean to."

I'm shocked. Not at the bald facts of her confession, although of course all abuse is shocking. But I'm shocked at her coming out with it like that. To me, her real estate agent, of all people. Down here on the beach.

But then, why shouldn't she tell me? Why *should* she keep such horrors to herself? Why should anyone?

"That's horrible," I say, cringing at the lameness of my response.

"I didn't want the house in the first place," she says. "It's a millstone around my neck. I just want to be rid of it." She sniffs. "I don't want the money, either. I'm giving it all to a charity for victims of abuse."

Her eyes slide toward me. She almost smiles. "He'd have hated that."

She takes a woolen hat out of her coat pocket and pulls it down over her head, stuffing her hair in at the sides.

"I'll drop the keys off later," she says. Her voice is brisk again. Businesslike. It's as if the last minute never happened. As if she hasn't just disclosed the deepest part of herself.

"I'm heading out of town this afternoon. I doubt I'll be back until a few days before closing."

She holds out her hand—a stiff and formal gesture. "Goodbye, Miss Critchley."

"Goodbye, Mrs. Marchant."

We shake hands, then she strides off across the sand, head down, looking like a woman on a mission to get the hell out of this place as fast as humanly possible.

18

ABOUT HALF AN HOUR AFTER I GET TO WORK, MICHAEL SENDS
me a text message asking if I'm still okay to meet him for
lunch at one. He's about to leave the city.

I check with Dave and he says he'll be back in time.

"I'm off to do a couple of appraisals first," he says, pulling on his jacket and grabbing his iPad from his desk. "The
office is all yours." He winks at me. "Don't do anything I
wouldn't do."

When his hand is on the door handle, he stops and turns
around. "I meant to tell you," he says. "Susan Marchant
dropped her keys off about five minutes before you got here.
She actually smiled at me." He shakes his head. "People always surprise you, don't they?" And with that he is gone,
striding off toward his car.

I've taken several calls, chased two escrow agents who
have been dragging their feet, and commiserated with a client whose sale has just fallen through when I get an email
notification on my phone.

It's from Liz Blackthorne with "Apologies to All" as the
subject line.

Dear Book Club Friends,

I'm really sorry but I won't be able to make our next meeting, or indeed the one after that. Is it possible that someone else could host this time? I will be in touch about future arrangements.

Regards

Liz x

PS Enjoy your *Frankenstein*.

That's odd. Liz's emails are usually much chattier. This sounds far too formal, and what does she mean, she'll be in touch about future arrangements? It's almost as if she's preparing the ground for leaving the group altogether, but surely not.

Everyone knows it's *Liz's* group. She's always at pains to say we don't need a leader, that ours is a *collaborative* book club, but Liz *is* our leader. If it weren't for her keeping us all on track, it would turn into a free-for-all, with everyone going off on tangents and Barbara dominating every discussion, not to mention Maddie and her endless anecdotes, and Karen and her insatiable curiosity about everyone's love life, or lack of one.

I tap out a quick reply.

Sorry to hear that, Liz. Hope everything's okay? Maybe we can meet for coffee soon?

Love Jo xx

Maybe I should give her a call and see what's up. I've been meaning to, ever since seeing her in the street the other day. She looked so distracted and, what with this email, now

I'm wondering whether something bad has happened. A family emergency, perhaps.

But her phone rings unanswered. Oh well, I don't have time to worry about it right now. If she doesn't respond to my email, I'll drop by later. See if she's all right.

MICHAEL IS ALREADY SEATED WHEN I ARRIVE. IT DOESN'T surprise me in the least that he suggested Leonard's. It's the latest addition to Flinstead's culinary venues—one of those stylish hipster restaurants that's more suited to Tribeca or LA than a small seaside town past its best. He looks good against all the exposed brickwork and steel. Edgy and urban and impossibly attractive.

There's a bottle of sparkling wine in a bucket on the table. He isn't normally one for romantic gestures, although *Joanna the Brave and Beautiful* was pretty cool. But then, ours isn't your typical romance. At least it hasn't been, till now.

I raise my eyebrows. "A quick lunch, you said. I won't be able to drink much of that. *Some* of us have to go to work, you know."

He leans forward to kiss me. This feels like a date and I'm awkward in a way I wouldn't be normally, aware of the dark circles under my eyes and my bitten nails. I've been gnawing away at them even more since Sally Mac decided to follow me on Twitter. Which I *have* to tell him about. But not yet. He looks so happy and relaxed. I don't want to spoil things.

I tell myself his good mood is because of us. Because of me. That working on the Sally McGowan book is entirely coincidental.

"You look tired," he says.

Okay, so maybe he needs to work on the romance thing.

"Still beautiful, though," he adds, and pours me half a glass of Prosecco.

We chink glasses and Michael hooks his foot around my ankle, works it up my calf. If I didn't have to go back to work this afternoon, I know exactly where this celebration would end. Is that why I'm so eager to agree to this latest plan of his? Because of something as basic and animal as sex? It says something that I know more about the geography of his face and body than I do about his mind, but then we've always skated around the edges of our inner lives. Letting each other in just as far as was needed and no farther. Why *is* that? How have we let that happen?

While we're eating, we discuss the practicalities of him moving in. What he's going to do about his apartment. How much stuff he'll bring over. I can't quite believe this is happening.

"I thought I'd rent it out on Airbnb," he says. "That way, I only have to bring my clothes and personal bits and pieces. Leave all the bigger stuff there."

It's a good idea, I know it is. It'll be quicker than subletting it and there's no room for any of Michael's furniture in my cottage. But that annoying little voice has started up again. Because it's also more temporary, isn't it? Easier for him to move back in when he's had enough of playing house with Alfie and me.

I can't hold the words in much longer.

"You *are* sure this is what you want? That this isn't just because of . . ." I silently mouth the name: *Sally McGowan*.

The effect is instantaneous, as I knew it would be. He

sets down his fork and stares at me as if I've accused him of something monstrous.

"What do you take me for, Joey?"

His voice is a little louder than it needs to be. The buzz of chatter around us dims, or maybe I'm just imagining that, being overly self-conscious because this is a private conversation in a public place.

My chest is tight with emotion. I should never have said it. But now that I've started, I can't stop. I have to let my worries out before it's too late and arrangements have been made. I can't let a romantic lunch cloud my vision. It's too important. This is my future. Alfie's future. He'll be devastated if Michael moves in, only to move out again a few months later. He won't understand.

I'll be devastated, too. I know that now.

"It just seems a bit . . . unexpected, that's all. One minute we're jogging along like we always have, then I tell you about that rumor and all of a sudden you want to move in."

"Look, I'll admit it might seem that way," he says. He exhales slowly, pushes a piece of chicken around on his plate with his fork. "But honestly, I've been wanting to ask you for months." He puts down his glass and looks directly into my eyes. "Years, if you must know."

Now it's my turn to stare. "Years?"

"You've always been so fiercely independent. I thought if I asked for more, you might . . . I don't know, pull up the drawbridge completely."

I clasp my hands on my lap. Is he actually saying what I think he is? That he's been too scared to tell me how he feels? That I've basically been pushing him away all this time?

"I . . . I always assumed you . . ." My voice breaks. Any second now I'm going to start crying over my pasta. I shut my eyes tight and focus on my breath. "I always assumed you wanted the freedom to just take off whenever you liked."

Michael reaches across the table and strokes my cheek with his finger. "What a couple of idiots we both are."

"You can say that again."

"What a couple of idiots we both are."

I laugh through my tears. "Shut up and finish your chicken before it gets cold."

"See?" he says. "That's what I've always loved about you, Joanna Critchley. Your kind, gentle manner."

When the waitress asks us if we want any dessert, Michael's foot starts working its way up my calf again. There's only one dessert we both want now, but that's going to have to wait till tonight. We shake our heads and ask for the check instead.

As we leave the restaurant and step out onto the street, we're like one of those soppy couples in a romantic movie. The bit at the end where, after all the misunderstandings and confusion, all the tears and the heartache, they've finally found each other again and are about to live happily ever after.

But then the shouting begins.

19

street. Voices raised in anger. A gathering crowd.

"What's happening over there?" Michael says, already pulling away from me.

I recognize Sonia Martins's white complexion and dark hair from here, see the fury on her face.

I tug at his arm. "I was going to tell you. Someone's been sticking pictures of Sally McGowan on the window of the New Age shop and saying the woman who runs the store is her."

Michael curses under his breath, and before I can stop him he's crossing the road. There's no choice but to follow him. When we get there, two women are jabbing their fingers at her and flinging accusations. One of them is the woman with the greasy ponytail from the other day. She's wearing the same gray sweat suit and she's with a pasty-faced woman with a whining toddler in a stroller. They're calling Sonia Martins a child murderer. A filthy, dangerous monster who should be locked up forever.

Sonia snatches the bits of paper they're thrusting under her nose and rips them into pieces. "How dare you spread these vicious lies!" she shouts. "How dare you! Get away from here or I'll call the police."

"You can't tell us to go away. This is a public street."

"Yeah, we have more right to be here than you do."

Suddenly Michael's taking control of the situation. Steering Sonia Martins into her shop, telling the crowd that the show's over and that he's known this lady for years and can categorically vouch for the fact that she is *not* Sally McGowan. The expression on Sonia Martins's face is caught between gratitude and confusion, and she allows Michael, and now me—for what else can I do but tag along?—to accompany her into the shop.

Sonia is shaking all over. She fumbles in her pocket and brings out the keys. Turns the key in the lock and flips the CLOSED sign, sags against the glass.

"Thank you," she says to Michael. "I should call the police. It's a crime what they're doing, isn't it? Making false accusations? This could ruin my business." She glances nervously out of the window. "If it hasn't already."

A few people are still standing around, peering in at us, but most of them have moved on.

"Can we make you a cup of tea or something?" Michael says.

"No, no, I'm fine. Thank you for what you said out there. That was kind, considering we've never even met."

Michael gives a little shake of his head, as if to say, *It's nothing.* Her eyes dart toward me. "I've seen you before, though, haven't I? You're a customer." She narrows her eyes. "I saw you yesterday as well. I must admit, at the time I thought maybe you had something to do with . . ." She spreads her hands in the air—a gesture of hopelessness. ". . . with all this."

Michael throws me a sharp look.

"Me? No, absolutely not. I did see the pictures stuck on the window that first time. I was going to take them down, but then the man from the shop next door came out and removed them."

"Chris, yes. He called me. I was hoping it would all go away, that it was just someone's idea of a nasty joke."

"I can help you refute this rumor," Michael says.

Ah, so that's what he's up to. I should have known. Michael Lewis. Never one to miss the chance of firing off some copy. Anything to get a byline. Even in a two-bit local rag.

He reaches into his back pocket and pulls out his wallet, takes out one of his business cards. "Michael Lewis. I'm a freelance journalist. The sooner you can get your side of things out there, the better. We can nip this thing in the bud, but we have to act fast."

Sonia's face has changed. She clenches her fists at her sides. "So that's what all this is about. A story in a paper! Get out of here! Get out now!"

She pushes past us and unlocks the door, stands there with it open. "Go on. Leave now before I call the police and have you arrested for harassment."

"No," Michael says. "You don't understand. This is just going to get worse. These things always do. We need to get something in the paper as soon as we can. It's the only way you're going to—"

"Get out. Both of you. Now!"

"Come on, let's go," I say. "I'm sorry about this, Sonia, I really am. Michael?"

Michael puts his card on the counter and follows me out.

"Call me if you change your mind" is the last thing he says to her as she slams the door on us.

"For Christ's sake, Michael. What's wrong with you? You could see how upset she was."

He's walking so fast I can barely keep up with him.

"I really fucked that up, didn't I? What was I thinking, pushing my card on her so soon?" He slows his pace to let me catch up. "Why didn't you tell me about this before?" An accusing tone has crept into his voice. "I could have come up earlier and talked to her. She's never going to give me an interview now."

He swerves to get out of the way of a group of giggling teenagers. This isn't how the afternoon was meant to pan out. Our lovely, romantic lunch ruined, and all because of this stupid, stupid rumor.

"How do you know for sure she *isn't* McGowan?"

"Because she hasn't run away. And anyway, it doesn't tie in with any of the information I've received."

"What do you think will happen now? Will she pack up and move again, even if the rumor's attached itself to someone else?"

"I've no idea, but there's a good chance she will. Just to be on the safe side. If I could write that woman's story, do a piece about false accusations and what's happened to other innocent people in similar cases, it might all blow over in a few days. But if she won't even talk to me . . ."

"Maybe she *will* talk to you once she's calmed down."

Then I remember something Maddie said, the day she cornered me on the playground. Something about feeling bad about passing the information on because she knew Liz was friends with Sonia Martins.

I slip my hand into Michael's and give it a squeeze. "I

know someone who's friends with her. The woman who runs my book club. Perhaps I can ask her to put in a good word for you. It's worth a try, isn't it?"

"Yes, it is."

He stops walking and draws me into his chest, wraps his arms around my shoulders, and holds me close.

"Sorry I snapped at you." His breath is warm on my neck. "It's not the end of the world, what's happened. I can still get a story out of the false-accusations thing. With or without Sonia Martins. But preferably *with*."

"And *I'm* sorry I didn't tell you about the pictures."

20

AS SOON AS I GET HOME FROM WORK AND PUT MY KEY IN THE door, I'm aware that the house already smells different. It smells of Michael, and it's a nice smell. Not so much a fragrance, although there is, perhaps, the tiniest hint of aftershave in the air. It's more his own unique scent and possibly the fact that the house isn't empty, like it usually is. An occupied space always smells different from an empty one.

He's hunched over his laptop in the back room, typing up notes, preparing the ground for a possible interview with Sonia Martins and checking facts about previous incidents of false accusations. Innocent people hounded out of their homes and jobs, driven to suicide in one tragic case, and all because of a rumor that's taken hold.

"Any luck with your friend?" he says.

"Her phone keeps going to voicemail, but I'll pop by there later. I have to pick Alfie up now from his after-school club. Are you coming?"

He twists his mouth and I know that he's torn. Torn between wanting to surprise Alfie and needing to carry on with his work. This is what it's going to be like from now on. I have no illusions about that. Being a freelance journalist is tough, even for someone like Michael, who has tons of experience and contacts. Besides, chasing stories is in his blood. I've always known that.

He snaps his laptop shut and stands up. "You haven't told him anything yet, have you?"

"No. I thought we'd tell him together."

"Good idea." He pulls me into his arms and hugs me for so long it's me who pulls back first.

"Do you really think McGowan's gone to ground?"

He sighs. "I've been thinking about that. She'd only go to all the hassle of moving if she thought she was in real danger, and at the moment she isn't. Not if the finger's pointing at someone else. I'm still going to try and put a pitch together for a book. Even if I don't manage to find her, there are other angles I can use."

I bury my face in his neck. I still haven't told him about the Twitter thing, and I should. I should tell him right now. Get it all out in the open. I don't want there to be any secrets between us. We've wasted enough time as it is. But after all the drama of this afternoon I don't think I can take it if he reacts badly. And anyway, there haven't been any more tweets. It's just someone messing around. It has to be.

ALFIE CAN BARELY CONTAIN HIS EXCITEMENT WHEN HE SPOTS his dad standing next to me. He's already thrilled that it's the Friday of a holiday weekend, but this is the icing on the cake. I'm aware of some of the other mothers' curious glances at Michael as he hoists Alfie onto his shoulders. It's the first time they've seen him, although Michael tends to draw admiring glances wherever he is. I'm sure that's one of the reasons he's managed so well since going freelance. Out of all the dads at the school playground, he's definitely the best-looking, although of course I'm biased in that respect.

Not that his good looks and boyish charm worked their magic with Sonia Martins. But maybe they will, given time. If I can just speak to Liz . . .

"Are you staying tonight, Daddy?"

I look up at Alfie sitting on those broad shoulders, thrilled to be seeing his daddy again so soon.

"Yes," Michael says. "I'm . . ." He catches my eye, suddenly unsure of what to say.

"Daddy's coming to stay with us to work from Flinstead for a while," I say, which seems the most sensible explanation. For now, at least.

Alfie roars with delight and sticks both arms in the air in a gesture of triumph.

"Be careful, Alfie. Hold on tight!"

I might just as well be talking to myself.

LIZ'S FRONT-DOOR BELL RESOUNDS DEEP WITHIN THE HOUSE. It's one of those long chimes with eight notes. I wait, expecting any second now to see the shape of her walking toward the frosted-glass panel in the door. I've never dropped by unannounced before. I hope she doesn't mind. As for asking her to put in a good word for Michael with Sonia, I've no idea what she'll say. She might even blame me for what's been happening. Me and my big mouth.

I glance at the windows of her front room, but the blinds are closed. Perhaps she's in the bathroom. I press the bell again. As the last dong vibrates and there's still no sign of her, I step closer to the door and peer through the patterned frosting. It feels wrong doing this, as if I'm spying on her, intruding on her personal space, and yet I feel sure she's in. I don't know why. It's just a feeling I have.

The corridor with its dark-green-painted floorboards stretches to the back of the house. I see the fuzzy silhouette of the half-moon console table she keeps her phone on, and the old-fashioned umbrella stand next to it. My gaze drifts past the newel post and the balusters of the staircase on the right to the arrangement of photos on the wall. Arty black-and-white shots of old storefronts and houses. There's no sign of her coming downstairs, and I'm starting to feel really uncomfortable now. What if her neighbors can see me? One of them might come and investigate. They're big on Neighborhood Watch around here.

I step back. She's out. She must be.

I walk up the path to the sidewalk, pausing at the gate to take one last look. A shadow flits across one of the upper windows that stare back at me. A disconcerting blink.

I suppose it could have been a strand of my hair caught in the breeze. Or one of those annoying dark spots or filaments that sometimes float across my field of vision.

And yet I'm sure it wasn't. I'm sure it was Liz, watching me from upstairs.

When I first got out, I was terrified. It felt like I was wearing a sign with my name on it in big black letters for all to see. The only time I felt safe was when I got back home and locked myself in my bedroom, when I drew the curtains and wedged the chair under the door handle. Only then did I relax. I was used to being locked up.

I got braver as time went on. Learned how to walk down a street without trembling every time someone walked toward me. Learned how to speak to people in stores. The trick is not to act too shy and awkward. Inhabit your own body, they told me. Own your own voice. But don't get too confident, either. Don't draw attention to yourself. Appearing normal is a balancing act. Tip too far one way or the other and people start to notice you. The loud woman. The timid woman. The beautiful woman. The ugly woman. The woman who's always smiling. The woman who never smiles. You have to find the middle ground and stick to it.

Age helps. It's definitely gotten easier, the older I've become. Middle-aged women are virtually invisible. Isn't that what they say?

But now the cloak is starting to slip. The net is closing in on me. And I'm tired of running scared all the time. Tired of being the hunted.

They want a monster. I'll give them a monster.

21

KAY LIVES TWO DOORS DOWN FROM FATIMA. I GIVE THE EXTE-
rior of the house a quick visual sweep. It's a modest shingled
townhouse that needs repainting. If Kay were selling her
house, I might say something like "within walking distance
of all Flinstead amenities." When a house doesn't have much
going for it appearance-wise, it's practicalities you have to
focus on. Practicalities that will sell it in the end. That and a
reasonable price, of course.

Alfie hops from foot to foot on her doorstep. He's been
restless ever since Michael got a call about his apartment
and had to shoot off. We'd been having a great holiday weekend till then, relaxing together, the three of us, walking on
the beach and playing games. But the sooner he gets tenants
installed the better. Then I remembered Kay's offer of bringing Alfie to see her tropical fish.

She opens the door wearing a striped cook's apron. Her
face breaks into a welcoming smile. "Good timing," she says.
"I've just baked some chocolate chip cookies."

Alfie shoots in past her legs and into the living room.
"Where are the fish?" he demands.

"Alfie, that's very rude. You don't just run into people's houses without being asked. Come back and take your shoes off."

Kay laughs. "It's fine. Really. Come on in and I'll put the kettle on."

Five minutes later I'm sitting in Kay's front room watching her pour the tea. It's too weak and watery for me, but I don't like to say anything. The décor is dated and as far from minimal as it's possible to be. Patterned 1970s carpet, chintzy overstuffed chairs, and little end tables that gleam with polish. *In need of some updating.*

I have a sudden flash of recall: my grandparents' living room. Me perched on the edge of the sofa, a plate of peanut butter sandwiches balanced on my knees, and Granddad's guide dog, Pepper, a chocolate Labrador, sitting at attention in front of me, waiting patiently for a dropped crumb. Nana would be in one armchair, her permed hair sprayed into a silver helmet, and Granddad would be in another. I can still see those opaque eyes that veered and rolled in their sockets. I couldn't stop looking at them. Even though I knew he would never see again, I always prayed for a miracle.

Kay's curtains match the sofa, just like Nana and Granddad's did—although their house was much messier than this—and there's a scalloped valance with a fringe. Glass-fronted display cabinets stand on either side of the small tiled fireplace, teapots in one, porcelain figurines and framed photographs in the other, one of which I recognize as Ketifa in her school uniform.

The aquarium has pride of place on the sideboard. Alfie perches on a stool in front of it, his eyes glued to the magical underwater scene playing out before him. I've never seen him sitting so still.

"It's Nemo and Marlin," he says in wonder as two orange clownfish glide past. Kay crouches down next to him and points out some of the others. "See that yellow one at the bottom, the one with the funny mouth? That's a yellow watchman goby. And look at the shiny gold one next to that rock. You'll never guess what that one's called."

Alfie taps his finger gently on the side of the glass, and the fish darts away and disappears into the fronds of a plant.

"It's a licorice gourami," Kay says.

Alfie giggles. "Grandma likes licorice."

"And so do I," Kay says, ruffling Alfie's hair. "But I wouldn't want to eat my lovely gourami."

I sit on the armchair opposite and notice how natural she is with him. He seems to have taken to her instantly. Probably because she's talking to him in a very sensible, matter-of-fact way and not using that silly high-pitched voice some people use when talking to children.

"Here, let me show you something," she says. She eases herself off the floor. Then she walks over to a table by the window and picks up a chart with pictures of different tropical fish and their names underneath.

"See if you can find any of these in my tank," she says, spreading it out on the carpet. Alfie leaps off his stool and studies it intently.

Kay and I try not to laugh as we watch his little head bob from the poster to the tank and back to the poster again. A wistful expression steals over Kay's face.

"I'd love to have been a kindergarten teacher," she says. "I think I'd have been good at it."

"What stopped you?" I say.

She laughs, but there's a bitter edge to it. "It wasn't really an option, dear."

"Why's that?"

She shrugs. "Oh, you know how it is. Didn't work hard enough at school. Married too young. Had Gillian." A shadow passes over her face. Then she smiles, becomes brighter. "Talking of Gillian, let me show you some photos."

She unlocks the door of one of the display cabinets and lifts out two framed photographs, brings them over for me to look at.

A tanned, freckle-faced young woman with dark-blond hair streaming in the breeze beams at us from a wide expanse of white sand, the turquoise ocean in the distance. She's leaning in toward an extremely good-looking young man in a pair of board shorts.

"That's my Gillian," Kay says. "With her husband, Carl."

"What a lovely couple."

"And these two little terrors are my grandchildren, Callie and Marcus," she says, smiling indulgently.

"They're gorgeous. How old are they?"

"Callie's three. And Marcus is six."

"Ah, so he's the same age as Alfie," I say, knowing full well what's going to happen next and, right on cue, Alfie's head spins around. "I'm six and a *quarter*," he says, indignantly.

Kay laughs. "That quarter makes all the difference, doesn't it?"

"What's in there?" Alfie says, pointing to a basket on the floor by Kay's chair.

Kay sets the photos on the coffee table and lifts the basket onto her lap. She unties the bows securing the lid. "This," she says, proudly, "is my sewing basket."

"Mommy uses an old cookie tin for her sewing things," Alfie says.

I laugh. "Yeah, a couple of old needles and a few spools

of thread. I can just about sew on a button, and I even manage to mess that up sometimes."

Kay takes out a beautifully embroidered needle case and strokes it with her thumbs. "I learned from my mother," she says. "Before . . ." Her breath catches. She unpops the case, which opens like a book. ". . . before she got ill and couldn't hold a needle anymore."

Alfie watches with interest as she turns each felt page to reveal different-sized needles neatly inserted in each one.

"And of course, we learned at school. The girls did needlework and the boys did woodwork." She grins. "None of this gender equality in those days."

Alfie's attention returns to the fish tank, and my mouth arranges itself into the obligatory smile. Kay and I don't really have much in common, but she's a nice woman. I don't mind sitting and looking at her photos and drinking tea with her. It's a neighborly thing to do, and Alfie's just loving those fish. He's particularly taken with the little skull embedded in the sand at the bottom. Tiny fish like turquoise slivers keep darting in and out of the eye sockets. It's mesmerizing.

"To be honest, I'd like to be a bit handier with a needle." I lower my voice. "Alfie's been invited to Liam's Halloween birthday party next week. I'll probably end up ordering some overpriced crap online."

Kay puts the basket on the floor and reaches for her teacup. "Why don't I make something for him?"

"Oh no, that wasn't what I meant at all. I couldn't possibly . . ."

"It wouldn't take me long." Kay's gaze settles fondly on Alfie. "Unless, of course, your mom wants to run something up?" She looks pensive all of a sudden. "I know I would, if Marcus or Callie were around."

I laugh. "The only thing my mom could run up is a hill."

Kay pats my knee. "That's settled, then. All we need to do now is decide on the outfit."

"Darth Vader!" Alfie shouts. "I want to go as Darth Vader."

Kay's brow creases as she thinks. "Have you got any black clothes, Alfie?"

"Yes," I say. "You've got your black sweatpants and a long-sleeved black T-shirt, haven't you?"

Alfie nods. "I've got black gloves, too."

"And your new rain boots," I say. "They're still nice and shiny. They'll look just like Darth's boots."

"Excellent," Kay says. "I've got an old tablecloth we could dye black and I'll make a cloak out of it. I'll put some padding in the shoulder part, give him some bulk. It'll be easy. Then all Mommy will have to do is pick up a mask. By this time next week, you'll have a costume for the party."

"Kay, that would be amazing. Thank you *so* much."

But she doesn't respond. She's lost in a reverie, gazing at Alfie. Poor Kay. She must really miss her grandchildren.

22

KAY SURE CAME THROUGH WITH THE COSTUME. HERE WE ARE, October 31 already and for once, Alfie can't wait to get to school. He'd have happily gone in yesterday if it hadn't been a teacher training day. And with Michael off again on another of his fact-finding missions, I'm relieved that Alfie is distracted by Halloween, otherwise he'd be asking me a whole bunch of questions about when Daddy's coming back.

"Have you seen the funny picture on the bulletin board?" Fatima says as she meets us on our way across the playground. "It's really good. Someone has photoshopped the first-grade class photo for Halloween. Made all the kids look like zombies and skeletons. Miss Williams has a pair of devil's horns."

She laughs. "I can see by your face, Joanna, that you're not a great fan of Halloween."

I lower my voice. "It's the thought of spending this evening at Debbie's house with fourteen six-year-old boys high as kites on too much food coloring and sugar. Then we have to tramp around in the cold knocking on people's doors. I can't wait."

Fatima laughs again.

"Come on, then, Alfie," I say. "Let's go and see what you look like as a zombie."

The hall has that smell peculiar to elementary schools everywhere. Sneaker soles and modeling clay. School lunches and glue. The musty reek of all those little bodies. Alfie tugs me toward the L-shaped area outside Mr. Matthews's office. There's a small crowd clustered in front of the bulletin board, pointing and laughing. We wait till there's space to squeeze in, and take a look.

Good grief. They've really gone to town with all this. The normally professional head shots of each member of staff have been doctored to include witches' hats and hideous warts and bloodstained fangs. Mr. Matthews, the principal, has had his eyes whited out, but he still manages to look as sexy as ever. I'm sure I'm not the only mom to have had the occasional fantasy about getting summoned to his office for being naughty.

Alfie is pointing to his class photo and shrieking with laughter. "Look, Mommy. Look!"

"Oh my goodness!" I say. Someone must have spent ages doing this. Each child's uniform has been replaced with some kind of Halloween outfit. My eyes scan all the little zombies and vampires and skeletons for Alfie. Normally, it's easy to pick him out, with his distinctive frizzy hair, but their faces have been altered to make them look paler and more ghoulish. If my memory serves me right he's in the second-from-the-back row over to the left.

"There I am!" he shouts excitedly. "Can you see me, Mommy? Can you see me?"

At last, my eyes pick him out, and my heart stops. My breath freezes in the back of my throat. I can't quite believe what I'm seeing. No skeleton costume or zombie suit for Alfie. He's still in his school uniform, but his white shirt is splattered with blood and there's a knife sticking out of his chest.

I try to swallow but can't. I make myself look at every child in the photo, work my way systematically along each row to see whether any of the others have knives sticking out of them, but none does. A tight pressure spreads across my chest like a band. My heart races. Why has he been singled out like this? Why is Alfie the only one with a knife sticking out of him? What kind of school would put something like this up on their bulletin board?

Alfie has started staggering like a zombie with his fists clenched around an imaginary knife in his chest. The other kids are copying him and laughing.

"Who did this?" I ask one of the dads standing next to me. My voice comes out shrill and accusing, and I'm aware of my entire upper body stiffening in rage. "Who made this photo? Was it one of the teachers?"

He gives me an odd look. "Why? What's wrong with it? It's only a joke, right?"

I hear a muttering behind me. The phrase "one of the PC brigade" reaches my ears and I swing around, furious. "So you think it's perfectly acceptable for my son to be shown with a knife sticking out of his chest, do you?"

"Now, hold on a minute, honey. No need to go nuts over it. It's only Halloween. It's not like it's real. Jeez, some people."

The door to Mr. Matthews's office swings open and Mrs. Haynes, the school secretary, comes out. "Everything all right here?" she says.

"No, it isn't all right. I want to speak to the principal."

She opens her mouth to say something, then closes it again. "Why don't you come and sit down and tell me what the problem is."

People are staring at me. They're gathering around as if I'm some kind of spectator sport. Alfie's lurching around with a couple of boys, in a world of his own. He's still pretending to be a zombie, oblivious to the scene I'm causing. I grab his arm and pull him to my side. My jaw tightens and I look Mrs. Haynes in the eye, keep my voice as low and calm as I can.

"I need to speak to Mr. Matthews. About that photo on the bulletin board. It's very important."

Mrs. Haynes presses her lips together. I see her glance at someone beyond my shoulder and I know she's weighing up her options and deciding that, actually, it'd be better for everyone concerned if she just took me straight to Mr. Matthews before this all gets out of hand.

Tears have started to pool in my eyes.

"Of course," she says. "If you wait here for a moment, I'll let him know you'd like to see him."

She's using that slow, deliberate tone of voice people use in tense situations. What she really means is, *I'll just let him know that a hysterical mother wants to come and rant at him.* She's probably taken one of those courses: How to Deal with Angry Parents.

While I'm waiting for her to come back Teri appears at my side, a worried look on her face. "What's going on, Joanna? What's happened?"

I tell her about the photo and she charges off to look at it. She stands in front of it for a while before walking slowly back to my side, but by this time Mr. Matthews has come out of his office and is speaking to me in that low, well-modulated voice of his.

"Mrs. Critchley, would you like to come into my office? Do you want a cup of coffee or something?"

"No," I say. "No, thank you. And it's *Miss* Critchley. Not Mrs."

"I'm sorry," he says, and I catch the fleeting look that passes between him and Teri.

"Joanna, shall I wait with Alfie outside?" Teri asks. "I've got a PTA meeting at eight so if you're not back by then, I'll take Alfie to his classroom for you, okay?"

"Yes, yes, please," I say, and I watch her leading him away. He looks back at me over his shoulder as if to say, *What's happening, Mommy?*, but I'm too upset to reassure him right now.

Mr. Matthews's office smells of coffee and aftershave. He gestures for me to sit down and closes the door behind us.

"That photo," I say. "I need you to explain."

Mr. Matthews rests his fingertips on the desk in front of him and takes a breath.

"Celebrating Halloween can be a divisive topic," he says, and pauses. He looks like he's trying to think of something diplomatic to say. He must think I disapprove of it on religious grounds.

"No, you don't understand. I'm not *anti*-Halloween. But I'm strongly opposed to you singling out my son in that hideous way."

Mr. Matthews frowns. "Excuse me a moment. Let me go and get the photo in question."

While I'm waiting for him to return my breathing slows. What am I doing in here? Am I overreacting? Letting my imagination run away with me again? If it weren't for all this business about Sally McGowan and all the things I've been reading about her—those stupid tweets—I wouldn't even be giving this a second thought.

Maybe I didn't look closely enough. Maybe there were more children with gruesome Photoshop additions. Maybe in my shock, my eyes skimmed over them, seeing only Alfie in that horrible, blood-spattered shirt. That knife. Maybe there *were* other children still wearing their recognizable school uniforms, just like Alfie, with blood splatter on their shirts. No knives in their chest, but even so. It's just a horrible coincidence. A random click of a button on a computer.

It's not as if Alfie was in the least bit upset about it. He loved it, didn't he? The way he was staggering around like a zombie in the hall with the other boys. And now I've made a complete fool of myself. Ruined his moment of gory glory.

Mr. Matthews returns a few moments later with the photo and sits down to give it his full attention. I watch his eyebrows move closer, see the lines on his forehead deepen in a frown. He's figuring out what to say to me. He looks up then and places the photo on the desk between us. I close my eyes, mortified with embarrassment. I'll have to apologize for making a scene and get out of here as soon as possible.

And then Mr. Matthews begins to speak. "I'm extremely sorry about this, Miss Critchley. I can see exactly why you're so distressed about it. The thing is, nobody actually knows who did this. Mrs. Haynes said she found it under the office door when she came in this morning and assumed one of the parents had left it there as a joke. She showed it to the other staff before assembly and they all thought it was really clever. None of them noticed the . . ."

He pauses and looks down at the photo. "None of them

noticed how Alfie was made to look so . . . different from everyone else."

He leans back in his chair and sighs. "This should never have been put on the bulletin board. I can only apologize."

It takes a moment or two for his words to register in my brain. So it wasn't created by a staff member. Mrs. Haynes found it slipped under the door this morning. Which means they have no idea where this picture came from.

My mouth goes dry. I can barely swallow. Mr. Matthews doesn't think I'm making a fuss over nothing. He isn't just trying to placate an overprotective mother. He's visibly disturbed at what he's seen. Because someone *has* singled Alfie out.

The knot in my stomach twists tight. Out of a class of thirty children, someone has deliberately chosen to depict my son with a knife plunged into his chest.

23

"BUT I WANT TO TELL JAKE AND LIAM ABOUT MY DARTH VADER costume," Alfie wails, tugging at my arm to slow me down.

How typical that the first morning he's shown any kind of enthusiasm for going to school, here I am hauling him back home again.

"Sorry, darling, but we've got to do something else today."

I'm walking too fast for his little legs. He's almost having to run to keep up with me, but I won't slow down. I can't. Not till I get us safely home.

"But you said if I don't go to school, the police will come." His voice is high and wobbly. He's on the verge of tears.

"You're right, I *did* say that, and if you stay at home every day, then I *will* get into trouble, but this is just for *one* day, Alfie. I've forgotten something very important I have to do."

"What, Mommy?"

I wrack my brain, trying to think of something. I hate lying to him, but there's no way I'm going home without him; I'd be worried sick. Whoever brought that photo in walked into the school unchallenged. Which means it must have been somebody dropping off a child, or someone who works there. A teacher? Mrs. Haynes or her assistant? A janitor? It could have been anyone. How can I leave him there on his own when I don't know who is doing this, or what they're capable of?

You think your children are safe at school, but are they? Are they really?

"I can still go to Liam's party, can't I? Can't I, Mommy?"

Oh hell. The party. I can't keep him away from that, not when he's so excited and Kay's gone to all the trouble of making his costume.

"Don't worry about the party, Alfie. I'll figure something out, I promise."

By the time we get home Alfie is sobbing. What kind of mother am I, not letting him go to school with his new friends, practically dragging him along the street in my haste to get home? It's a good fifteen minutes before I manage to calm him down, and even then he's sulky and withdrawn.

"I want Daddy," he says, his lower lip jutting out.

"Daddy had to go into the city today to do some work. You know he did. He'll be back tomorrow."

"I want Grandma, then."

I sigh. "If you're a good boy and play quietly for a little while, we'll give Grandma a call and see if she wants to come over. Okay?"

Alfie nods. His bottom lip has started to quiver.

I pull him onto my lap and give him a big hug. "And of *course* you can go to Liam's party."

Alfie leaps onto the floor and does a silly dance. I'm forgiven. At last.

I exhale slowly and go into the kitchen to make some coffee and call in to work. Dave says not to worry when I lie to him about having to take Alfie to the doctor's, but he can't be thrilled about me taking the day off. I feel dreadful letting him down, but what choice do I have? I promise him I'll make the time up as soon as I can.

The doorbell startles me. For a couple of seconds, I consider ignoring it. I'm not expecting anyone, so it's probably a door-to-door salesperson. They'll go away in a minute. But Alfie is already peeking through the mail slot and shouting for me to come and answer the door.

My relief when I see Kay standing on the doorstep with a red lightsaber in her hand is so overwhelming that I dissolve into nervous giggles.

She steps inside, waving it about. "Every Sith Lord needs his own lightsaber," she says, passing it into Alfie's eager little hands. "But you need to be careful with it. Because this one is made out of cardboard tubes, duct tape, and contact paper."

Alfie runs upstairs with it, making lightsaber humming noises.

Kay follows me into the kitchen, laughing. "I thought he'd be at school."

I'm about to tell her the same lie I told Dave, but before I know what's happening my eyes have filled up with tears and I'm telling her everything.

"Now, look here," she says, when I've finished. "Whoever created that photo *isn't* Sally McGowan. It can't be." She takes the pot of coffee from my hands and starts pouring it into the mugs. "From everything I've read about her, she's a reformed character now. A woman trying to put her past behind her and get on with her life."

I let her get the milk from the fridge. The state I'm in, I'd probably slosh it all over the counter.

"But what if she isn't? What if she's somehow wangled a job at the school?"

Kay stirs the coffee. "They do police checks, honey. That could never happen."

"Yes, it could. If she's changed her identity, she won't be showing up on FBI records, will she?"

A frown furrows Kay's brow. "I'm no expert on these things, honey, but I'm sure she wouldn't be allowed to get a job in a school. In any case, it was a long time ago. She was just a child."

We go into the living room and sit down with our coffees.

"You're right. I mean, why would she put herself at risk just because of a rumor?"

I put my mug on the table between us. "But the fact remains that somebody *did* make that horrible photo. Somebody chose to show my son with a knife sticking out of his chest. And maybe whoever it is is also the person who's following me on Twitter."

Kay frowns again. "What do you mean?"

I pull my phone from my bag. "Someone called Sally Mac is following me. She tweets quotes about rumors."

Kay pulls a puzzled face. "Sally Mac?"

I nod and click on my followers, hoping she won't still be there, that I was right about it being a random coincidence and that Sally Mac, whoever she is, has realized I'm not going to follow her back and has unfollowed me and moved on to someone else. Someone who enjoys reading her silly quotes.

No such luck. There she is, although her tweets seem to have dried up. There aren't any new ones, as far as I can see.

Kay peers at my phone. "Let's get this into perspective,"

she says. "I don't *do* Twitter, but as far as I can see someone's trying to scare you. Think about it, Joanna. It's Halloween tonight. This is just someone's idea of a sick joke. Maybe it's one of the other mothers. You know what they're like."

I shake my head. "Surely they wouldn't do something like this. I mean, the Twitter thing I can just about understand, but that photo . . . it was horrible."

Kay presses her lips together and sighs through her nose. "I wasn't going to say anything about this, but . . ."

"Say anything about what?"

She clears her throat. "Fatima had a really hard time last year."

"Why? What happened?"

Her lips twist. "Debbie Barton said some nasty stuff. Slightly, you know . . . *racist.*"

"Oh God, really?"

"It only happened once, and Fatima challenged her about it. So did I." She gives a wry laugh. "Of course, Debbie acted all upset and offended. Said she'd only been joking around and Fatima had gotten it all wrong. It all blew over in the end. They're friendly with each other now. After a fashion." Kay sips her coffee. "Although they've never babysat for each other."

"Are you saying that Debbie might deliberately be trying to freak me out because she's a racist and I've got a mixed-race son?"

Kay wrinkles her nose. "I'm not pointing the finger at anyone in particular. I'm just saying that it's more likely to be something ignorant like that, rather than . . . well, rather than anything else."

I'm trying to get my head around the implications of what Kay has just said when the phone rings.

"Hello, darling." Mom's voice sounds all weak and croaky. "Any chance you could take Sol out for a walk later? I've come down with some kind of virus. I feel awful. All aches and pains."

"Oh no. You poor thing. Of course I will. I've got Alfie at home with me today, but we'll drop by in a bit."

"Why isn't he at school? He's not still having problems, is he?"

Oh God. If she thinks I've put Alfie in any kind of danger, I'll never hear the end of it.

"No, no. He's fine. It's a long story, Mom. I'll tell you later. You get yourself off to bed and I'll let myself in with the spare key."

When the call is over Kay stands up. "Sounds like you're wanted somewhere else, honey," she says. "I'd better get going."

From upstairs comes the sound of Alfie, still making lightsaber noises in his bedroom.

"Thank you so much for making that for him. He loves it."

When Kay is halfway down the path, she stops and turns around. "Can I give you some advice?" she says. "Stop worrying about that silly Twitter account and the photo. It's a Halloween prank, that's all."

I nod. She's right.

"By the way, hon, if you ever need anyone to look after Alfie at short notice, say if your mom can't do it, or she's not feeling well, you know you can always knock on my door. I'm usually in. Save you going through the babysitting circle every time."

"Thank you, Kay. That's really, really kind of you."

24

AFTER MUCH SOUL SEARCHING, I DECIDE THAT I'LL TAKE ALFIE
back to school after lunch. I can't justify keeping him out all
day, and it'll look bad if he goes to Liam's party when he
hasn't been at school. Besides, now that I've spoken to Kay, I
feel much calmer. She's so kind and levelheaded. Of course
it's a Halloween prank. Not a very nice one, admittedly, but a
prank nonetheless. It has to be.

Alfie is delighted when I tell him we're taking Sol for a
walk. He seems to have forgotten all about being upset with
me earlier. That's the great thing about children. They live in
the moment and, right now, he's happy. Which means I am,
too.

At Mom's, I call through the mail slot before using the
spare key. This is the first time I've had to use it and Sol is
confused and excited, running back and forth between the
hall and Mom's bedroom, and barking nonstop.

At last he settles down and pads off to his basket, closely
followed by Alfie. I perch on the end of Mom's bed.

She heaves herself upright. She looks terrible. "Sorry
about the mess. I didn't feel up to tidying."

Alfie tries to catch them, but every time he approaches they blow away and he groans with laughter.

I'm laughing at this, laughing *with* him, and pulling my woolen hat out of my pocket because my ears are freezing, when Maddie bobs into my sight line. She's walking fast, chin parallel to the sand, her slightly bent arms swinging rhythmically, almost mechanically, at her sides. She's power walking. I've seen her do this before. She's so *in the zone,* she almost mows me down.

"Oh hi, I didn't even see you there," she says. Her face is pink from exertion, and a fine sheen of sweat coats her forehead and upper lip. She crouches down to retie the laces of her sneakers, and I can't help noticing how fit she looks. It's humiliating that a woman in her late fifties is in better condition than I am. I really must start doing some proper exercise.

When she straightens up, she laughs. "Look at you, all wrapped up, and here's me, sweating like a pig." She pulls the collar of her sweatshirt away from her and lets it ping back to create a draft on her neck. "Actually, I'm glad I've bumped into you. There's something I wanted to tell you."

I brace myself for what's coming. If it's more of the same about Sonia Martins from Stones and Crones, I'm not sure I want to hear it. I glance over at Alfie and Sol, who are examining what looks from here like a large dead crab. At least I hope it's dead, because Alfie has just lifted it up with his fingers and, if it isn't, he's about to get a nasty pinch.

"It's about my friend, from Pilates."

"The probation officer?"

"No, another one."

Oh God. What's she going to come out with this time?

If only I'd swerved out of her way and let her power walk past me.

"She's buying my neighbor's house. It's being sold by Pegton's, so you probably know it. In fact, it was me who first told her it was up for sale."

"Whereabouts?"

"Maple Drive. Number twenty-four."

So Anne Wilson is one of Maddie's friends. "I'd forgotten you lived there," I say.

"Yes, I'm right next door at number twenty-two. The thing is . . ." She sighs. "I wish I hadn't said anything now. I mean, she might have found the place on Zillow, of course. But if I'd kept my mouth shut, chances are someone else would have put an offer in before she got around to viewing it."

"You don't want her living next door to you?"

"Not really. Not now. I've found something out about her, you see. Something that's made me—how can I put it?—reevaluate our friendship."

I don't ask what, because I know she's going to tell me anyway.

"I've known her for ages. We used to work in the same office—that's how we first met. Then Martin did some tax work for her husband, Graham, and we started going out for meals together, the four of us. We even went away together once. To Miami. Not the most successful of vacations, but that's another story. Then Anne discovered Graham was having an affair and they split up. I didn't see much of her for ages because she got a little odd. You know how some women get when their husbands leave them for someone else. Really bitter and vindictive. I mean, I'm not saying I wouldn't be absolutely furious if Martin had an affair, but

I wouldn't stalk the other woman and make her life hell. I wouldn't become completely obsessed with her, to the point of making myself miserable. At least, I hope I wouldn't. I hope I'd have more self-respect." She sniffs. "I can't vouch for what I would or wouldn't do to Martin, of course."

I glance over Maddie's shoulder. Alfie is now throwing a stick into the shallows and Sol is lumbering dutifully after it.

"But then I started seeing her again at Pilates and she'd stopped going on and on about it. She really seemed to have turned a corner and put it all behind her. I'd gotten my old friend back at last. And she has a new boyfriend now. A lawyer. Although, between you and me, he's got a bit of history, too."

She mimes someone taking a swig of drink. "Another sort of weakness altogether, but he's sober now, thank God."

"Yes, she was with a man the first time she viewed the house. Tall, silver-haired."

"That's him. New man. New house." Maddie giggles. "New face, too. Anne's always been vain."

"So why don't you want her moving in next door to you?"

"Because one of our mutual acquaintances has just told me that the woman Graham left her for is the woman who owns that New Age shop I was telling you about. Sonia Martins."

I stare at her, my brain racing with this new information.

"The woman you thought might be Sally McGowan," I say.

Maddie blushes. "It isn't her. Sonia Martins was born here in Flinstead. Her mother's lived here for ages. I didn't realize that when I told you. I didn't know." She shakes her head. "The thing is, now that I know it's her that Graham had the affair with, I'm convinced that Anne is behind this horrible vendetta against her and, worse still, that it's all my fault. Because I was the one who told her about the rumor. It's exactly the kind of thing she'd do. I thought she'd moved on from all that vindictiveness, but clearly she hasn't."

Maddie twists her fingers in front of her and stares out to sea. "I can't prove it was her, but I'm certain it was, and I really don't want her living next door to me. Not now that I know what she's done."

She turns to face me. "You know the shop window got smashed last night?"

"Oh my God! No!"

"It was being boarded up when I walked past just now. Oh, I'm not saying it was Anne who did that. But these things take on a life of their own, don't they? She just lit the fuse and stood back." Maddie sighs. "I shouldn't say this, not with you working at Pegton's, but I really hope the sale falls through. Whenever I see Susan Marchant now, I keep telling her she must be nuts to want to sell such a beautiful house, but she just looks at me as if *I'm* the nutcase. I can't blame her, of course. She'll need the money, won't she?"

"Well, actually, no, she won't. She's going to give it to . . ." I clear my throat. I've no right to start blabbing about Susan Marchant's charitable intentions. I've already caused enough trouble by passing on the rumor about McGowan—none of this would have happened if I'd kept my mouth shut.

Maddie gives me a questioning look, but luckily Sol starts barking—the perfect excuse to turn away and see what he and Alfie are up to. But Sol is standing alone at the water's edge and Alfie is nowhere to be seen. My heart skips a beat. I scan the beach. He must be here somewhere. I only just saw him throwing a stick.

"What's the matter?" Maddie asks.

"I can't see Alfie. I can't see him anywhere." My chest tightens with fear.

"Don't panic. He can't have gone far."

We both turn toward the sea at the same time, but there's no sign of him. Alfie wouldn't have gone in the water. Not in this chilly weather. I just know he wouldn't, and even if he had, he'd have come running back the minute the cold water reached his knees. Besides, it's so shallow on this stretch of beach.

A memory from the news ages ago comes back to me. Two little children arriving for their vacation on a Florida beach. Running into the sea excitedly, never to be seen again. Not alive, anyway. But Alfie wouldn't do that. Not on a day like this.

"Alfie? Alfie?" I shout as loud as I can, but my voice is lost on the wind. Now I'm running. Running toward the wooden breakwaters and the next stretch of beach, but there's no one else down here. No one except Maddie and Sol and me.

"I'll go the other way," Maddie shouts, and she jogs off in the direction of Mistden Pier, calling Alfie's name as she goes.

Sol is still barking. "Where is he, Sol? Where's Alfie?"

I follow the direction of his gaze and see a woman in a pale-blue jacket striding purposefully along the boardwalk. She appears to be holding on to something with her hand.

And then I see it. A little shock of hair, bobbing in and out of view behind the seawall, and I'm suddenly so dizzy I think I'm going to faint. It's the top of Alfie's head.

25

IT'S LIKE ONE OF THOSE NIGHTMARES WHEN YOU'RE BEING chased and you can't run fast enough. Except this is no dream. This is really happening, and I'm the one who's chasing. My feet sink into the wet sand and the muscles in my calves pull with the effort. I have to reach the steps up to the boardwalk, but the sand gets drier the nearer to them I get and it's harder and harder to run. It feels like I'm moving in slow motion.

Whoever has Alfie could be halfway up the cliff path by now. If I don't catch up with her, she could be across the parking lot and into a car in minutes. My heart pounds. What was I thinking, taking my eyes off him? Standing around listening to more of Maddie's silly gossip.

At last, I reach the wooden steps and take them two at a time, using the metal handrail to haul myself up. I can just about see them up ahead, following the line of the cabanas. The woman in the blue jacket and Alfie, trotting along beside her. I can't believe he's doing that. I've told him a million times not to go with strangers. I scream his name, but the noise that reaches my ears is reed-thin. A whisper on the wind.

Now I'm running on the hard concrete. Sprinting, or trying to, the colors of the cabanas whizzing past in my peripheral vision. For one terrifying second, I almost lose my balance and topple over face-first, but somehow I keep going. I haven't run like this for years, and it hurts. It really hurts.

The distance between me and Alfie shrinks. I've almost caught up with them, but still he can't hear me shouting his name. This wind, it's impossible. The woman in the blue jacket is tall and slender. I'm sure I've seen that straight black hair before. It's someone about my age. I can tell from her clothes and the way she's moving. The occasional blurred flash of her profile as she glances down at Alfie. Who is she? How dare she take my son? And is it my imagination, or has she just started walking even faster?

"Alfie!" I scream and, this time, thank God, his head turns and his tearstained face breaks into a massive smile. He drops the woman's hand and charges toward me, barreling into my legs and almost toppling me.

I sink to a crouching position and wrap my arms around his body, hugging him tight. When I look up, Karen is standing in front of me, her face etched with concern. She looks different somehow.

"I found him all alone on the sand," she says. "He was crying his eyes out."

"He wasn't all alone! He was with me, and Sol. Where were you taking him?"

Her jaw tightens. "To the school. I don't know your phone number and I didn't know what else to do. I didn't want to call the police . . . I . . ."

"But didn't you see me talking to Maddie?" My voice is ragged from all the running, not to mention blind panic. "We were right there. You *must* have seen us." I hold Alfie by the shoulders and peer into his face. "Alfie, darling, couldn't you see Mommy? I was right there the whole time. You were playing with Sol, weren't you?"

His lower lip trembles. "I threw his stick and another dog took it so I ran after it." His face crumples. "I couldn't see you anymore. I couldn't see Sol, either. The beach looked all different."

He starts to wail and I hug him to my chest again. He's still so small and vulnerable, and the beach is huge when the tide's out. How much bigger must it seem to someone Alfie's size?

"Oh, Alfie. What have I told you about running off?"

"We looked for you everywhere," Karen says. Her face is stricken. "You didn't tell me Mommy was wearing a hat, did you, Alfie?"

"She wasn't," he says, his voice muffled by my coat.

"Oh, darling. I put my hat on when my ears got cold." I look up at Karen. "It's new. He's probably never seen me wearing it before. I didn't think."

Now that Alfie is safe in my arms and my breathing's returned to normal, I start to cry. How could I have let this happen? I was so engrossed in what Maddie was telling me about Anne Wilson, I must have forgotten to keep checking on Alfie and Sol. In fact, where the hell *is* Sol? He'll be going berserk by now. Mom'll never forgive me if I've lost him. She dotes on that dog almost as much as she dotes on Alfie. I run to the seawall and scan the beach from left to right.

Then I see him, plodding along next to Maddie—they're some way in the distance still, but I recognize Sol's lumbering gait and Maddie's lithe, Lycra-clad figure. I didn't realize how far I'd run. Now Maddie's waving at me. She's bringing Sol up to meet us. My eyes fill with tears and Karen touches me gently on the arm.

"I lost Hayley once. In Target. I only took my eye off her for a second, and when I turned around she was gone. A sales assistant found her by one of the checkouts, looking for candy." She sighs. "Joanna, I'm so sorry I didn't see you, but I've broken my glasses. They're being repaired and I don't have a spare pair."

That's why she looks different. She's almost crying now. "We tramped up and down for ages. I should have waited for longer, but I'm supposed to be taking my mother to a doctor's appointment in ten minutes. I didn't know what else to do. If it was summer, there'd have been a lifeguard, but . . ."

"It's all right, Karen. Honestly. I'm just grateful you looked after him."

She squeezes my hands, and for a couple of seconds we look into each other's eyes. Two women united by the common bond of motherhood and the terror of losing the only thing in the world that really matters. Our children.

26

MRS. HAYNES IS ALL SWEETNESS AND LIGHT WHEN I TAKE
Alfie back to school. She must be worried I'm going to make
a complaint about that photo. To be honest, I haven't entirely
ruled it out. Just thinking about it makes me nauseous. Who
would have done such a thing?

But Mr. Matthews has already apologized and it's been
removed from the board. Besides, I'm not sure what good it
would do to lodge a complaint now. I might just end up with
a reputation as a troublesome parent. One who needs to be
handled with kid gloves.

Or maybe it's the presence of Sol that's softened her up.
Dogs have that effect on people, and Flinstead is a dog lovers' paradise. When Alfie went to school in the city, dogs
weren't allowed anywhere on school premises.

"I've seen this lovely fella before," she says, fondling
Sol's ears. "He's a big old sweetie, aren't you, you gorgeous
boy?"

Ugh. Now she's letting him lick her face. I've never understood how people can do that. Don't they know where
those noses and tongues have been? Once, when I took

Sol out for a walk, I had to stop him eating another dog's shit.

Mom just laughed when I told her and proceeded to give me a mini lecture on the different types of coprophagia, as it's called. Autocoprophagia is when they eat their own poop; intraspecific coprophagia is when they eat another dog's poop; and interspecific coprophagia is when they eat poop from another species of animal altogether. Funny the things that stick in your mind. I bet Sol would indulge in all three if he had his way.

"Okay, Alfie. Shall we say goodbye to Mommy now?" Mrs. Haynes says.

I give him a hug and kiss the top of his head. "See you this afternoon, darling."

"Mommy, remember it's Liam's birthday party!" he calls over his shoulder as Mrs. Haynes leads him away.

I give him a wave. "Of course." The incident at the beach earlier had wiped it clean out of my mind. Still, at least he's not upset anymore.

I watch until he and Mrs. Haynes disappear through the door that leads from the hall to his classroom. I don't like leaving him after what's just happened, but this is a good school. A *safe* school.

MOM'S STILL FEELING AWFUL WHEN I TAKE SOL BACK. SHE looks as white as her sheets, and the tip of her nose is all red from where she's been blowing it.

"Keep away from me," she warns in a croaky voice. "I don't want you and Alfie coming down with this, too. It's horrible. I was feeling fine yesterday."

She reaches for her glass of water and empties it.

"Here, let me get you some more," I say. "Are you sure you don't want anything to eat?"

She grimaces.

"I could come by again this evening if you like, after the party."

"What party?"

"Didn't I tell you about it? I'm sure I did. It's one of Alfie's classmates. He's having a birthday party after school. A costume party."

Mom groans. "Don't tell me—Halloween?"

"'Fraid so. I did what you said and made friends with some of the other moms."

She nods. "I hope you've gotten him a good costume. You don't want him to be the odd one out."

I stare at her in disbelief. This is the woman who used to tell me that pretty dresses were a complete waste of money and fashionable shoes were bad for my growing feet. "If you need a certain pair of shoes to fit in with the right crowd, Joanna, it's the *wrong* crowd," she used to say.

"You should see your face!" she says now, and laughs. "I know what you're thinking, but it's different when you're a grandmother. You'll find that out one day. At least, I hope you will."

I wonder whether this is a good time to tell her about Michael moving in. If I don't tell her soon, Alfie's only going to blurt something out, and then I'll feel bad for keeping it from her. I sit down on the edge of the bed. I'll probably end up with her cold now, but so be it. I need to be straight with her.

"Mom, there's something I have to tell you. Michael's asked if he can move in with me and I've said yes."

I look at my reflection in her dressing-table mirror and then, obliquely, at hers. She's folding her hankie into a small square, gathering her thoughts.

"Well," she says at last. "If you feel in your heart that it's the right thing to do, and if you're absolutely sure it's what you want." She sniffs. "All I want is for you to be happy, Jo. You know that, don't you?"

Her eyes are wet, and though this could be the effect of her cold, I don't think it is.

"Of *course* I know that. And I also know you've always thought he had commitment issues." I stare at my knees. "I've never told you this, Mom, but he asked me to marry him once."

She gasps. "And you turned him down?"

"Yes."

"Why?"

"Because I didn't want it to be just about Alfie." I sigh. "And I guess it had something to do with Dad, too. I couldn't bear the thought of Michael turning out just like him and letting us down."

Mom unfolds her hankie and blows her nose.

"I know how much it damaged your self-esteem, Mom, and I didn't want to—"

"End up an embittered old woman like me?"

"That's *not* what I was going to say."

She laughs. "You're right, though. It *did* damage my self-esteem, and I'm sorry if I passed on my own insecurities about men to you. That wasn't fair."

"I just wish he hadn't been such a shit."

"You and me both, darling."

I squeeze her wrist. "But I'll promise you: If Michael

doesn't step up and commit to us, like he's said he will, I'll end it for good."

Mom nods in approval. *She* could never move on, but I'm stronger than her. I can.

I just hope I don't have to.

27

SARTRE, OR RATHER A CHARACTER IN ONE OF HIS PLAYS, famously said that "Hell is other people." I know that statement's not quite as simple as it sounds, and I don't have the necessary philosophical knowledge to unpick it. But at this precise moment, I'm taking it at face value. Hell is indeed other people, especially the people sitting in Debbie Barton's sunroom drinking Prosecco, and even more especially their children, who right now are being entertained by a balloon sculptor in the room next door and making so much noise my head feels ready to burst.

My eyes drift from the faces that surround me and into the dining room beyond the French doors. A vast diamanté-framed mirror reflects the lush green of the garden, and a glass chandelier twinkles from the ceiling. Debbie's husband, Colin—a plumber, I think she said—is sitting at the table having a beer with Karen's husband, Rob. The two of them look out of place in what is the most bling-filled, girlie-inspired décor I've ever seen. Lots of purple and pink. Furry pillows and sparkly accessories. "Amusing" wall plaques with quotes. I wonder how much input Colin had in all this.

Not much, by the looks of things. I bring my attention back to the conversation going on around me. It's becoming more and more like an episode from one of those reality-TV shows—*The Real Housewives of Flinstead-on-Sea*. Tash will have a field day when I tell her about it.

To be fair, Debbie did say I could go home and come back later, but given the day I've had there's no way I'm leaving Alfie on his own. After all, how well do I really know these people? They seem friendly enough, but after what Kay told me this morning . . .

Every now and then Karen and I catch each other's eye. From the look on her face, she's finding all this as tedious as I am.

I lean toward her. "How's your mother?"

She frowns in surprise.

"You said earlier you were taking her to a doctor's appointment. I hope you weren't late."

"Oh no, no," she says. "Well, we were a little bit, but it didn't matter. You always have to wait about twenty minutes past your appointment time, don't you? She's . . . she's fine."

Karen takes a sip of her Prosecco and stares into the middle distance. Her expression has changed. I remember her mother's face as she looked back at me over her shoulder, that time they waved at me through the window of Pegton's. She didn't look fine to me. Oh dear, I wish I hadn't said anything now.

Around us, the chatter has turned to what's been happening at Stones and Crones. The brick through the window and what it all means. Whether there's any truth to the allegations.

Karen closes her eyes and sighs. She opens them and catches me staring at her. "How are you doing with this month's book-club read?" she says. "I'm finding it a bit heavy going, to be honest. All those stories within stories."

"What book is it?" Debbie asks before I've even had a chance to answer.

"Mary Shelley's *Frankenstein*," Karen says.

Debbie pulls a face, as if to say, *What a bore*. "I'm surprised nobody's come to Liam's party dressed as Frankenstein."

Karen and I exchange a glance. A fleeting moment of mild amusement. I've misjudged her. I see that now. She might have been a little intrusive that time at book club, but maybe she was just trying to be friendly. I've certainly got more in common with her than with this crowd and, after what happened at the beach this morning, we seem to have reached a new understanding.

"Frankenstein is the name of the scientist who *creates* the monster," I tell Debbie, immediately wishing I hadn't. No one likes a smart-ass. "Although everyone gets it mixed up."

"You could argue that he's the *real* monster for abandoning his creation," Karen says.

I nod. "Or for creating him in the first place."

Debbie makes a face. "Cut it out, you two. You're not at your book club now."

Laughter erupts from the room next door.

"He's good value for the money, that balloon guy," Debbie says. "Very good-looking, too."

Murmurs of agreement ripple through the group. Someone makes a joke about him being good at manipulating latex and they all shriek with laughter.

"Speaking of good-looking men," Cathy says, lowering her voice a little so that Colin and Rob don't overhear, "I couldn't help noticing that rather gorgeous man you were with just before the holiday weekend, Joanna." She smiles. "Is he your *baby daddy*?"

I bristle at the phrase. I don't mind the question behind it. I've no problem confirming that Michael is Alfie's father. Why would I? But the term *baby daddy* has a nuance to it I don't like, implying as it does that his only significance is biological. And the way she said it, too, as if it were in quotes. Would she have said that if Michael weren't black?

I detect a slight lowering of voices around me, as if the others don't want to be blatant enough to stop talking, but neither do they want to miss out on my answer.

"He's Alfie's dad, yes. He's also my partner." It feels odd saying this out loud. I usually say something like, *He's Alfie's dad and my best friend,* but if I say that now, it might invite further questions, and my instinct in situations like this is to shut down the line of inquiry as politely and efficiently as I can. Besides, things are different now. Michael *is* my partner.

"Oh, I didn't realize," Cathy says. "I thought you were single."

I smile. There's a slight pause in the conversations going on around me, like white space on a page, and then, when my silent smile continues, the voices resume. Pitter-pattering over the awkwardness until the moment is washed away. Borne aloft on a tide of trivia.

"Okay," Debbie says. "I think it's time to quiet things down a bit in there." She gets up and goes over to a sideboard, from which she draws a large box wrapped in shiny silver paper. "Any volunteers for music control in Hot Potato?"

Karen's hand shoots up so fast she almost knocks Teri's Prosecco to the floor.

Debbie points to her iPad on the coffee table. "I've got a playlist set up on Spotify. Just click on Spooky Tunes."

We all troop into the adjoining room, where balloon animals are being brandished like weapons and bashed over a sea of heads. Karen's and Teri's daughters, Hayley and Ruby, are the only girls in the group, and it's interesting to see how they've taken themselves off to a quiet corner and are playing an entirely different game that involves trotting their animals along the back of the sofa in a sort of dance routine.

Alfie's hair is damp with sweat and his eyes have a manic gleam. I perch on the end of a sofa as far too many mothers try to organize the children into a seated circle. Colin and Rob have wisely stayed in the dining room. At last, the *Ghostbusters* theme tune starts up and the potato is on the move.

TWO HOURS LATER, AFTER A DISMAL HALF HOUR TRAIPSING along dark, wet streets while our hyperactive offspring knock on strangers' doors and ask for treats, I'm desperate to get home. But when Karen and Rob ask me in for a cup of coffee—well, just Karen, really—and I realize they live in The Regal, I can't resist. It used to be a fancy hotel in its day and I'm dying to see what it's like.

One of the apartments on the upper floors with a terrace and a view came up for sale recently, but the owner withdrew it before I got a chance to take a look. Karen and Rob's place, disappointingly, turns out to be in the more modern extension, but I can hardly change my mind now. And besides, she did let Alfie win the main prize in Hot Potato.

Karen ushers me into a warm, square-shaped living room. It might not be as big as I'd been expecting, but it has a homey feel to it. Hayley scrambles up onto the lap of an older woman curled up on one end of a large sofa with a laptop. The same woman I saw with Karen outside Pegton's. She's dwarfed by a white, fluffy bathrobe, and she's wearing a pink beanie and slippers.

"Meet my mother," Karen says. "This isn't her usual attire, but then it is Halloween, right, Mom?"

I cross the room toward her, hand extended. She can't get up, not with Hayley hogging her lap. She shakes my hand. Her wrists are tiny, her face gaunt.

"She's charming, isn't she, my daughter?" Her voice is surprisingly gruff. The pink hat and the fluffy slippers had me expecting something a little softer. More feminine.

"Learned it all from you, Mother dear," Karen retorts. It's just mother-daughter banter, but I sense a slight tension between them. It must be a strain for Karen and Rob, having her mother stay with them in this small apartment. I can't help noticing that Rob's disappeared into the bedroom and closed the door behind him.

Karen plucks a DVD from a basket on the floor, and before long Hayley and Alfie are sitting cross-legged in front of the TV, enthralled by the opening scenes of *Frozen*.

Karen beckons me into the kitchen. "Let's go have some coffee. Mom'll keep an eye on them. She loves *Frozen*."

As I follow Karen out of the room, I glance back at the three of them: a somewhat disheveled Darth Vader and his ghostly bride, and the thin woman in the oversized bathrobe, tapping away at her keyboard.

LATER THAT NIGHT, WHEN I'M STRETCHED OUT ON THE SOFA watching mindless TV, I reflect on the day. All that terror I felt this morning when I saw that awful photo, and my panic at losing Alfie—it's all faded away. If I never hear the words *Halloween* and *trick or treat* again, I'll be happy, but at least Alfie enjoyed himself, and I'm glad I went back to Karen's apartment. I have a feeling we're going to be friends after all.

I reach for my phone to check whether Michael's been in touch and, sure enough, there's a text.

How was the party? Bet Alfie stuffed himself with candy.

For the next couple of minutes we bat messages back and forth, neither one of us wanting to be the last to sign off. I know I should tell him about the photo, and the incident on the beach this morning, but it seems too much for a text and I'd rather tell him face-to-face. Eventually we say good night and I toss the phone onto the cushion beside me. Then I pick it up again and go onto Twitter. Just one last look at Sally Mac before I delete my Twitter account for good. Now that Michael's moving in, I won't be so bored in the evenings.

She's still there, and . . . oh . . . she's posted another tweet.

I stare at it, unable to process what I'm seeing. The sound of the TV recedes and an iciness trickles from the back of my neck all the way down my spine. I must have misread it. Please, God, let me have misread it.

But I haven't. The words are still there and the message is clear:

Look what you've started. You and your big mouth. I'm watching you. I'm #WatchingAlfie.

I wear my sneakers with the bouncy soles so that I don't make any noise. Tonight, I wait till the last of the evil clowns and walking dead have cleared the streets, till the late-night dog-walkers have long since turned in, and then I slip into the darkness. Feel its cold embrace on my skin. Inhale the purity of its breath.

In a small town like Flinstead, and on windless nights like this when the sea is soft and flat, the silence is profound. Even after all these years, the thrill of having the streets to myself never leaves me. This is my time—Sally's time.

Inevitably, I'm drawn to the beach. It's even darker down there, unless it's a clear night when the moon is shining. The freedom I feel when I'm on the sand, unobserved by human eye, is exhilarating. I'm not scared of the dark or the immensity of the ocean. I'm not scared of anything down there. It's like I'm moving through a dreamscape, at one with the universe.

Weightless. Immortal.

Invincible.

Tonight, though, I stick to the streets. Most of the houses are in complete darkness as I pass them, but one or two still have a light on in a downstairs room. I conjure up scenes hidden from view. A young couple making love on a sofa, giggling when the springs squeak; an old man drifting in and out of sleep in front of the TV; a nursing mother, head drooping as the baby suckles, husband snoring upstairs.

I'm so jealous of their ordinary lives I could scream. I could pick up this stone here and hurl it through a window. Shatter their peace and tranquility. Make them as scared as me. Just for a little while, so they know what it's like.

They'll never know what it's like.

At her house, a faint orangey glow is just visible at the bedroom window.

28

IT'S PAST MIDNIGHT BEFORE I DARE TO GO TO BED. I MUST
have checked the locks on every window in the house at least
three times, and I've drawn the bolts across on the front and
back doors, which I don't usually bother with, as long as
they're locked. I can't shake the image of someone watching
me from the street. *Watching Alfie.* A shiver runs through me.

When I go into the kitchen to get myself a glass of water,
the blackness of the window above the sink scares me. If
there were someone out there, they'd see me as I turn on the
tap and wait for the water to run cold. Why haven't I put a
blind up yet?

I'm being stupid, I know I am, but even the sight of the
knife block sitting on the counter unnerves me. I remember
Mom telling me something she'd read about in the paper
once, a horrible story about an intruder using one of the
homeowner's own kitchen knives to attack her when she
confronted him. She always hides her knife block in a cabi-
net now.

When she first told me this, I thought she was being a

little paranoid, but now I remove each of the knives and hide them in a drawer under my kitchen towels.

Upstairs in my bedroom, I try calling Michael again, but his phone keeps going to voicemail. I've been leaving messages and texting him ever since I saw the tweet.

Call me as soon as you get this message.

Something horrible has happened.

I have to talk to you.

Maybe he's asleep already. He did say he might drop in to the gym after work. Perhaps he was tired. Or maybe he went out for a drink with one of his friends and hasn't checked his phone yet.

I know what Mom would think if she knew he wasn't returning my calls.

After tossing and turning for goodness knows how long, I get up and go into Alfie's room. I lift his comforter as gently as I can and slip into bed next to him, wrap my arms around his warm, sleeping body, and breathe him in. The sound of my heart beats loud in my ears.

I know, deep down, that whoever sent that tweet is just messing with my mind, just like I know that Michael isn't playing around. But still, I won't sleep tonight.

IT'S A WHILE BEFORE I REALIZE THAT THE DISTANT RINGING noise isn't part of my dream but is coming from my phone in the next room. I ease myself out of Alfie's bed so as not to wake him. The watery gray light coming through the gap in his curtains means it's early dawn. So I must have slept a couple of hours, at least.

It's Michael. "I'm outside. I didn't want to ring the bell in case it woke Alfie."

The sight of him on the doorstep with his big leather duffel on the path behind him is balm to my frayed nerves. His arms enfold me in a long, close hug. He must have woken early and seen my messages, driven here as soon as he could.

I tell him about the photo at the school first, and I can see from the skeptical expression on his face that he thinks I'm overreacting.

"You say some of the other kids were made to look like zombies?"

"Yes."

"And how did you know they were zombies?"

"For God's sake, Michael! I know what a zombie looks like! Their faces were gray and their eyes all weird and bloodshot. And they had oozing wounds. You know, the usual zombie stuff."

"So I don't see how Alfie having a knife sticking out of him is any worse than that. It's a classic Halloween image, isn't it?"

"Well, Mr. Matthews thought it was inappropriate. He agreed it was odd that Alfie had been singled out in that way."

Michael raises his eyebrows. "He was probably just saying that to defuse the situation. Come on, Joey. You can't really think there's anything more to it than that, can you?"

I reach for my phone and go onto Twitter. "Wait till you see this, then."

But when I click on my followers the Sally Mac account has vanished. She's not following me anymore. I search for her username, but there's no trace of her.

"That's weird. She's gone."

"Who's gone?"

I tell him about Sally Mac (@rumormill7) and the tweets she's posted. His eyes narrow. Then I tell him about the Watching Alfie hashtag and they narrow farther still.

"That's sick," he says.

"You don't think it's her, do you? That she's somehow gotten wind of the fact I've been spreading this rumor?"

Too late, I realize what I've said.

Michael stares at me. "What do you mean, *you've* been spreading the rumor?"

My cheeks burn with embarrassment. Embarrassment and shame. "When I first heard it, before I even mentioned it to you, I talked about it at my book club."

Michael rolls his eyes.

"I was trying to deflect attention away from Jenny, one of the other members, because Karen was quizzing her on her love life and Jenny looked really uncomfortable. It was the first thing that came into my head. I've regretted it ever since."

"But you haven't told anyone what I found out, have you? Nobody knows I'm planning a book about her?"

"Nobody knows about the book, but—"

"But what?"

"The week after book club, one of the women—Maddie— told me she'd been talking to a friend of hers from Pilates who used to be a probation officer and told her all this stuff about witness protection. Maddie put two and two together and came up with five. She convinced herself that Sonia Martins from Stones and Crones was Sally McGowan."

Michael shakes his head in disbelief. "So all that's because of you, too."

"Oh, so I'm responsible for Maddie blabbing to her friend, am I?"

He sighs. "No, of course not. But that's how these things get out of control. They spread like wildfire."

"Anyway, she doesn't think it's her anymore. Apparently, the husband of another one of her friends at Pilates ran off with Sonia Martins, so now Maddie thinks her friend has started this false rumor about her out of revenge." I clench my toes. "Someone put a brick through the shop window the other night."

"For Christ's sake," Michael says under his breath.

"I know. The whole thing's ridiculous."

"Anything else you want to get off your chest?" He's looking into my eyes. He knows there's something I'm not telling him.

I take a deep breath. This isn't something I want to admit, but if we're really going to make our relationship work I have to be honest with him.

"I might have mentioned what you said about her being moved to a dry town."

He sighs deeply and looks away.

"Why?" he says at last. "Why would you do that? I didn't think you were a gossip."

"I'm *not*. It's just that . . . Alfie's been having problems making friends. Nobody was sitting next to him at lunchtimes. I didn't want him to be miserable. I didn't want him to be the victim again, not after what he went through before. All that horrible name-calling he had to put up with. And I've been finding it hard, too. The other mothers already know each other. I feel like the new girl at school."

"So you thought gossiping to them would help."

"It *did* help. They asked me to join the babysitting circle. And Alfie got invited to Liam's birthday party. I've been trying to pour cold water on the story ever since."

I've been looking at my hands while I've been telling him all this, but now I lift my head and force myself to meet his eyes.

"You don't think it's Sally McGowan, do you, Michael? This Sally Mac person on Twitter?"

"Hardly," he says. "I would think having a Twitter account is the very last thing she'd want to do. It's probably another one of the mad-mommy brigade."

He wipes a stray tear from my cheek with his thumb. It's a tender gesture that makes me cry even more.

"It can't be a coincidence that the account's been deleted the day after Halloween, Joey. It was a malicious joke, that's all."

"I hope so. I really do."

He enfolds me in his arms again. I'm glad I've finally told him. It feels like a weight has been lifted.

"Twitter is full of twits," he says. "Twits and trolls and people with something to sell."

"So I guess I fall into the twit category."

He laughs. "You said it."

29

THAT EVENING, AFTER MICHAEL'S PUT ALFIE TO BED, WE
search online for the documentary I read about a while
back—*In Identity Limbo,* written and presented by Martin
Knight—but we're only able to find short clips of it on You-
Tube. Excerpts from interviews with protected persons, shot
so you can only see the silhouettes of their profiles talking,
or where their faces are deliberately blurred, their voices dis-
torted.

While some are grateful for their new identities, others
say they wish they'd never agreed to leave their old lives behind. The strain of living a lie, of continually having to be on
guard, has exacted a terrible toll on their mental health. One
of the interviewees, Peter—not his real name, of course—
explains how hard it is not to screw up when you first take on
a new identity. What worked for him, he says, is including a
small element of truth somewhere in each of his lies, something to lend them authenticity.

Then a psychologist cites the "illusion of truth" effect,
whereby the more times something is repeated, the more it
is believed. Like rumors, I think. So what happens in the end

is that people start believing their own fictions and their old lives become less and less real to them.

It makes sense when you think about it. I told a lie once, when I was a teenager. Said I'd lost my virginity to one of the boys who worked on Mistden Pier, when all we'd really done is make out and feel each other up. I lied to fit in with the right group of friends. Or rather, the wrong group of friends, but I couldn't see that at the time. We talked about it so often, dissected all the details, I honestly felt like it had really happened. The fantasy seemed far more real than the awkward fumbling that actually took place.

All the people interviewed in these clips are those whose testimony has put gang members behind bars. Either victims of violent crime or ex-criminals-turned-informers. Of course, the likes of Sally McGowan wouldn't be afforded that level of protection, not in the States, anyway. So we end up watching an old documentary about McGowan instead. It was made in the late 1970s and may well have been groundbreaking in its day, but it now looks and sounds really dated.

We sit close to each other on the sofa, Michael's laptop resting across our knees, and watch as black-and-white footage of Dearborn and Chicago in the 1960s is interspersed with interviews of people who knew Sally as a child. Students and teachers at the school she attended. Neighbors and people involved in the original investigation into her case and the trial itself. The general consensus is that she was a headstrong child, intelligent beyond her years. A leader, not a follower. According to some of them, Sally had a tendency to be a bit of a bully. Hardly surprising, considering her background.

The music alternates between mournful and menacing, and the sonorous male voiceover is thick with doom. I'm sure I've seen some of these shots before, probably in those documentaries I sometimes watch. The ones that focus on a particular block or house and show the changes through time. Grubby children playing unsupervised in the street. Housewives leaning on broom handles, gossiping. Boarded-up stores and derelict houses. The standard it-sucks-to-be-poor footage.

And then, of course, there are the lingering close-ups of Sally McGowan's young face.

"What do you see when you look into those eyes?" Michael says, pausing the film for a moment.

"I'm not entirely sure," I say. "I mean, I know what I *think* I see."

"Which is?"

I consider his question. "At first I thought she looked defiant. Fearless, almost. There's an incredible self-assurance about her, don't you think? A knowingness. My mother would say she looks like she's been here before. An old soul in the body of a child."

Michael wrinkles his nose. "I think she looks scared and is trying to hide it. Mind you, I'm not sure what you *can* tell from a photograph. A millisecond after the camera shutter opened and closed, her face might have changed."

"You're right. We're just projecting what we know about her onto that one frozen image."

"I was looking at photos of myself as a child the other day," Michael says. "Wondering whether someone would be able to pick out my adult face, having only seen me as a little boy." He laughs. "I don't think I've changed that much, to be honest."

"Are we talking physically here?"

He pinches my thigh in response.

"Apparently, for women, the most changes occur between when you're young and when you're middle-aged, whereas in men it's between middle and old age," he says.

He sits up and takes my face in his hands, runs his fingertips along my cheekbones and temples as if he's a cosmetic surgeon, sizing me up for his next procedure.

"We're not just talking skin here, it's the facial bones that change shape. The eye sockets enlarge, the angle of the lower jaw drops, and the tip of the nose dips downward."

"Such a lot to look forward to," I say.

"You lose the deep fat pads in your cheeks, too, and your eyelids start to droop, which makes the eyes look smaller." He grins. "I reckon you've got another ten years."

"You rat!" I grab his wrists and make him slap his own face with his hands. The laptop nearly slides onto the floor and we catch it just in time, laughing.

"You've really looked into this, haven't you?"

"Just idle googling, that's all."

"And all this happens earlier in women than men? Typical. We always get the short end of the stick."

We contemplate the face on the screen before us. The face I've come to know so well in the past few weeks. And the more I study it, the more it becomes what it actually is: just the face of a ten-year-old girl looking into the lens of a camera, as she was no doubt instructed to do. A child being processed through the criminal justice system.

But this was no ordinary child. This was a child who'd committed a monstrous crime.

Would Sally McGowan have turned out differently if she'd been nurtured by a loving family, if she hadn't been abused by her father and traumatized by her upbringing? If you can call it that—by the sounds of it, it was more like a downbringing. I guess we'll never know the answer to that question. And yet, she has never reoffended. Despite her dreadful past and her unthinkable crime, people believed in her ability to change and grow, to move beyond the horrors of her past. They must have, or else she wouldn't have been given help to relocate.

And now, somewhere out there, possibly in this very town, if Michael's sources are correct, her anonymity may finally be coming to an end. Because of people like me. And people like Michael, who, for all his faux outrage at my gossiping, has been guilty of fueling all sorts of false or unsubstantiated stories in his time. It's how he makes his living.

He presses PLAY and the video resumes. Now we're looking at photos of her parents, Jean and Kenny McGowan, the details of their faces slightly blurred. But there's no mistaking the look of fear in Jean's eyes and Kenny's belligerent swagger as he strides toward the cameraman. I wouldn't mind betting there was a nasty confrontation after that picture was taken. Kenny's hands look enormous. One of them is clenched into a fist. A fist that looks ready to swing.

"Surely he should have faced prosecution," I say. "He might not have murdered Robbie Harris, but he abused and tortured Sally for most of her young life. Everything I've read points to him being violent with the mother, too. Why did they believe him when he said it was Sally who inflicted the cuts and bruises on her skin? Everyone knew he was a violent drunk and a bully."

"It was a different world back then," Michael points out. "People didn't talk so openly about stuff like that. Maybe they couldn't bring themselves to admit such things could happen."

I think of what Susan Marchant told me about her father, and shudder. Even when abuse like that stops, its effects last a lifetime. The memories never fade. I see Susan's face on the beach, the pain behind her eyes. Something niggles at the back of my mind, then elbows its way to the front. What if Susan's doing what "Peter" did and embedding a germ of truth in a lie? McGowan *was* horribly abused by her father, after all. As Maddie would say, it makes you wonder, doesn't it?

The documentary is over now. Michael closes his laptop and stands up. He's doing that thing he always does when he's thinking hard about something: pushing his tongue into the flesh below his lower lip. It makes him look like an idiot, but I'll never tell him that because I've grown quite fond of it over the years.

"I could kill for a drink," he says. "I think I'll run out and buy something."

"Don't bother. I've got a bottle of red wine. And I'm sure there's some brandy, too."

"But I really want a whiskey," he says. "The store's open till ten, isn't it? I'll only be a few minutes."

As the front door closes behind him I run upstairs to the bedroom window without turning the light on and peer behind the curtain. Michael isn't a real drinker. And since when has he drunk whiskey? I'm sure he only said that because he knows I don't have any and it's given him the excuse to leave the house.

I watch him saunter away. As he crosses the street by the lamppost, he pulls his phone out of his pocket. By the time he reaches the other side, he's already talking to somebody. One of his sources, perhaps? He doesn't want me to listen in on the conversation because now that he knows I've told people about his dry-town theory, he doesn't trust me anymore.

I let the curtain fall back. I suppose I can hardly blame him for keeping things close to his chest.

I go downstairs again and dial Liz's number. She must be home by now. She's always telling us how she's a homebody at heart and how she hates going out in the evenings. If I can just persuade her to speak to Sonia Martins, maybe, just maybe, Sonia will grant Michael an interview. I need to undo some of the damage I've done.

30

I FEEL HER BEFORE I SEE HER. A PRESENCE AT THE FOOT OF the bed. An irresistible force that draws my eyes toward her like a magnet. At first her face is blurry, ethereal, like an impressionist portrait. Then she comes into focus and my heart stops. It's her. It's Sally McGowan!

She throws her head back and her face splits open in a scream of manic laughter. I'm hypnotized by the back of her throat and the small, soft piece of flesh that hangs there, quivering. As her arms stretch toward me, they're pale as bone. Nausea surges through me like a monstrous wave that refuses to break. Her hands are smeared with blood and I know, with terrifying clarity, that it's Alfie's blood.

She's killed my baby.

When I wake, I'm sitting bolt upright and Michael is shaking me by the shoulders. "It's just a dream, Joey. A nightmare. It's all right. You're safe now. You're safe. I've got you."

I scrabble to free myself from the covers. My skin is cold and clammy and my limbs don't seem to work properly. "Alfie! Where's Alfie?"

"Shh. Alfie's fine. He's asleep in his bed."

"Have you looked?"

"No, but where else would he be?"

I'm fully awake now, and though I know it was a night-mare—of course it was a nightmare—the horror still clings to me like a shroud. I have to go and see him for myself.

I push open his bedroom door and there he is, curled on his side in his *Star Wars* pajamas, his lips stuck together in sleep, his chest rising and falling, rising and falling. I lean over him and inhale the familiar baby scent of his skin. His hair curls damply against the curve of his cheek. I smooth it back with my fingers, hook it around his little pink ear. He wrinkles his nose and chews air, but only for a second. I haven't woken him. I crouch beside the bed, not yet ready to leave his side. Unwilling to tear myself away. No, not unwill-ing. Unable. I'm physically unable to remove myself from this room. As if he's a newborn baby all over again, and if I'm not here to see him breathe, then maybe he won't.

Michael appears in the doorway, stark naked. He looks like a bronze statue, the way he's just standing there, stock-still.

"Come on, Joey," he whispers. "Back to bed. I'll give you a massage."

"I HAVEN'T HAD A NIGHTMARE LIKE THAT FOR AGES."

"Shh," Michael says, his breath warm on the back of my neck as he lies on his side behind me. I feel the heat of him. He circles my shoulder blades with his fingertips, then traces the contours of my spine. His fingers are feathers.

"Think of something nice," he says. His voice is gravelly and low. His lips graze my ear and I shiver. Bits of the dream linger, but as his fingers continue their journey over each bump of my vertebrae, the horror recedes and we have slow, gentle sex that morphs, seamlessly, into something faster, more urgent. I don't even remember changing position, but here I am, on my knees, left cheek pressed into the pillow, the weight of his hands on my hips, his fingers digging into my flesh.

It isn't till we're finished that we notice Alfie, standing solemnly by the side of the bed, his pajama bottoms all twisted, a puzzled expression on his face.

"What are you doing, Mommy?" he says.

I suddenly remember an incident from when I was about his age, walking in on my mom and dad. How overly happy and surprised they were to see me. How Mom's cheeks were all flushed and Dad carried me back to my own bed and whistled a tune to me till I fell asleep. It's a bittersweet memory, tainted as it is with what came afterward. Did he whistle his other children to sleep like that? I wonder.

Afterward, when we've told Alfie how we wanted to swap sides of the bed and, instead of being sensible and getting up, Daddy thought he'd just clamber over me, when we've told him how hot we were and how we had to take off our pajamas to get cool, and Alfie, the little innocent, has accepted both explanations, had a drink of water, peed, and gone back to bed, Michael and I surrender to giggles under the covers, stuffing our fists in our mouths to keep quiet.

But later, when we migrate to our separate sleeping positions—Michael on his back, me curled on my left side, the pillow pulled down at an angle under my shoulder—the memory of my nightmare returns and echoes of dread haunt me long into the night.

———

I WAKE TO THE SOUND OF THE SHOWER AND THE BURBLE OF
the radio. Michael's side of the bed is already cold. *Michael's
side.* How quickly it has become *his* side in my head.

I stretch like a cat, arms and legs extended as far as they
can reach, and yawn, noisily. The shower has stopped and
Michael appears, one towel fastened around his hips like a
short skirt with a revealing split up the side, another hanging around his neck like an untied scarf.

"You sound like a Wookiee," he says. Then: "Are these
the biggest bath towels you have?"

"Yes." I lean across and try to whip his skirt away, but
he's too quick for me and grabs me by the wrists.

He grins. "Don't start something you can't finish. Alfie's
up and about."

Downstairs, it feels like we're in one of those hipster
breakfast cereal commercials: black stay-at-home dad, white
mom all dressed up for work, and mixed-race son sloshing
milk into his cereal bowl. Even the sun is shining. The dread
that's been hanging over me these past few days hasn't exactly gone, but it's retreated to a small dark closet in my
mind and I've shut the door on it.

"I've got a couple of showings to do this morning. One
of them's near where Liz lives, so I'm going to pop in afterward and see if I can talk to her about Sonia Martins. I tried
calling her again last night when you were out, but her phone
was busy."

Michael nods. "Do you want me to take Alfie to school?"

"Yes!" Alfie shouts.

I smile. "I could get used to this."

Michael winks at me. That slow, lazy wink. I wonder if
he knows how effective it is. The physical sensation it always

prompts. I don't ever want him to wink like that at someone else.

I try not to think of him leaving the house last night and talking on the phone. If this is going to work, I have to trust him. And I do. I can't complain that he's betrayed me in the past, because he hasn't. It was an open relationship and it was what we decided, right from the start. Like I told Mom, nobody forced me to go along with it, and I can't pretend it didn't suit me just as much as it suited him. You can't be betrayed by a man who's made you no promises.

But it's different now. He's told me it's different, and it is. It has to be.

31

LOCKED DOORS AND TOUGH LOVE: LIFE
INSIDE GRAY WILLOW GRANGE

By Susan Piercy

SUNDAY, AUGUST 21, 2016
The Observer

As 12-year-old Carl Bargiel faces sentencing for a violent
and unprovoked attack on a teacher, we ask what happens
inside a juvenile detention center.

Gray Willow Grange is a boarding school with a difference. The pupils don't get to go home for weekends or
holidays, at least not till their sentence is drawing to a
close and they have satisfied the parole board that they are
no longer a threat to society.

This is where Sally McGowan was sent after killing
five-year-old Robbie Harris and where other notorious
child criminals have been imprisoned: Those we know
about, and those we don't. Children who have killed or
tortured. Children, in short, who have committed the
most atrocious crimes.

Dr. Winifred Quilter, criminologist and director of the Malcolm J. Cottee Foundation, a charity dedicated to the rehabilitation of child offenders, explains that children who commit violent crimes almost always share the same set of risk factors: poorly educated and unemployed parents who are often substance abusers or who suffer from a variety of mental health problems; family structures that have broken down; emotional and/or physical abuse and/or neglect; witnessing domestic violence; and sexual abuse from an early age.

"These are children who have been given no boundaries for acceptable behavior," says Dr. Quilter, "and whose dysfunctional parents offer wildly inconsistent approaches to discipline, ranging from complete indifference to the harshest of beatings and humiliation."

Nigel Gildersleeve, warden at Gray Willow Grange, agrees. "We have to start from scratch with these children. Many of them are malnourished and have never even eaten at a table or used silverware. They have no concept of what it means to take turns. They cannot empathize or interact appropriately with others because no one has ever empathized or interacted appropriately with them. They have fallen behind at school because teachers can't cope with their disruptive behavior. If you want these children to be rehabilitated, you have to try to undo years of damage before you can even *start* to address the nature of their crimes. Subjecting them to harsh punishment merely reinforces the violence already instilled in them. They need structure and nurturing. Tough love, in other words, and yes, that sometimes includes rewards for good behavior."

"Children's brains change and develop, particularly

during puberty," says Dr. Lavinia Molyneux, a psychiatrist who works with children and adolescents. "Therefore, with the right treatment, we can and frequently *do* effect a marked change in their behavior, with many going on to do well academically and become responsible, law-abiding citizens."

There will, of course, always be exceptions: a subgroup of children who develop into psychopaths and continue to offend as adults. "But it would be counterproductive," says Mr. Gildersleeve, "to change the methods we have developed over years of experience and research just to satisfy the public's appetite for retributive justice in one or two exceptional cases."

ART THERAPY AND TABLE TENNIS, JUKEBOXES AND POOL, TRIPS TO THE BEACH—THIS IS WHAT YOU GET FOR MURDERING A CHILD
By Katie Hamlin

SATURDAY, JUNE 12, 1976
DAILY NEWS

Pictures of Sally McGowan laughing and playing pool in her prison have outraged the grieving family of little Robbie Harris, so brutally and callously murdered by McGowan just seven years ago.

"It makes my blood boil seeing her enjoying herself without a worry in the world while my precious angel is cold in his grave," says a tearful Sylvia Harris from her cramped living room.

According to Deirdre Mason, a former Gray Willow cafeteria worker, inmates regularly get to play games and watch TV. "And the food is far better quality than my kids get for their school lunches," she says.

"They're not being punished for the terrible things they've done," she continues. "It seems like they're getting things they don't deserve. One-to-one lessons, some of them, and all those activities most hardworking parents couldn't afford."

Sylvia Harris can only shake her head in despair. "Where's the justice for my little Robbie?" she asks.

I'm parked outside a condo complex on the esplanade. It's called, somewhat unimaginatively, Sea Breeze Court, and I'm waiting to show two different couples around number 33, whose owner has, sadly, died.

Trawling for articles about Sally McGowan is something I seem to do automatically now. Especially at times like this, when I have nothing much else to do. I just find myself typing her name in the search bar and seeing what comes up, scrolling down until I find something I haven't yet read.

I wonder what Michael's up to. I do worry about his methods sometimes. How he finds things out. I'm not so naïve as to believe it's all strictly aboveboard. I just hope it's not illegal enough that he'd get into trouble if he were found out. In one of the articles I've read there was a quote from some Russian author and journalist who argued that the tabloid press is more effective than the FSB in tracking people down. But it's not as if Michael's doing this to reveal McGowan's identity. He just wants to write a book about her. Make a name for himself as a serious writer. Make a bit of money at the same time.

I dread to think what the Harris family will make of that.

Exploiting their tragedy for his own ends—that's what they'll say. Their private grief once more made public property. And Sally McGowan the center of attention all over again when, really, it should be Robbie Harris we're remembering. Little Robbie Harris. The boy who lost his life.

Number 33 Sea Breeze Court is boxy and bland. The previous owner's furniture looks like it came from a much bigger, grander house. It's totally unsuitable for a small condo like this. But still, the view is the selling point, and the neat concrete balcony with room for two chairs and a table and a couple of potted plants. Not that you ever see anyone sitting on their balconies. Not even in summer. At least, I never have.

I unlock the balcony door and stand aside so that Mr. and Mrs. Frankis can go out if they want to. Mr. Frankis steps outside and peers down onto the manicured lawn below.

"I like the gardens," he says.

Mrs. Frankis stays where she is. There's no way she'll agree to buy this condo, whatever Mr. Frankis thinks. You only have to look at her face.

"As you can see," I say, "it's a perfect spot for morning coffee, or for evening drinks, watching the sun go down."

"How much are they asking for this?" she says, finally walking out and peering at the house next door. The one that's boarded up. Only now I notice someone's pried the boards off the front door and smashed a pane of glass. Probably some bored teenagers breaking in on a dare. That's going to turn her right off. I know it is.

"It's listed at four hundred and sixty thousand dollars," I say. "There's already been a lot of interest. I think it will go pretty fast."

She doesn't respond, although her left eyebrow says more than enough. I'm wasting my time here. The sooner we can go through the motions of inspecting the two bedrooms, the better. My next couple is waiting outside. With any luck, both showings will be over in another ten minutes and I can drop in to see Liz without Dave wondering where I am.

When Mr. and Mrs. Frankis have gone, I go down to greet Mr. and Mrs. Enright, or Steve and Fiona, as they insist I call them. Steve and Fiona *love* the condo. Fiona can see past the heavy mahogany furniture and hideous curtains and envisages something clean and minimal. The kitchen will have to go, she says, but except for that it's perfect. They lean their elbows on the balcony wall and enjoy the view.

"I can just see us sitting here drinking G and T's on a sunny evening," Steve says.

Good old Steve. He's doing my job for me. And they're so enraptured by the ocean that neither of them has mentioned the derelict house next door.

Annoyingly, they then spend ages chatting in the second bedroom. Mainly about whether they'll have a bed or a sofa bed in there. Or possibly a futon. It's a good sign when people start discussing what furniture they'll put where, as if the condo is already theirs, but I'm not in the mood for it today.

At last, they leave, with promises to be in touch before the end of the day. I check my watch. If I hurry, there's still time to call on Liz.

32

THIS TIME, I DON'T LOOK AT THE UPSTAIRS WINDOWS. I WALK
deliberately up the path and ring the bell. I step away from
the door and wait, but, as before, she doesn't come. The
blinds at her front room windows are still closed and, as I
peer through the window in the door, I see what looks like
mail lying on the mat.

Something is wrong. I feel it in my bones. A shiver runs
down my spine. Maybe she's fallen and broken something.
Maybe she can't get to the phone and has been lying there
for days. For all I know, she could be dead.

I should knock at the houses on either side, her neighbors'. Maybe they know where she is and can put my mind
at ease. But just as I'm about to go next door, I notice that her
side gate is ajar. Last time I came it was locked. I'm sure
of it.

I push it gently, but it's stuck fast on the concrete. It's
very old and the wood is rotting in places. The hinges must
have come loose.

"Hello!" I call through the gap. "Liz, are you there?"

Silence.

With one hand on the latch, I use the other to grip the side of the gate and lift it clear of the ground. It swings open and I walk through into the side passage, calling her name as I go.

No answer.

Her backyard is long; it must be at least a hundred feet. Like her house, it reflects her personality. Creative and idiosyncratic. Slightly hippie-ish, with its wind chimes and garden Buddhas, its profusion of colored terra-cotta pots and abundant borders that spill over onto the gravel path that meanders between them. No manicured lawn and neat flower beds for Liz.

A rickety wheelbarrow heaped with bags of compost has been left out, a discarded pair of gloves sitting on top, and at the far end of the garden is an old shed, wreathed in ivy. She must be in there. No wonder she can't hear me.

But when I reach the shed I see that it's padlocked shut. I glance back toward the house. She must have gone inside for something. If she looks out of the window, it'll give her a shock, seeing me prowling around her yard.

I retrace my steps until I'm standing outside her back door. I knock as loud as I can. I call her name. Where the hell is she?

I try the handle of the door and it opens, so I stick my head inside and call into the house. "Liz? Liz, are you there?"

The house feels ominously still, almost as if no one's at home, but she must be. She wouldn't have gone out and left the back door and the gate open. She must have been doing some gardening and then come inside to use the bathroom. That's why she can't hear me. I can't just barge in and go upstairs. It wouldn't be right. I'll wait by the gate until she comes down. I don't want to frighten her, but I do want to talk to her. Not just about the Sonia Martins thing, but about book club and whether she's okay. That email of hers is still on my mind, and the way she was that time I saw her on the street. Distracted. Harassed-looking.

Minutes pass and she doesn't come out. Perhaps she's not going to. Perhaps she's doing something else now and has forgotten all about the unlocked gate. I go back to the front door and ring the bell again, but still she doesn't come. This is ridiculous. I take my phone out and dial her number, hear it ringing in the house. It rings and rings without switching to voicemail. Reluctantly, I end the call and go back around the side.

Maybe I was right all along and she's fallen somewhere. For all I know, the house has been unsecured for days. Maybe I just *assumed* the gate was locked the last time I was here because it was pulled closed. Now that I think of it, I didn't even *look* at the gate.

In the kitchen, I touch the kettle. It's stone-cold. I walk through into the hallway and on toward the open door of the dining room, where, not so long ago, we all sat laughing and drinking wine. An unexpected sensation of dread comes over me, for it was in here that I passed on the rumor about Sally McGowan.

A disturbing thought buzzes in my brain like a fly as I peer around the door. I want to swat it away but it keeps coming back. I call out to Liz again, but once more there's no reply. The room is empty, so I make my way toward the front door and the living room, which I've previously only glimpsed in passing. But that, too, is empty.

I'm at the foot of the stairs now. "Liz, it's me. Joanna. Are you there?"

I peer up toward the landing, but I can't hear anybody moving around. The stairs creak as I make my way, slowly, tentatively, upstairs. Sunlight streams in through the front door and through the banisters, striping the glass of the framed black-and-white photographs hanging on the wall.

The silence is oppressive, and I don't like the way I'm trembling. I shouldn't be snooping around Liz's house like this. I hardly know her, not really. Maybe I should just leave and phone the police, get them to check it out. Yes, that's exactly what I should do. But still my feet continue to climb upward. Why? What am I expecting to find?

Upstairs, I'm more convinced than ever that something bad has happened. I've never seen inside any of the bedrooms before because, whenever I've used the bathroom on book-club nights, the doors are closed. Just like they are today. I open them one at a time; bracing myself for what I might find. Liz lying injured on the floor. Unconscious. Maybe even . . .

The bathroom is empty and so are the two bedrooms at the front of the house. My muscles tense. There's only one place left where she can possibly be. The back bedroom.

Hardly breathing, I turn the handle and push open the door. My eyes roam each corner of the room. It's not a bedroom at all—it's an art studio. Several unfinished paintings are stacked against the wall. There's an old oak table she obviously uses as a desk. It's cluttered with jars of pens and pencils, big pots of paintbrushes and piles of newspapers and scrapbooks and photocopied clippings. Coils and slivers of paper litter the surface of the table and the floor beneath.

The closed blades of scissors of various sizes have been stuck into lumps of Blu-Tack and ranged in order of height along the side of the table.

I sag against the doorframe. This isn't an episode of *Murder, She Wrote,* and Liz isn't lying facedown in a pool of blood. Nor is she hanging from a beam. She's just slipped out to the store or something and forgotten about the unlocked gate and back door. She's an artist. They have a tendency to be absentminded, don't they? I almost laugh.

I must get out of here. Now. If she comes back and catches me in her studio, I'll be mortified. Would she believe me if I told her I thought she'd fallen?

I'm just about to leave when I spot an unusual painting leaning against the wall. It's nothing at all like her other stuff. This is an incomplete self-portrait. Unflattering to the point of ugly. I can't resist staring at it, this brutally honest depiction of a Liz I've never seen before yet instantly recognize, even in this raw, unfinished state. There's something odd about it, though. It looks as if it's created out of something other than paint.

I step a little closer and see that I'm right. Of course. That explains all the cutouts on the floor. It's made out of tiny scraps of paper, some white, some black. The black bits are used for the shaded areas of her face—the hollows under her eyes, the pupils of the eyes themselves, the sunken cheeks, and the nostrils. Such a labor-intensive process. It must have taken her ages just to get this far with it.

Then my eyes snag on the headline of one of the newspaper clippings on the desk and my heart does a weird little flip. *"I still remember the blood,"* says child killer Sally McGowan's *former friend and neighbor Margaret Cole.* It's the same article I read online. It's been printed from the internet, and right in the middle, where the picture of Sally McGowan's face used to be, is a hole.

Blood thunders in my ears. Are those scraps of paper that make up Liz's self-portrait what I think they are? Are they cut from images of Sally McGowan's face?

The floorboards behind me creak and I spin around. Liz is standing in the doorway, a carving knife in her hand.

33

THE KNIFE CLATTERS TO THE FLOOR. LIZ STARES AT ME.

"Joanna!" she says. "What are you doing in my house?"

I open my mouth to explain, but all I can think of is the self-portrait behind me and how it's been made.

I swallow hard, eyes glued to the knife on the floor.

"I thought you were an intruder," she says, picking it up.

My whole body stiffens.

"I thought someone had broken in."

"I've been calling you for ages," I say at last. "I sent you emails. I was worried about you so I came by and . . ."

She's staring at me through narrowed eyes. The knife hangs loosely in her hand.

"You didn't answer the doorbell, so I . . . I went around the back. The gate was open. I called out for you. You weren't in the yard and the shed was locked up. The back door was unlocked. I thought maybe you'd . . . I thought maybe you'd fallen somewhere."

Her shoulders sag as she exhales.

"Oh dear. I was around the back of the shed, weeding."

She raises her finger to her earlobe. "I don't have my hearing aid in."

"I didn't know you were deaf."

She frowns. "I'm not *deaf*, I'm just a bit hard of hearing. Come on," she says, turning to leave the room. "Let's put some coffee on. We're lucky we didn't give each other a heart attack."

I follow her downstairs. Why isn't she saying anything about the portrait? She must know I've seen it. My face was only a couple of inches away from the canvas when she came into the room. And she must know I've seen the clippings on her desk.

Thoughts slide about and crash into one another in my head. Could this mean what I think it does? Is Liz Blackthorne Sally McGowan? Why else would she make a self-portrait out of pictures of a child killer? Is it Liz who's been sending me those threatening tweets? Did she alter the class photo, too?

My knees tremble. I touch the handrail for support, the palm of my hand sticking to it as I concentrate on setting each foot down. My eyes slide to the black-and-white photographs on the wall and it's like I'm seeing them for the very first time. One is of a stocky man in a striped apron standing outside a butcher shop, legs apart, arms folded. Another is of a little girl in a cotton dress and knitted sweater pushing a toy baby carriage along a dirty street.

My stomach contracts into a tight little ball. Some are shots of rooftops, a whole sea of them all jutting up against one another, and, in the distance, huge industrial chimneys belching smoke. Others are of children crouching at curbsides or clambering over burnt-out cars. Children clustered near decaying buildings.

They're just like that documentary Michael and I watched the other day. Why didn't I notice them before?

Liz is at the bottom of the stairs now, and I'm just a few steps behind. If she were to turn around and run up at me with that knife, I wouldn't stand a chance.

She turns and walks toward the kitchen. I could open the front door and leave. Tell her I've just remembered I have to be somewhere else. Tell her I'll call her later. But I don't. I follow her into the kitchen and watch as she opens a drawer and drops the knife inside, pushes it shut.

I breathe out. She switches the kettle on, then unscrews a metal French press. She opens the drawer again. I take a step back, but she's just getting a spoon out. She fills the press with three heaped dessert spoons of coffee. She plucks two pottery mugs from one of the open shelves above the counter.

This is Liz. Liz from book club. Clever, funny Liz, with her love of books and art and conversation. This isn't Sally McGowan. It can't be. And yet . . . I know something's coming. This fussing over coffee is just a prelude. I sense it in the way she's moving. Slowly. Deliberately. She's playing for time. Working up to it.

She puts the French press and two mugs on a tray. "Do you take milk and sugar?"

"Just milk, please."

She's almost at the fridge when she freezes. "Oh." She makes an apologetic face. "I don't think I have any milk. Sorry."

"That's fine. I'll drink it black."

"Are you sure?"

"Yes."

"I taught myself to appreciate black coffee when I was at art school," she says. Her voice is warm and friendly, as if this is any old day and we are just two friends having coffee. I try to tell myself that this *is* any old day and that we *are* just two friends having coffee. I haven't found a disturbing self-portrait in her studio and a pile of newspaper clippings about Sally McGowan.

"It went with the territory," she says. "Along with copious amounts of red wine and lots of bed-hopping."

She smiles and hands me the tray. "Why don't you carry this into the dining room and I'll cut some cake."

I take the tray and, as I turn, feel the weight of her gaze on the back of my neck. Why am I still here? I need to get back to work. Dave will be wondering where I am.

When I've put the tray on the dining room table, I take my phone out of my pocket and speed-dial the office.

"Sorry, Dave, I've been held up at Sea Breeze Court. Should be with you in about twenty minutes."

"No worries," Dave says. "It's nice and quiet this morning. See you later."

While I wait for Liz to come in with the cake, I study the pictures on the wall. Her paintings. They are fierce and abstract. Kaleidoscopic swirls of color and form. Which is what makes the realism of the self-portrait upstairs all the more striking.

"Some people don't *get* my kind of work."

I didn't hear her come in. She's standing next to me, so close that our shoulders almost touch.

"I don't know much about art," I say, afraid she'll hear my heart beating.

The weird thing is, I don't know if I'm genuinely frightened of her or whether it's just a heightened awareness that I *should* be frightened, and that's producing the same physical sensations. I feel like I'm a character in a movie. None of it is *really* happening. But it is. It is.

"I really like these, though," I say. "I don't know what they're supposed to represent, but they draw me in."

"That's why I prefer not to give my paintings titles," she says. "If you read the title of a painting, it directs your thoughts in a particular way, and I'd rather people drew their own conclusions."

She pushes down the plunger on the French press. "I have my own private titles, though."

What, I wonder, is her private title for the unfinished portrait upstairs? Will she tell me? Will we even speak about it? We have to. We can't just drink coffee and eat cake. We can't just have an intellectual conversation about the meaning of art when there's a giant elephant in the room.

I take a chance. "You've heard what's been going on at Stones and Crones, I suppose."

Liz takes a bite of her cake, washes it down with a mouthful of coffee.

"I have. And it sickens me. Poor Sonia."

I squirm in my chair. Does Liz hold me responsible for what's happening with her friend? I want to tell her that it's almost certainly Maddie's friend Anne Wilson who put those pictures up, but then it will look as if I'm trying to dump the blame on her when, actually, Maddie wouldn't even have known about the rumor if I hadn't blurted it out in the first place.

And how do I know for sure that Maddie is telling the truth? Maybe Maddie hates Anne Wilson for an entirely different reason. Maybe Anne has been flirting with Maddie's husband and it's Maddie who's the vindictive one. After all, how well do I really know Maddie? How well do we know anyone, come to that?

If only I'd never said anything at book club. If only I hadn't told Cathy and Debbie what Michael told me about the dry-town theory, then Cathy wouldn't have told everyone at the babysitting circle meeting and none of this would be happening. Without fresh gossip, the rumor would have fizzled out by now.

"Michael and I tried to help her," I say.

Liz widens her eyes. "Michael?"

"Yes, Alfie's dad. My . . . my partner. He's living with me now."

Liz goes very still. "How does he think he can help her?"

"By writing an article about false accusations. Making it clear she's *not* McGowan."

"You mean, he's a reporter?"

"Yes."

Liz presses her lips together. Something about her has changed. There's a strange sensation in the pit of my stomach.

"We were wondering if . . . if you'd speak to Sonia. Try to persuade her to talk to Michael. She got very angry when she found out he was a reporter. I can't say I blame her, but Michael says it'll get worse. There've been cases where people have been hounded out of their homes because of false rumors."

"I know," she says. Her voice is clipped. She won't meet my eyes.

I want to tell her I feel bad for passing the rumor on. I

want to tell her it was only that once. At book club. But knowing me, I'll go red when I say it. My face always lets me down when I'm lying, and then she'll know I feel guilty. Better to say nothing. I'll only end up tying myself in knots. And besides, another question burns in my mind.

The question I don't dare ask her.

34

"YOU NEED TO KNOW SOMETHING ABOUT ME," LIZ SAYS.

I brace myself. This is it. She's going to tell me who she is. Our eyes meet briefly, then we both look down at our coffees. Part of me doesn't want to hear what's coming next. I want to get away from her. Away from this house. Back to Dave in the office. Back to normality. But another part knows I'm staying. I have to know the truth. Not just because of Michael and his book—my God, what he wouldn't give to be here now—but because I'm curious. I *need* to know.

"I don't live like other people," Liz says. "I like my solitude. It's the only way I can work." She pushes her mug away from her and folds her arms on the table. "It's not that I don't *want* to see other people. I do. But only when I'm able to socialize. When I feel up to it. It sounds a bit pretentious to say it's because I'm an artist, but . . ." She twists her mouth into an odd little smile.

". . . it's because I'm an artist."

I wait for her to continue. I have the feeling that, if I speak, I'll break the spell of her confession. If that's what this is.

"When I'm working on a project, it consumes me," she says. "Nothing else matters. Nothing. The normal niceties of social interaction. Commitments like book club." She points to her disheveled hair and smiles. "Personal grooming. It all falls by the wayside. This morning was the first time I've done something else. I needed to get out in the fresh air, do something physical. And I never remember to lock my back door."

She takes a sip of coffee. "It's nice to know you were concerned about me, Jo," she says. "And I'm sorry I frightened you with the knife."

I make myself smile and nod. When is she going to mention the portrait? Surely she's not going to leave it like that?

"I'll speak to Sonia," she says. "But I doubt very much she'll give Michael an interview. Sonia's a very private person. Like me." Her eyes narrow. "Sometimes it's better to let things run their course. People will tire of it soon enough, when they see her getting on with her life, when she refuses to rise to the bait. A story in a paper will just fan the flames, in my opinion. Sonia needs to carry on as if nothing has happened."

I can't hold my tongue any longer. I have to ask her about the portrait.

"The project you're working on at the moment . . ." I say. The words hang in the air between us.

Liz gives me a sharp look.

"Is it that self-portrait I saw in your studio?"

She straightens her spine. "I don't usually talk about things I'm working on. Not until I've finished them," she says, gathering up our plates and mugs, signaling that the conversation is over. This part of it, at least.

"Can I ask you something else before I go?"

I've crossed into forbidden territory. I don't know what the hell I'm doing but, now that I've started, I can't stop.

Liz leans back in her chair and scrutinizes my face. She blinks several times.

"I saw the clippings," I say. "I know what the bits of paper are." My breath catches in my throat. What comes out is barely even a whisper. "You're not . . . you're not *her,* are you?"

A faint smile plays at the corners of Liz's lips. I can't believe I said that. Can't believe I'm sitting here asking Liz from book club if she's Sally McGowan. I ball my fists between my thighs.

"Did you ever see the painting *Myra,* by Marcus Harvey?" she asks.

Myra Hindley murdered five children in England in the 1960s—her name makes me shiver. "No, but I vaguely remember reading something about it once. Didn't someone throw paint at it?"

"It was vandalized, yes. It caused a huge controversy when it was hung at the Royal Academy. Not just because of the subject matter, but because it was made up of prints taken from the cast of a child's hand. People thought it was an outrage. The victims' families wanted it removed to protect their feelings. Even Myra Hindley herself wanted it taken down, but it wasn't. It stayed for the duration of the exhibition, and rightly so, in my view. Art *should* divide opinion. It *should* provoke emotion. Art should make us *think*.

"When you told us about the rumor, I was interested to see the different reactions in the group. It got me thinking about the case. I couldn't *stop* thinking about it. That's how I know an idea's got legs. When it doesn't let me go."

"But . . . but why is it a *self*-portrait?"

"Remember Nietzsche?" Liz says. *"He who fights with monsters should be careful lest he thereby become a monster. And if thou gaze long into an abyss, the abyss will also gaze into thee."*

She fixes me with her eyes, and though I want to look away, I can't.

"There's darkness in everyone's soul," Liz says. "That's what my portrait is all about. We're *all of us* capable of evil thoughts and evil acts under certain circumstances. I'm an artist, Jo. This is what I *do*."

"I didn't mean to accuse you, I . . ."

"You didn't accuse. You asked."

"Same thing, isn't it?"

She clasps her hands together in front of her chin, her elbows on the table. Her eyes flash. "What if I'd said yes?" she says.

I laugh, except the noise that comes out of my mouth sounds more like a whimper.

It's only when we've said goodbye and I'm walking to my car that it occurs to me she didn't actually say no.

35

WHEN I GET BACK TO THE OFFICE, DAVE IS WITH A CLIENT. I slide into the chair behind my desk and switch on my PC, immerse myself in routine tasks. Anything to push the last half hour to the back of my mind.

Do I believe what Liz just told me? Is that really what her portrait is about? An exploration of the monster in all of us? It has a ring of truth about it. Artists do get obsessed with certain subjects. I watched a PBS series—*What Do Artists Do All Day?*—and it was a fascinating insight into the creative process. But the way she reacted when I mentioned that Michael was a reporter—I wasn't imagining that. I know I wasn't. Something about her changed.

When the client leaves, Dave leans back in his chair and clasps his hands behind his head.

"Steve Enright phoned. I think they're going to make an offer on Sea Breeze Court, but they'd like another showing first. I've made an appointment for two P.M. Is that okay?"

I need to stop thinking about Liz and force myself to focus on something else instead. There are corrugated patches in the armpits of Dave's shirt—old sweat stains. Couldn't I find something more palatable to focus on?

"Fine," I say, and make a note of the time in my calendar. "Have the Frankises gotten back with any feedback?"

"Yes. Mrs. Frankis has concerns about the house next door. You know, the abandoned one. She's worried it'll attract squatters."

"I'm surprised it hasn't, to be honest. It looks like someone's already had a go at breaking in."

"I keep meaning to reach out to the town council about that. Find out what's going on. Oh, by the way, that woman came back. The one who was asking about a job."

"Kay?"

"Something about wanting to know how the party went. Was Alfie's costume a success?"

Shit. I meant to knock on Kay's door and tell her how well it went, thank her again for her help. I've been so preoccupied with everything that's been going on, I forgot all about it. She went to so much trouble for Alfie and me. The least I could do is get her a thank-you card and a box of chocolates or something.

THE HOURS THAT FOLLOW DON'T SO MUCH DRAG AS STAND still. It gets harder and harder to stop the events of the morning piercing through the shield I've erected in my mind. Insistent little stabs that won't be shut out, however hard I try to block them.

Dave's wife, Carol, drops by at about one thirty with a couple of chocolate eclairs in a box.

"Thought you two might like a little treat," she says.

She pops in all the time. Dave says she's paranoid about

him running off with someone else and, ever since he told her I live alone with Alfie, she always seems to be on her way to or from an appointment at the hair salon or the dentist's, or filling in time before meeting a friend for coffee. Maybe now that I've told Dave that Michael's moved in, she'll ease off a bit. *If* he tells her. I think he's secretly thrilled to be the subject of such misplaced jealousy. And of course, the eclairs are always welcome.

I sink my teeth into the chocolate, enjoying the fresh cream and choux pastry that flood my mouth. Carol is sitting at her husband's desk, leaning in toward him and having a private confab in hushed tones. She does this a lot. It's her way of marking her territory, and I don't usually take any notice, but today I hear the words "Stones and Crones" and "the police" and my ears prick up.

"They've been in the shop for ages," she says.

I pretend to be doing something on the computer, but really I'm just moving the cursor around and listening to their conversation.

"I can't believe she's that child killer, can you? But then, how would we know?"

She's talking normally now, her suspicion of what Dave and I might get up to when she's not around temporarily replaced by this latest turn of events, and I think of what Liz said earlier, about people getting tired of it if they see Sonia Martins moving on with her life, refusing to rise to the bait. It's not happening yet.

Dave sighs. "I hope to God she's not, or we'll be besieged by the press and every other Tom, Dick, or Harry who wants a piece of the action."

"Maybe she's called them herself," I say. "To make a complaint about the false accusation."

Carol swivels around to face me. "It doesn't look good, though, does it? The police in her store for everyone to see. People will draw their own conclusions. I can't see her doing much business after this, can you?"

"You never know, business might improve."

Carol gives me a blank look.

"She means more people will go in the store to get a look at her," Dave says.

"And buy a set of runes while they're in there," I quip.

Dave smirks, but Carol is pursing her lips.

"Anyway," she adds, "how do you know it's a false accusation?"

Relieved that it's almost time for my appointment with the Enrights, I stand up and make moves to leave.

"If there was any truth in the rumor, I doubt she'd still be here." I pull on my coat and hook my handbag over my shoulder. "Okay then, I'm off to sell a condo."

"Try not to mention we may have a child killer in our midst," Dave says drily.

Carol glares at him.

MY CAR IS POINTING TOWARD THE OCEAN, WHICH MEANS I have to drive past Stones and Crones. A police car is parked up on the left, a few doors away from the shop, but even though there's no one behind me and I'm driving quite slowly, I can't see what's happening inside because the window is still boarded up.

I do see Kay, though. She's waiting to cross the street up ahead, hovering between two parked cars. I stop to wave her across but she doesn't see me. Her eyes are locked on the other side of the road, on the boarded window of Stones and

Crones. Then she spots me through the windshield and does a little jolt of recognition. She raises her hand to say hello.

Now a van is right behind me and I have to drive on. As I glance in my rearview mirror, I see Kay staring at the police car. Her face is blank. Immobile. Like a mask.

36

"IT'S SO UNLIKE ANY OF HER OTHER PICTURES. THAT'S WHAT made me notice it."

Michael pours oil into the frying pan and starts browning the onions. He hasn't spoken yet, but he's listening intently as he prepares our chicken curry. It's nice to be cooked for, to enjoy a civilized meal in the evening instead of eating with Alfie at five, which is what I always used to do. It changes everything, having another adult in the house. Especially one who likes cooking.

"I couldn't believe it when I realized it was made out of scraps of paper. But when I saw where the scraps of paper came from . . ."

Michael chops a clove of garlic and tosses the pieces in with the onion.

"How did she react when you asked her if she was Sally McGowan?"

"Calmly."

I tell him what she said about the Myra Hindley painting, and he nods.

"I remember it being on the news when I was a teenager," he says.

"She said something about darkness being in all our souls and that we're all capable of evil. That's the idea behind the portrait. The message she's trying to convey."

Michael tips the saucer of spices into the pan, and a delicious aroma fills the kitchen. "Not sure we're all capable of plunging a knife into a little boy's chest," he says. "But still, I think I see what she means."

The diced chicken and canned tomatoes are going in now. I marvel at his ability to do all this at the same time as having a thoughtful conversation.

"But there's more to it than that," I say. "She was *too* calm. I mean, how would you react if someone more or less accused you of being a notorious criminal? She's hiding something, I know she is. And she definitely reacted when I told her you were a journalist."

Michael pauses in his stirring. Only for a beat, but it's enough to tell me he thinks it's significant.

"*How* did she react?"

"It's hard to describe, but her face sort of closed down for a few seconds. She got very quiet, and then she said it was unlikely Sonia would speak to you."

"That's not an uncommon reaction. Loads of people distrust journalists. We're up there with realtors as the nation's most detested." He laughs. "We're going to be a popular couple, you and I."

I open the bottle of wine we bought earlier and pour out two glasses. Michael puts the lid on the pan and adjusts the heat. Then we take our drinks into the living room.

"And then there are those photographs on the wall by the stairs."

"What photographs?"

So I tell him about those, too, and how they reminded me of the documentary we watched.

"How old is Liz?"

"I don't know. I've never asked and she's never said. I'd say she's probably in her late fifties. It's hard to tell, though. Her hair is completely white so I guess it's possible she's older."

Michael's glass is midway to his mouth when he pauses.

"I know someone whose hair went white overnight when they were forty," he says.

"What's Liz's last name?" he asks, a few seconds later. "Has she ever exhibited any of her art?"

"I'm not sure. She might have. It certainly deserves to be exhibited. It's very good."

He picks up his laptop from where he's left it on the table. "Let's look her up. See if there are any pictures of her work."

"Blackthorne," I say. "Her name is Liz Blackthorne."

His fingers pause over the keyboard. He frowns.

"What?"

"Nothing. Just . . . nothing. Let's see what's online."

He types her name into the search bar and finds various Liz Blackthornes but not the one we're looking for. He tries Elizabeth Blackthorne and E. Blackthorne, and at last we find her listed on a few art-related and gallery websites as E. K. Blackthorne. There is a thumbnail photo of her on one of these sites with examples of her work and brief descriptive passages next to each one. None of them is titled. Then we find a blog of hers called *Art in a Seaside Town*.

"Look," I say. "It says she graduated from the Art Institute of Chicago. Doesn't say when, though. Still, at least we know she's not McGowan. She'd never have stayed that close to the Dearborn area, would she? Not if she didn't want to be recognized."

"No, I don't suppose she would." There's a concentrated look in Michael's eyes, as if he's trying to calculate an impossible sum.

"And the Chicago connection explains those photographs."

"Maybe."

He snaps the laptop shut and returns to the here and now. Something in his demeanor has changed. He thinks it's her. I know he does.

He heads for the door. "I'm just going to check on the curry and put the rice on." He grins. "Must be nice being waited on hand and foot. I wonder when it's going to be my turn."

I laugh, but as soon as he's gone that horrible photo of Alfie with a knife sticking out of his chest appears behind my eyes. It's always there. Waiting to catch me off guard. Could Liz have doctored that photo? How would she have gotten hold of the digital image? No, Kay and Michael are right about that. It was a Halloween prank by one of the other mothers. Nothing to do with McGowan—well, not directly.

The Twitter account, though. All those literary quotes. Now, that *could* have been Liz. Trying to scare me into shutting up about that rumor.

37

IT'S TWO THIRTY-SEVEN A.M. AND I'M WIDE AWAKE. I'M ALSO alone in the bed.

After supper we started watching a movie, but neither of us could concentrate so we finished the wine and had an early night. We tried to make love as quietly as we could so as not to disturb Alfie. I don't remember much after that. I must have fallen asleep really fast. All this sex is tiring me out.

I get up and open the bedroom door. Perhaps Michael's just in the bathroom, but he isn't, so I creep downstairs to see what he's doing. The light's on in the dining room, and the door is closed.

His head jerks up as soon as I go in.

"Hey, you," he says. "I didn't wake you, did I?"

I shake my head. "What's up? Can't you sleep?"

"I'm always the same when I'm in the middle of a new project," he says. "I can never switch off."

He opens his arms and I sink onto his lap, rest my head against his neck.

"That's more or less what Liz said to me yesterday," I say.

He stiffens slightly and I sit up. The look that passes across his eyes is fleeting and subtle, but there's no mistaking it. The mere mention of her name has affected him in some way.

"You think it's her, don't you?"

"I don't know what to think at the moment," he says. "My head feels like a jigsaw that's missing a key piece."

He gestures to the papers spread all over the table. Pages and pages of scrawled notes. Hole-punched reports with Post-it markers sticking out at the sides.

"But it's got to be somewhere. I just need to find it."

He nods toward his laptop. "I spoke to the *Flinstead and Mistden Gazette* earlier. Take a look at this and see what you think. It'll be on their website tomorrow." He squints at the time display at the bottom of the screen. "Well, later *today*, actually. It's a much shorter version of the article I really wanted to write. Maybe I can pitch something about false accusations to one of the bigger papers."

LOCAL SHOPKEEPER'S VIGILANTE TORMENT

A false rumor is jeopardizing the livelihood of local shop-keeper Sonia Martins.

On Wednesday, October 18, a photo was stuck to the window of her popular New Age gift shop, Stones and Crones, falsely implying that she was child killer Sally McGowan.

Her shop was targeted again when a brick was thrown through the window. The incident happened sometime between 12:30 A.M. and 6:30 A.M. on Tuesday, October 31. Police are appealing for witnesses.

Flinstead police chief Bob Sanderson said: "All necessary background checks have been completed and I can confirm that this rumor is completely untrue. Sonia Martins is a respectable member of our community. She was born in Flinstead and her mother has lived here all her life.

"We are a small town," he said, "and rumors like this spread quickly. I would urge whoever is doing this to think very carefully about their actions, as the consequences can be serious."

Sonia Martins is so distressed by recent events she has even considered leaving Flinstead.

"I know most people don't believe it, but some very clearly do, and I no longer feel safe, either in my home or my place of work. I just want whoever is doing this to stop."

There have been four previous cases of women falsely accused of being McGowan, one of which ended tragically in suicide.

Anyone with information on the incident in Flinstead should call the Flinstead Police Department.

"So you've spoken to Sonia already? Why didn't you tell me?"

He shrugs. "It slipped my mind. Sorry. She had second thoughts after the brick was thrown."

"I'm not surprised, poor woman! Let's hope that's an end to it now."

"Come on," Michael says, gathering up his papers and stuffing them into his briefcase. "Let's try and get some sleep."

IN THE MORNING, I FEEL AWFUL. IT'S A GOOD THING IT'S MY day off and that Dave point-blank refused my offer to go in and make up for Tuesday. But there are tons of things I need to do today. I've got to pick up some things for Mom, who's still under the weather, and I want to get a card and a thank-you present for Kay. And then I need to catch up on some laundry and ironing and change the sheets. All I really want to do is go back to bed and sleep for a week.

"Tell you what," Michael says. "You go have a nice bath while I take Alfie to school."

I give him a hug. "I knew there was a reason I let you move in."

"What, apart from the great sex and my superior cooking skills?"

"Hmm, that might have had something to do with it. How do you feel about coming to Mom's with me later?"

He laughs. "Now you're pushing your luck."

"Sol will be pleased to see you," I say. "I thought we could take him out for a walk."

He kisses me on the nose, then the forehead, and, finally, the mouth. He tastes of toothpaste.

"Maybe your mom'll be pleased to see me, too," he says.

"Now who's pushing their luck?"

MOM'S WATCHING *HOUSE HUNTERS* WHEN WE ARRIVE WITH her groceries. She's all bundled up in sweaters and wearing a woolen hat.

"The heat's not working," she says, taking the bag from Michael. "None of the radiators are getting hot enough."

Michael touches the one in the hall. "They probably just need bleeding."

"Yes, I realize that," she says. "Except I can't find the little key."

I follow her into the kitchen while Michael makes a fuss over Sol in the front room.

"Do you have to be quite so *terse* with him?" I say when we're out of earshot. "I thought, after our conversation the other day, you'd start cutting him some slack."

"Sorry, I didn't know I *was* being terse," she says. Tersely.

Michael appears in the doorway. "I could do it with a screwdriver if you've got one," he says.

Mom looks at him in surprise. "Oh, I didn't think of that."

She rummages in a drawer. "What one would be best?"

Michael selects one and goes back into the hall. Then he comes back for a dishcloth. "Don't want dirty water dripping on your carpet, do we?"

I help Mom put her groceries away, while Michael goes around the house on bleeding duty. We hear him singing while he works.

"Thank you for doing that," she says, stiffly, when he comes back.

Michael doffs an imaginary cap. "Always at your service, Mrs. C.," he says, and Mom almost smiles at him. At least she's trying.

Just before we leave she calls out from the living room: "Michael, I don't suppose you'd ever consider joining the Flinstead church choir, would you?"

He widens his eyes at me in horror and it's all I can do not to burst out laughing.

"I couldn't help noticing you're a rather good baritone and we only have three men and one of them can't even sing."

Michael winks at me. "Not sure a church choir's really my thing, Mrs. C. But I'll give it some thought."

By the time we get to the end of the driveway, Sol plodding ahead of us on his leash, we can't hold the laughter in anymore.

"It's progress, though, you have to admit."

"Hmm," Michael says. "That kind of progress, I can do without, thank you very much."

38

KAY ANSWERS HER DOOR AFTER THE SECOND RING OF THE doorbell. She looks slightly flustered, but she quickly recovers.

"Hello, dear," she says. "Sorry about that, I was just saying good night to Marcus and Callie on Skype. It's nine o'clock at night where they live."

"I hope I didn't interrupt you."

"Not at all. We've been chatting for ages and those kids need to get to bed. Gillian lets them stay up far too late, in my opinion. Come in and have a cup of tea with me. I've got some delicious carrot cake that needs eating."

"That's very kind of you, Kay, but I really just wanted to bring you this."

She takes the gift bag and peers inside. "Chocolates. How lovely. You shouldn't have," she says, wagging her finger at me, but I can tell she's pleased.

"Sorry I missed you when you stopped in to Pegton's. I've been meaning to thank you properly ever since the party. Alfie looked amazing as Darth Vader."

"It was my pleasure, sweetheart. Now, are you sure you won't have some tea?"

I'm not really in the mood for one of Kay's watery teas, but she's already standing aside for me to go in and I don't like to say no. Not after she's been so kind.

"Okay, then. But I can't stay long."

Kay's living room looks exactly as it did the last time I was here. Every surface gleams. It smells the same, too—lemon-scented furniture polish.

I'm watching the tropical fish when she returns a few minutes later with a tray. "Here, you slice the cake, and I'll bring the teapot in."

As I'm pushing the knife through the icing on top of the carrot cake, I catch sight of my reflection in the screen of Kay's laptop, which she's left open on the coffee table. It's a really old model, but then I don't suppose she can afford to buy a new one. Not if she's struggling to find another job.

My hair's sticking up at a weird angle and I rake my fingers through it. Then I notice something odd. There's no built-in webcam in this laptop, yet she just said she was finishing a Skype call with her grandchildren. I look around to see if there's a portable one she might have unplugged just now, but I can't see one anywhere.

How odd. Perhaps she just uses Skype as a free telephone, without the video function.

Kay comes back in with another tray. "It's such a joy, seeing their little faces," she says. "Marcus has just learned his three times table. He's so smart for his age. And Callie can count to twenty. Well, almost."

"Do you have one of those portable webcams?"

A strange expression flickers over her eyes. Her neck reddens. She lifts the lid of the teapot and gives it a stir.

"Yes, that's right, dear." She smiles. "All high technology here, you know."

A pulse pounds in the side of her neck. She's lying. There's no portable webcam. She can't possibly have been Skyping Marcus and Callie just now. And didn't she tell me a while back that they live in Melbourne? I'm no expert on time zones, but I'm pretty sure it's the middle of the night over there.

Why would she lie about something like that?

"Guess what?" she says. "I've found a job. In the garden center in Mistden. I'm starting next week."

Why do I get the feeling she's deliberately changing the subject?

"That's great. Well done."

She pours the tea. I notice her hand is trembling.

"Are you all right, Kay?"

"I'm fine, honey," she says, but she isn't. I can tell.

"I saw Alfie's dad this morning," she says brightly. Too brightly. "He's very handsome, isn't he? He looks like that British actor everyone says should be James Bond."

"Idris Elba?" I laugh. "I'm not going to tell him that. It'll make him even more bigheaded than he already is."

"What does he do for a living?" she says.

"He's a freelance journalist."

Kay puts her cup down. It rattles against the saucer. "Is he staying with you at the moment, then?"

"Yes. Actually, he's moved in."

"I thought you said you liked living apart." She sounds almost annoyed, as if I've let her down in some way.

"We did. But, well, things have changed. He wants us to give it a real shot."

"That's fantastic, honey." She smiles, but it doesn't quite work. There's a strange look in her eyes, as if she's some-place else in her head. That same masklike expression I saw on her face yesterday, when she was staring across the road at the police car.

"Yes, yes, it is." I take a few bites of my carrot cake and realize I haven't eaten any breakfast. No wonder I'm so hungry.

"More tea, dear?"

"No, I need to get going. Lots to do today."

"Of course. Me too."

As I reach the end of her path, the mailman is just about to turn in and deliver her mail. He looks in a bit of a hurry so I offer to take the letters from him and go back to hand them to Kay, but she's already gone inside and shut her front door. That's odd. Before, she's stood on the step and waved goodbye.

I push the letters through her mail slot and can't help noticing that they're all marked RETURN TO SENDER and that the addresses have been slashed through with a thick black line. They are all the same. An address in Melbourne, Australia.

39

WHEN I GET HOME, EXPECTING TO SEE MICHAEL WHERE I LEFT him, hunched over the dining room table surrounded by his papers, the house is empty and the table has been cleared. There's a note propped against the kettle in his large, confident handwriting.

Something's come up. Got to go back to the city. Will call you. Michael xx

I read it again, as if it might somehow have changed from these three curt sentences into a message that tells me something useful. Like *what* exactly has "come up" and *why* has he had to go back to the city and for how long? Surely he could have given me a little more information. Like when he's planning on coming back. Will it be later today? Tonight? Tomorrow? I don't need every detail of his itinerary, but does he have to be so infuriatingly *cryptic*?

I dial his cellphone but it goes straight to voicemail. Of course it does. He'll be driving. I don't leave a message. I'm sure he'll text me when he arrives, although why didn't he call before he left? He knows I always have my phone on me.

What was the great rush? Surely a couple of minutes wouldn't have made much difference.

I wander into the living room and flop down on the sofa. He's left his sweatshirt screwed up on the back of the armchair and a dirty mug and plate on the coffee table. There are toast crumbs on the rug, where he's been eating in front of the TV. Not a lot of crumbs, admittedly, but enough to piss me off.

The trouble is, I've spent so many years living on my own that I'm not used to sharing my space with a man. I've got Alfie, of course, but that's different. Alfie's a child. I'm being unreasonable, I know I am. It's been wonderful having Michael here all the time. Cuddling up to him in bed. Going for walks with Sol. And that curry last night was delicious. I just wish he'd spoken to me before leaving.

Two hours later and he still hasn't been in touch. I've tried calling him at least seven times and sent him I don't know how many text messages. Earlier today I heard him promise Alfie he'd pick him up from school, but there's no way he'll be back in time. What am I going to tell Alfie when he asks where his dad is, or if he'll be home for dinner? Is this what it's going to be like from now on? Michael getting so engrossed in his work, he forgets about everything else, Alfie and me included?

Maybe he thinks he can just carry on like he always has, answerable to no one but himself, squeezing Alfie and me into whatever time he has left on the margins of his real world. The world that matters to him most: his work. The irony is that he really does have another woman on his mind now: Sally McGowan.

The phone rings. This had better be him.

"Hi, hon. I thought it was time for one of our heart-to-hearts. I'm in Panera in between showings."

Tash's voice is like a blast of normality. A welcome respite from the worries churning in my head.

"Which one?"

"Church Street."

I can just picture her sitting on one of the brown leather chairs with a large latte and a blueberry muffin, watching the hustle and bustle pass by the window, and I wish, more than anything, that I was there, too, enjoying a break in the middle of the day, complaining about work and planning our next night out.

"How's life in Pleasantville?" she says.

"Not so pleasant. Although Michael's moved in with me, so it's not *all* bad."

"*Whaaat?* When? Why didn't you tell me?"

"Because it only just happened. Except now he's gone off to the city and hasn't told me when he's coming back."

"Whoa. Back up a bit. Tell me *everything*."

So I try to summarize what's been going on in the last few weeks, rumor and all (although I don't mention the Liz thing, just in case it really is her), right up to finding Michael's note.

"Wow!" Tash says. "And here I was thinking the most exciting thing to happen in Flinstead was your mother's neighbor winning Biggest Zucchini at last year's state fair."

"Very funny."

"Seriously, though, let's tackle the easiest issue first. If Michael says he'll call you, then he will. Men are hopeless when it comes to sharing their plans. Tommo's exactly the same. It's like getting blood out of a stone sometimes. To be honest, hon, it's going to take you both time to adjust. I mean, I know you've known each other for ages, but this is different. You're living together now. It's more like a brand-new relationship in that respect."

"Well, that's just it," I say. "For me, that's exactly what it feels like. But what if he's just taking it for granted that I'll be here with Alfie, picking up the pieces? Because that's how it's always been."

"So it's up to you to set some new ground rules. Talk to him, Jo. Men aren't like us. They don't pick up on things, and if they do, nine times out of ten they pick the wrong thing. You have to spell it out for them." She laughs. "Preferably in words of one syllable. And if you've got one of those neon lights, make damn sure you flash it a few times to ram the point home."

Good old Tash. She always manages to say the right thing. Michael's obviously just tied up in something. He *will* phone me eventually, and then we'll talk. And if we can't talk then, if he's chasing another one of his leads or doing whatever it is freelance journalists have to do these days to keep their heads above water, we'll make a time to talk soon. I'm overreacting. Dashing off at a minute's notice is all part of his job. I should know that by now.

"As for this other business," Tash says, "I don't know *what* to think. If sending ominous tweets threatening a child is someone's idea of a Halloween prank, they sound like a really nasty piece of work. Maybe your friend Kay's right and it's the woman from the babysitting circle. What's her name?"

"Debbie."

I don't go into the business with Kay, either. There's only

so much you can cover in one phone call and I don't want Tash to think I've landed in a nest of vipers. Besides, I have to pick Alfie up soon.

"I'd be tempted to bring it up next time you see them all at the coven," Tash says. "See whose face goes red. Then you'll know who it is and you can steer clear of them in future."

"The fact is, Tash, it could be anyone. That's what's so horrible about it."

40

NO SOONER HAVE I PUT THE PHONE DOWN ON TASH THAN IT rings again. This time it *is* Michael. About time. He's probably just looked at his watch and remembered his promise to Alfie.

"Joey, listen. Can you get on a train and meet me downtown?"

"You're kidding! What on earth for?"

"I need you to do me a big favor. I need you to speak to Liz with me."

"Why would I need to get on a train to do that? She's just around the corner."

"No. She's staying at a Holiday Inn here. She's attending an artists' convention. I've just watched her check in."

"My God, Michael. Are you *following* her?"

He sighs. "Look, I didn't tell you this, but she and I have been in touch. I was given her name by someone I know, that ex-hack I told you about."

"Wait a minute. What are you talking about?"

He takes a deep breath. "I was given the name E. K. Blackthorne as a possible lead. She used to be an art therapist and she worked at Gray Willow Grange, the juvenile detention center where Sally McGowan was sent as a child."

"Why didn't you tell me this last night? Why did you pretend—"

"Please, Joey, just listen. I was told that she and McGowan had a good rapport, and that they'd kept in touch. I was told that . . ." He clears his throat. "I was told they were lovers."

"What the hell!"

"As soon as you started talking about the self-portrait you'd found in your friend Liz's studio, I had the strangest feeling that maybe she was the same woman I'd already interviewed. Then when you told me her last name was Blackthorne, I knew for sure. Up till then I knew her only as E. K. or Elizabeth Blackthorne. I got in touch with her via her blog. She agreed to do a short telephone interview about her work at Gray Willow Grange. What it was like. I didn't mention anything about wanting to track McGowan down. That would have scared her off. I just made out I was interested in writing a piece about the rehabilitation of child offenders and how we only ever get to hear about the failures and never the successes. She lapped it up."

"Go on," I urge.

"We got along really well. I'd done a lot of research into art therapy and its use with damaged children. You know, kids without the language or emotional skills to talk about the shit they've been through, how art therapists can coax stuff out of them. We agreed to meet to talk some more. She suggested a café downtown, so I met her there last week. You know, when I went back to deal with the apartment? I told her what I really wanted to do was to see if I could get enough material to write a book. I still didn't mention McGowan's name. I talked about other, more recent cases.

"Amazingly, it was she who brought her up. She said she'd heard from someone she used to know that McGowan might be interested in talking at last. It's always bothered her that the press never believed it was a game that went wrong. She told me McGowan wants to put her side of the story across in a way she couldn't when she was a child. Half the stuff about the abuse she suffered was never fully explored during the trial. It's no wonder the press savaged her. But McGowan's only willing to speak out if her and her family's anonymity is preserved."

"Her family? She's not still in touch with them, surely?"

"Her parents? I doubt it. No, I presume she meant the family she has now. Husband, if there is one. And she had a child. I didn't ask Liz if she was still in touch with her, and she didn't tell me, but I got the sense she knew that I knew. I felt like we were really getting somewhere and that, in time, if she trusted me enough, she might be willing to broker some kind of meeting."

"Why didn't you tell me any of this?"

"Because I didn't realize she was *your* Liz until you told me about her last night. I didn't even realize she lived in Flinstead. And then, as soon as you told me you'd mentioned my name in connection with Sonia Martins and that I wanted to interview her, I knew the game was up, and I was right. She contacted me this morning to say she was very sorry but she didn't think she'd be able to help me anymore. She said she'd made a mistake and the whole idea of talking to McGowan was a non-starter, that she had no clue where she was anymore, and that I should concentrate on the other cases I'd mentioned.

"She knows who Sally McGowan is, Jo. I'm convinced of it. I think she probably moved to Flinstead so she could be near her. Please come, Joey. She'll take one look at me and clam up, but if you're there, too . . ."

"But what about Alfie? School gets out soon. Why on earth didn't you tell me all this earlier, and I could have driven in with you?"

"Because I wasn't sure if she'd definitely attend the convention. It might have been a wasted journey."

"I can't ask Mom to pick him up. She's still feeling awful. You know she is."

He sighs. "Shit. I didn't think of that. Maybe you could get someone from your babysitting circle to look after him? Please, Joey. If I can find McGowan and talk to her, I *know* I'll be able to tell her story the way she wants it told. I won't do anything to jeopardize her anonymity."

He pauses. "I'll meet you at South Station," he says. "If you catch the next train, you can be here by three thirty."

There's a desperation in his voice I can't ignore. I feel myself wavering.

"Well, as long as I can find someone I trust to look after Alfie. Fatima, maybe, or Teri Monkton."

"What about Kay? You said she was great with him."

"She is, but . . . oh, I don't know. I'm not sure what's happening with Kay at the moment. I think she's been lying to me. Lying to all of us. I'd rather ask one of the others, to be honest. I'll figure something out. I'll shoot you a text in a little while and let you know if I can make it. Otherwise . . . otherwise, you're just going to have to try and talk to her yourself."

I KEEP MY FINGER ON THE BELL FOR THE THIRD TIME. FATIMA must be out. I glance over at Kay's house. She's said before that she'd be happy to look after Alfie at short notice and I know she'd say yes, so what's stopping me? Before this morning, I'd have had no qualms about asking her. Alfie would be more than happy to spend time with Kay and her tropical fish. And she'd probably spoil him rotten.

But something tells me it isn't a good idea. A vague sense of foreboding. There's something weird going on with her and her daughter. There must be. Why else would all Kay's letters be sent back? And why does Kay feel she has to lie about Skyping her grandchildren? It doesn't make sense. I'll have to give someone from the babysitting circle a call, see if they can help me out. I don't want to ask Debbie, though.

Just then, Karen walks by. She's on the opposite side of the street, and at first she doesn't see me. When she does, she crosses immediately.

"Hi. You recovered from that god-awful party yet?"

"Just about."

Why don't I ask her? Alfie's already familiar with her apartment. He seemed really at home there the other night, watching *Frozen* with Hayley. Although she does have her mother to look after at the moment.

"What's up?" Karen says.

"I was just wondering whether you could do me a huge favor and pick Alfie up from school this afternoon and look after him for a few hours. But I'm worried it's asking too much of you. You must have your hands full, taking care of your mom."

"Of *course* I'll pick him up. Actually, it's easier for us both when Hayley's occupied with a friend. She can be a little demanding otherwise, and Mom's always too nice not to play with her, even when I can see she's too tired and would rather not."

"You are a lifesaver! I hate to ask last minute, but I've got to do something in the city. I'll be back before seven. Seven thirty at the latest."

"Take as long as you like," Karen says. "Hayley will be thrilled. Did I tell you she thinks Alfie's her boyfriend? It's ever since they watched *Frozen* together."

I laugh. "I'm not sure Alfie realizes that."

"We're having hot dogs and beans for supper. Will he eat that? I can make something different if he won't."

"No, that would be perfect. Thanks, Karen. I'll phone the school and let them know. Let me give you my number."

Karen pulls out her phone and adds my name to her contacts. "I'll send you a text," she says. "Then you'll have mine."

"Thank you *so* much. I really appreciate it. I'll send you my mom's number, too, just in case of an emergency. She's not feeling well at the moment, or I'd have asked her."

"There won't be any emergency," Karen says. "Although Hayley will probably insist he watches *Frozen* again, so Alfie might *think* he needs rescuing." She glances over my shoulder and smiles. "Hi, Kay. How's things?"

I turn around to see Kay standing on her doorstep. She's rubbing at the exterior of her front door with a cloth. Oh no. Her face. She must have heard every word and be wondering why I didn't ask her. She'll see it as a deliberate snub. I know she will.

She waves the cloth at us and says hello. I open my mouth to give some sort of explanation, but she's already gone inside and closed her door. Oh well, there's nothing I can do about it right now.

41

SOUTH STATION IS JAMMED AND IT ISN'T EVEN RUSH HOUR. Up until four months ago, I'd lived in this city for almost fifteen years. It felt like home. Now it's as if I'm a visitor. I'm stunned by the number of people and the speed at which they walk, the cacophony of voices and sounds that bombards my ears. I feel like a country bumpkin, dazzled by the bright lights of the big city.

I gasp as Michael touches my arm. He's wearing his gray wool coat and looks suave and rugged at the same time. I think of what Kay said this morning, about him looking like Idris Elba, and smile. Then I remember that awkward moment earlier on, and the embarrassment that she heard me asking someone else to look after Alfie settles over me once again.

Michael kisses me lightly on the lips, then takes hold of my arm and gently steers me toward the subway.

"So where are we going again?"

"Kenmore Square. She's at the Holiday Inn. Her convention ends at four, so I thought we could have a drink in the bar and then wait for her in the lobby. Maybe it's best if you approach her first."

"What shall I say?" I'm not looking forward to surprising Liz like this. Not after what happened in her house yesterday. How is she going to react when she sees me?

"Let's figure it out when we get there. I just want you to reassure her of my intentions. Let her know she can trust me, and that Sally can, too."

"But why couldn't we have waited till she got home? Why do we have to stalk her like this?"

"Because it's easier for her to shut the door in our face if we doorstep her. Meeting her in a public place is better. Even if she walks away, we can walk alongside her. She might not talk to us, but she'll have to listen."

I suppose this is the dogged reporter in him coming out. The determination to make someone talk. To get his story at all costs.

We take the T and then, blinking in the early-November sunshine, walk to the hotel. It's as much as I can do to keep up with Michael's long strides. Within a few minutes, we're passing through the entrance of the Holiday Inn. I can't believe I've allowed myself to be talked into all this, although I have to admit it's exciting. I feel like a private eye. No wonder Michael's so cloak-and-dagger sometimes, if this is the sort of thing he has to do to find things out.

We wander through to the bar and Michael pulls out his wallet. "What do you want to drink?"

What *do* I want to drink? I'm running on adrenaline now. I can't think straight. The last thing I need is alcohol.

"A Coke, please."

Michael orders a Coke for me and a lager for him.

He gestures to a menu on the counter. "Do you want anything to eat?"

I shake my head. I feel nauseous and apprehensive now that I'm actually here. Michael pays for the drinks and we find a table in a quiet corner in sight of the large wall clock and the glass doors to the lobby.

"While I was waiting for you at the station," Michael says, "I started wondering why Liz shut down on me so fast. I was really getting somewhere with her."

"It's obvious, isn't it? When she thought you were just some journalist interested in the rehabilitation of child offenders, it was different. But now that she knows you're my partner and you want to interview Sonia Martins about the false-accusation thing, it's all a bit close to home."

Michael takes a swig of beer. "But maybe there's more to it than that."

"How do you mean?"

"What if I'm right and Liz knows exactly where McGowan is? What if she's somebody you both know and that's why she doesn't want to speak to me anymore? Because she's frightened you'll find out."

Something bad bumps around in my head. If Michael's right, then she and McGowan must have been scared out of their wits. Right from the start, when I first mentioned the rumor. Scared enough to want to stop it before it did any more damage? Scared enough to send me threatening tweets as Sally Mac? To digitally alter a school photo?

I don't know how computer literate Liz is, but she has a blog, so she must be reasonably savvy. But how would she have gotten into the school to leave a photo under the principal's door? Didn't Mr. Matthews say that Mrs. Haynes found it there when she came in? And how would Liz have known about the photo in the first place? She doesn't have anything to do with Perrydale Elementary. No, whoever left that photo must have had access to the school first thing in the morning, and except for the people who work there, that only leaves . . .

Something drops into my brain and sets off a ripple effect. When Teri Monkton found me waiting for Mr. Matthews and fuming with anger, I'm sure she said she was about to go into a PTA meeting. Could someone involved in the PTA have left the photo there when no one was looking?

Michael narrows his eyes. "What? What are you thinking?"

"I don't know. I'm starting to suspect just about everyone I know. It's stupid."

He pulls out his phone. "Here, take a look at these. I managed to get hold of some photos from one of my contacts. They're of Sally when she was a young woman."

He shows me three black-and-white pictures. Photos of old photos, so the quality isn't great. I study the first one. It's not an image I recognize from all my googling. She's holding a child in her arms, a toddler, and mouthing something at the person who's taking the photograph. Her face is contorted with anger. The toddler looks scared. She's clinging to the lapels of her mother's coat, her head tucked into the dip of her neck.

The second picture looks like it was taken at a farmers' market. Lots of stalls heaped with fruits and vegetables and handcrafts. A woman with dark hair in a bun is studying some apples. You can only see her profile, but I'm assuming this must be McGowan, too. She's holding the mittened hand of a young child. The same child who's in the first photo.

The third one is of a house at night. Now, this one I *have* seen before. The front window is smashed and a policeman is standing on the front path, his back to the house. The words CHILD MURDERER have been daubed on the door in paint. An involuntary shudder travels the length of my spine.

I look at them all again—the one of McGowan's profile as she reaches for an apple. Something about the bridge of her nose is vaguely familiar. I've never seen a photo of her from this particular angle. She *does* remind me of someone. But who? I press my fingertips to my temples. Maybe if I press hard enough I'll remember.

My eyes return to the toddler. A new thought is swirling around in my head, trying to make itself known. When it does, it's like a jolt of electricity. "Oh my God, Michael. Maybe it's the *daughter* I know. Sally McGowan's daughter!"

Michael looks thoughtful. "Well, that certainly widens the field."

"And if Liz knows McGowan, she'll know the daughter, too!"

A series of images like scenes from a movie flash before my eyes: the look on Liz's face when I first mentioned the rumor. Those wide, inquisitive eyes. The way she casually reached for an olive. *Too* casually, I see that now. The astonished expression on Karen's face and the way she stared at me at the babysitting circle when Cathy told me to tell everyone what I'd heard.

My spine slowly straightens. Another image presents itself. Karen and her mother peering in at me through Pegton's window. The mother's head turning to look back as they walked away. That peculiar expression on her face. Karen desperate to volunteer for doing the Hot Potato music. Deliberately letting Alfie win the main prize. Inviting us back to her home to meet her mother. She and her husband run a computer-graphics company. She'd have known exactly how to alter that photo, wouldn't she? And—oh my God!—she's the secretary of the PTA! If anyone could have left that photo before Mrs. Haynes arrived, it was her!

I think of Alfie in Karen's home right now and dread writhes in my gut. What did Karen say when I asked her why she was walking so fast with him that time? She said she was in a rush to take her mother to the doctor's. What if she was lying? What if she was trying to abduct him all along? What if Karen's mother is Sally McGowan and Karen told her it was me who passed the rumor on? They'd hate me for that, wouldn't they? For putting them at such risk?

Then I remember my nightmare: Sally McGowan standing at the foot of my bed, hands smeared with blood. How she looked . . . how she looked just like Karen! I stand up so fast I almost knock my chair over. It scrapes and wobbles on the floor.

"Oh my God, Michael. They've got Alfie! We've got to get back!"

"Who's got Alfie?"

"Hayley's mom, Karen. Karen has just picked our son up from school. I think she's Sally McGowan's daughter. She must blame me for spreading the rumor about her.

"Alfie's in danger, Michael. We have to leave now!"

42

"WE'VE GOT TO GET OUT OF HERE. WE'VE GOT TO CALL THE police. And Mom. I need to let her know what's happened. And the school." I grab my bag.

Michael stands up and puts both his hands on my shoulders. "Wait a minute. Let's think logically about this. Even if you're right and Karen is McGowan's daughter, why would she harm Alfie?"

"To punish me for spreading the rumor. Oh God! What if McGowan hurts him?"

"Joey, you're not making any sense."

"No, *you're* not making any sense. Why are you still sitting here when Alfie could be in danger?"

I run out of the bar and into the lobby. Michael races after me. Now I'm out of the glass doors and on the street again. It's started to rain and someone almost pokes my eye out rushing past with their umbrella. After the quiet of the bar, the noise of the traffic is loud and insistent. Too many people moving too fast. I'm in their way and I don't know what to do, where to go. I fumble in my bag for my phone.

Do I still have the Uber app on there, or did I delete it? Where the hell *is* my phone? It must be in here somewhere.

Michael grabs me by the arm, starts pulling me back toward the hotel. People are staring at us as if we're having a screaming argument right here on the street, but I don't care. I don't care what they think. All I want is to go home and get Alfie. Hold him in my arms and never let him go.

Michael's voice is in my ear. "Do you honestly think that, after thirty-six years of freedom, Sally McGowan—or her daughter—is going to do anything to jeopardize her anonymity? They're not going to hurt a little boy in front of Hayley. Why *would* they?"

If it weren't for Michael's hands on my arm and his eyes locking onto mine, holding them firm, I think I'd collapse in a heap on the sidewalk. I'm shaking now. Crying like a child.

"They wouldn't risk throwing their lives and contact with Hayley away just to teach you a lesson for spreading a rumor."

He holds me tight. "They'd disappear if they thought they were in danger. Move and start again somewhere else."

He's right. Karen's mom's dying. You only have to look at her to see that. She doesn't even *live* in Flinstead. She's just come to stay so Karen can take care of her. Liz has been in Flinstead for years and years. She said as much the first time I met her. If she moved there to be closer to Sally, that means Sally must have been there for years and years, too. Sally can't possibly be Karen's mother. I have it all wrong.

But if it's not Karen, then who is it? Who else could have doctored that photo and left it in the school?

Michael leads me back to the bar and buys me a brandy. He glances toward the lobby. "It's nearly four o'clock. Liz should be coming out of the convention soon. Let's sit here so we can keep an eye out for her."

"Show me those photos again," I insist when we've settled at a different table. I have a horrible feeling that Liz will take one look at us and disappear before we get a chance to speak to her. If he's right, and McGowan is someone Liz and I both know, then surely I'll be able to recognize her if I look hard enough. That nose is still bugging me.

Slowly, I scroll through them, study each one carefully. "Where did you say you got these?"

"From a contact of mine in the police. He managed to dig them out from the archives. They were never published, but . . . well, he owes me a couple of favors."

I don't ask why, or whether all this is something that could get him into trouble if it came to light. It's probably best I don't know.

"Are you sure they were never published?"

"Yes. A hundred percent sure."

"That's weird, because I've definitely seen the one of the house before. It must have found its way online at some point."

"I doubt it. These were never released to the press."

"But I've seen it. I know I have. It's almost as if . . ."

"Almost as if what?"

I'm imagining this. I must be. But it's almost as if I've seen this house in real life. As if I've stood in the same position as whoever it was who took this picture and seen it with my own eyes. But that's impossible. A mistaken sense of déjà vu, that's all. It happens sometimes. I suppose it looks a bit like my grandparents' house.

"When this picture was taken, she was named Sally

Holmes," Michael says. "She was married to a guy named Benjamin. In Iowa."

Benny. Benny and Sal.

Benny and Sal? That's odd. What made me think of that?

"Did he know who she was?"

"That's what I can't find out. Benjamin Holmes seems to have vanished off the face of the earth."

I swallow hard.

"Joey, are you okay?"

Why do I have a sudden memory of playing in that front yard? I'm going crazy. I must be. I'm remembering playing in Nana and Granddad's yard, that must be it. I think Mom has an old Polaroid of me sitting by a flower bed with my dolls. It's one of the few photos she has left from that time. Most of them were destroyed in the fire.

The fire.

Something weird happens to my insides. A hollowing-out sensation.

"What was the daughter's name?"

He checks a notebook in his pocket. "Lucy."

Lucy. No. No, it can't be. I close my eyes and take myself back to when I was a little girl, shrinking into my pillow, rigid with fear and confusion. A fireman's arms stretch toward me and he plucks me from my covers with his large gloved hands. His voice is kind in my ear.

"I'm taking you to Mommy and Daddy. Don't be scared. You're safe."

He carries me out of my bedroom and into the hall. I struggle in his arms, start to whimper into his jacket. He smells of smoke.

Now I'm in Mommy and Daddy's bedroom, but their bed is empty and the window is open. I feel the icy night air

on my bare arms and legs. Hear the clank of something hard
and metallic. Raised voices in the distance. People shouting.

I start to cry, but the fireman whispers in my ear. "Shh,"
he says. "You mustn't cry, because Mommy and Daddy are
waiting for you. You mustn't be scared."

And then I'm not cold anymore because something is
being wrapped around me. It feels like a big warm towel and
it's over my head, too. I cling to the fireman's jacket as he
climbs out of the window and onto the ladder.

Now he's running across the yard with me. I hear the
latch of the gate and his steps on the path at the back where
the garages are, and suddenly I'm in the ambulance with
Mommy and Daddy, and Mommy's arms are tight around
me and Daddy's voice is telling us it's going to be okay. It's
going to be okay.

I open my eyes. Michael is watching me, a wary expression on his face. I look at the photo of the house again.
"Where did you say this was?"

"It's in Coralville, on the outskirts of Iowa City."

Something ominous hurtles toward me. Something so
dreadful I can hardly bear to form the thought. But I have to.
I have to.

I force myself to take a sip of the brandy and almost
choke as it rasps against the back of my throat. No sirens.
There weren't any sirens. And why was the ambulance waiting on the access road at the back? Surely it would have been
at the front of the house.

It was Mom who suggested I join the book club. Mom
who gave me Liz's number. She said she'd gotten it from the
man in the bookstore, but . . .

Oh my God! I think it's *me* Liz is trying to protect. Me
and . . . me and Mom!

I feel like I'm dissolving. One realization gives way to another. A house of cards collapsing in on itself. It's not just photos of me as a child we don't have—there are none of *her*, either. All of them were lost in the fire, along with our personal possessions. But what if they weren't? What if they were deliberately destroyed?

My throat closes up. If this is true, then my whole life is a lie. My grandparents. Were they even . . . ?

"Joey, what's the matter? Talk to me."

Lucy Locket lost her pocket. Kitty Fisher found it.

It was my favorite nursery rhyme. That's why I named my imaginary friend after her. At least, that's what Mom's always told me. But if Mom had to be given another name, I'd have needed one, too. She'd have had to convince me I was called Joanna now.

Joanna, not Lucy.

I want to scream, but I can't. I can barely breathe.

This is a mistake. It must be. It's insane. Unthinkable.

How can my own mother be Sally McGowan?

43

I DON'T REMEMBER FINISHING THE BRANDY, BUT I MUST HAVE,
because the glass is empty.

"Let me get you another one," Michael says.

"No. I don't want another one." My voice sounds alien.
Disembodied.

I try again. "The fire was just a story they told me. To
make sense of what happened. To explain why we couldn't
go back."

Michael holds my hands in his. My breath judders at the
back of my throat, and he squeezes my fingers tight.

"Which means my whole life is a story. Everything I've
ever known is based on a lie."

Michael speaks at last. "You mean . . . ? Oh my God,
Joey." He lets go of my hands and leans back in his chair. "It
wasn't a fireman at all, was it? It was someone helping your
mother, bundling you out of the house."

I drop my face into my hands, press my fingertips into
my eyelids. Maybe if I press hard enough, the image of my
mother's face—Sally McGowan's face—will disappear. But it
doesn't. It gets sharper and sharper. How could I have missed

the resemblance? The narrow bridge of the nose. The shape of her mouth. It seems so obvious now. It's been staring me in the face. Literally.

"How could she lie to me like that? How could she pretend for all those years?"

Michael takes my hands again and holds them tight. "How could she not?"

"Maybe she lied to Dad, too. Is that why he left us?"

"I don't know, Joey. Only your mother can answer those questions."

"Maybe he wasn't such a bad guy after all. Maybe he just couldn't stomach what she'd done." I pull my hand away and clap it over my mouth as I start to retch. "I'm going to be sick—"

I make it to the ladies' room just in time. Fold over a toilet bowl and vomit. After the first acrid rush of brandy and Coke, all that's left is bile. It keeps coming up till there's nothing left and I'm dry-heaving, my whole torso cold with sweat.

Then I feel a hand between my shoulders. It's Michael, rubbing my back in circular movements. He helps me to my feet and over to a sink. The face that stares back at me from the mirror is gray, hair plastered to its forehead. It's like looking at a stranger.

Michael waits with me while I splash cold water onto my face and swill my mouth out. He pulls a wad of paper towels from the machine and hands them to me. A woman comes in and stares at us angrily. Stares at Michael. He leads me out into the carpeted corridor and back into the bar.

Michael asks for some water.

"Have a few sips of that."

But I can't. I doubt I could keep it down.

"I still can't believe it. None of it makes any sense. I don't even know who I *am* anymore."

Michael leans toward me and strokes my cheek with his finger. "You're still the same person, Joey. You're still *you*. That hasn't changed."

"But it has! Don't you see? I'm not Joanna Critchley. I'm not even Lucy Holmes. I don't know *who* I am."

Tears burn my eyeballs. I don't want to cry in the middle of this anonymous hotel bar that's fast filling up, but I can't help myself. My eyes can no longer hold the tears.

"My mother killed a child." Even though I'm whispering, the impact is the same as if I'd screamed the words out loud. I feel as though everyone has heard.

Somebody approaches our table. All I see is a pair of navy shoes with a Cuban heel at the bottom of green-trousered legs. The trousers are wide and silky and swish against her ankles. I can't bring myself to raise my head because I know whose legs they are and I don't want to see her face. This woman who's known all along. My mother's protector. Her lover, for Christ's sake!

She slides into the chair next to me. I see the skinny shape of her thighs, the bony mounds of her knees pressing up through the fabric of her trousers. She rests her left hand on my shoulder. It's the lightest of touches, but still I flinch. Some form of nonverbal communication flows between Michael and her—I sense its energy. Tap into its sad waves.

"Your mother loves you very much, Jo," Liz says.

"Not enough to tell me the truth." My voice is jagged. A shard of broken glass scraping on concrete.

"She wanted to. She knew she should, but she couldn't. She didn't want to lose you."

"Well, she's lost me now."

"No. You're in shock. You just need time to adjust. You won't think like that forever. I promise you."

I lift my head to look at her. The weight of it is almost unbearable. The muscles in my neck are as brittle as glass. They could snap at any second.

Liz's mouth is moving. She's forming words with her lips and tongue, but I can't hear them. There's a whistling in my ears and my back is slick with sweat. I'm going to faint.

Now Michael is pushing my head between my knees, telling me to breathe. I want to stay like this forever, hanging over my feet, blood pooling into the top of my head. I focus on my ankle boots. The scuff mark on the left toe. The tiny piece of dried leaf stuck to the side of the heel. Right now these boots of mine are the only thing grounding me to the earth. Everything else has crumbled away. I'm frightened that, if I sit up, I'll crumble away, too. Disintegrate into powdery dust. As if I never existed.

A murmuring swells in my ears. I'm aware of bodies clustering around our table. Other people's shoes. Concerned voices.

Then Michael's. "It's okay. Thank you. She'll be fine. She's okay. We've got this."

If it weren't for his hands on my shoulders, guiding me back up to a sitting position, I'd still be down there. Just me and my boots. Blocking out this strange new world.

I lift the glass of water to my lips and drink. I'm so thirsty all of a sudden I'm downing it too fast and it sloshes over the rim and down my chin. I set the glass down, so clumsily it almost topples and spills. I wipe my mouth with my hand. Liz digs into her bag and produces some tissues, hands one to me, and wipes the table with another one. Dries the bottom of my glass. There's a concentrated look on her face and her eyes are unnaturally wide, as if she's trying not to blink.

"There's so much I could tell you, Jo," she says. "So much I *want* to tell you. But it isn't my story. It's your mother's. You need to hear it from her, not me."

A tear slides from the corner of her eye. For a second or two it clings to her cheek like molten glass, then breaks free and rolls down.

"Forgive me," she says. "For the tweets." Her voice falters. "I didn't want to scare you, but I didn't know what else to do."

44

WE'RE IN MICHAEL'S CAR. I DON'T REMEMBER HOW WE GOT here. I have vague memories of walking—or rather being led, guided, *piloted* to an underground parking garage. Propelled along wet sidewalks. My body little more than a flimsy structure, supported only by the ballast of Michael's stronger, sturdier frame.

Liz isn't with us. I don't ask where she is. Don't want to know.

Michael drives through the darkening streets. Stops and starts in the endless flow of traffic. If I lean to the right, I can see myself in the side mirror. Dark hollows where my eyes used to be. Nothing is in the right place anymore. Even my internal organs seem to have shifted out of kilter.

We don't speak. There is nothing to say.

There is too much to say.

Alfie. He arrives in my mind like a thunderbolt. The shock of the last hour has erased him till now. Guilt slams into me so hard that, for a second, I think we've hit something.

Michael's hand shoots out to my thigh. "What is it?"

"I have to call Karen. Tell her we'll be late."

"Do you want me to pull over and speak to her?"

"No. Just drive. I'll do it."

I scrabble around for my bag. My phone. Stare at the locked screen in confusion. I've forgotten what to do. How to make it work. The cry takes us both by surprise. Curdles the air in the car. It's coming from me, spiraling up from deep in my belly. A tornado of anguish.

The turn signal ticks, but the stream of traffic on our right won't let up.

"Don't pull over. I can do it." My brain is working again. Telling my fingers what to do. Scrolling through my contacts till I come to the name KAREN.

"Karen, it's Jo." I gasp for breath. This is important. I have to pull myself together. Talk normally. Let her know we're on our way.

"Hi there," Karen says. All bright and cheerful. The tone of it grates, like an unexpected insult. "Alfie's had his supper. He's got quite an appetite, hasn't he?"

"Yes, yes, he has. Look, we might be a little late. The traffic, it's . . ."

"Hey, no problem. Really." A pause. "You okay, Jo? Only you sound a bit . . ."

"I've had some bad news." I screw my face up to hold the words back. The words playing in my brain in a loop. I've just found out my mother is a child killer. I've just found out my entire history is a fabrication, that I've been lied to since the day I was born.

"Joanna? Are you still there?"

"Yes, yes. I'm still here."

But am I? Am I really? *Someone* is still here, hunched in the passenger seat like a wounded animal. Someone pretending to be Joanna Critchley. Mother of Alfie Critchley. Daughter of . . .

"Karen, I have to speak to my . . . my mother. I'll be with you as soon as I can. I'm so sorry . . ."

"Take as long as you need. Alfie will be fine." She knows something bad's happened. I can tell by her voice. The way it's changed from bright and breezy to serious and concerned. "If he gets sleepy I'll make him up a bed on the sofa. Just do what you have to do. Okay?"

"Okay." It's hard to believe that, just a short while ago, I thought she meant Alfie and me harm. I thought she was Sally McGowan's daughter when, all along, it was . . . all along, it was me.

IT'S DARK NOW AND RAIN FALLS HARD AND FAST. MICHAEL puts the wipers on top speed, but visibility is poor. Headlights dazzle and distort in the windshield. Taillights bleed red. It's the worst time to be driving out of the city, but Michael is a good driver. Calm and steady. If he's frustrated at all, he keeps it hidden. He doesn't react when someone cuts in front of us, or when traffic slows to a snail's pace, picks up again, then slows. He just deals with it all. He just drives.

I'm dimly aware of the city draining into the suburbs through the rain-blurred windows, and then into dark nothingness. Vast chasms of black rearing up at us on either side and only the short span of road ahead, illuminated by the arc of the headlights.

It's all I've got, that short stretch of road. The only thing that's real. I can't take my eyes off it.

Michael puts the radio on to break the silence and the

sweet, raw voice of Ed Sheeran singing "Castle on the Hill" fills the car. An arm appears from nowhere to turn it off. It's mine, the finger already poised, but Michael beats me to it. It's too much. Too real and poignant. A love song for his hometown, and here am I, returning to mine. But everything has changed now. I've been dug up like an unwanted plant and tossed onto the soil, my roots exposed to the air.

My roots. I squeeze my eyes shut and try not to think of them. Diseased roots. Gnarled and foul. Kenny and Jean McGowan. The swagger and the fist. The fear and the shame. And Sally, their daughter. Sally, my mother.

The car is warm, the air stale. I open the window just a crack, rest my fingers on the top of the glass so that their tips are poking out into the night air. I used to do this as a child whenever we went on a long car trip. Mom at the wheel— a cautious driver, hands always in the ten-and-two position, gripping too tightly, her knuckles white from the strain—me slumped carelessly in the passenger seat. Gazing out of the windows. Daydreaming.

Cautious driver. Cautious woman. Cautious life. It all makes sense now. The pieces fit. She gives a good impression of having lots of friends and acquaintances from her choir, but now that I think of it, she's always kept people at bay. She's never allowed them to get too close. What did Michael say to me that time in the restaurant? That I've always been so fiercely independent, that he was worried I'd pull the drawbridge up if he asked for more. I've learned that from her, haven't I? I must have.

"Are you okay?"

The question reaches my ears at the same time as icy water shoots sideways through the gap and spits on my face.

Of course I'm not *okay*. I lean my head against the window and close my eyes. I'll never be *okay* again. The days of being *okay* are gone forever.

"I'll come in with you, Joey, if you like. Or do you want me to stay in the car?"

I haven't even thought about that. About what will happen when we get there. When I climb out of this car and enter that house. How will I drag myself from this warm, protective cocoon? Michael calm and steady beside me. The slanting pool of light beyond the windshield.

What will happen when I come face-to-face with her? What will I say? What will she?

If only Alfie were here in the car with us, we could just drive away and never come back. Start again someplace else. Leave it all behind us. Shed the past like an old skin. It's what *she* did, after all. And not just once.

We're getting closer now. The last leg of the journey. Familiar road signs. The ribbon of road no longer straight but bending. Full beam on. Full beam off. Villages glowing like clusters of jewels. Bars and restaurants. Dunkin' Donuts and gas station signs. Everything normal and where it's always been. The only thing that's changed is me. My past, present, and future. Warped beyond recognition.

The last town before Flinstead winks at us in the darkness.

Liz only calls in the dead of night. Most people dread a phone call at that time. For them it can mean only one thing: Something bad has happened. Something that necessitates immediate action.

An accident.

A tragedy.

A death.

So when I see her name flash up at five eleven on my caller-display screen, I know. I know something is up. The game I've been playing all my life. The game I almost won.

I know what she's going to say even before she says it and when she does . . . when she does, the words pierce my heart, over and over again. A thousand vicious stabs.

Joanna knows. Joanna knows. Joanna knows.

I won't leave the house tonight. I won't don my running gear and sprint through the streets like a ghost. I won't be drawn to the glow of her window like a moth to a flame. To the sweet warmth of her eyes and her mouth. To the hot bliss of her bed.

She cannot comfort me now. My dearest love. My Liz.

No one can.

The monster is out of its cage.

45

I'M SHAKING AS THE CAR DRAWS UP OUTSIDE HER HOUSE. *HER* house. Not Mom's house. Is it happening already? The separation?

Michael turns off the ignition and shifts in his seat to face me. He takes my hands in his and kisses them. His lips are warm and dry. His stubble grazes my flesh.

"Do you want me to come in with you?"

I shake my head. It's easier than speaking.

Her porch light is on. She doesn't usually put it on unless she's expecting someone, or if she goes out and won't be returning till late. She hardly ever goes out at night. She locks the doors early. Always has. Ever since I was a little girl and Dad left us. The doors were always locked by suppertime, and the curtains drawn. Now I know why.

"Nice and cozy," she used to say. "Just you and me, as snug as a bug in a rug."

My finger trembles as I press the bell. It doesn't work. I press it again, harder this time. The jaunty little tune that Alfie and I often dance to while we're waiting on the step is an affront to my ears. It comes from a happier, innocent time. It has no business striking its relentlessly upbeat message this evening.

I should have knocked instead. A somber rat-tat-tat. Too late now.

As soon as she opens the door and I see her face, I know she knows. Liz must have called ahead to warn her, and I'm glad. Glad she isn't greeting me in the normal way. The warm smile. The soft kiss on the cheek. The hug. Glad I don't have to find a way to broach the subject all on my own.

"I've been expecting you," she says, her eyes skating across mine and fixing on Michael's car, waiting outside.

She turns and walks ahead of me into the living room. A small glass of something amber-colored is sitting on the table by her armchair. She rarely drinks alone. At least, she never did. Although how am I to know what she did when I went up to bed? How am I to know what she does now, when I'm at home with Alfie and she is here, alone with her terrible secret? How am I to know anything about this stranger who calls herself my mother?

She inclines her head toward the sideboard. "Can I get you something to drink?"

My first instinct is to decline. I haven't eaten anything since lunch and after that first, rasping mouthful of brandy in the hotel, that searing sensation at the back of my throat, the rest of the glass slithered down only too easily.

"I'm afraid I've only got amaretto or sherry," she says, crouching at the sideboard and reaching into its depths.

"I'll have a sherry."

This seems wrong. Sitting down sipping sherry like a guest when she's about to confirm the worst possible news. Expand on the grisly detail, no doubt. Explain. But of course, I know exactly what she's doing. She's delaying the moment for as long as possible. She needs this time fussing with glasses and bottles, laying another coaster on the coffee table, shutting the sherry away in the sideboard. These are normal activities. Things one does when someone drops by for an early-evening drink. She's trying to stretch the illusion of normality till the last possible second. Maybe we both are.

The illusion of normality. That's all it's ever been. An illusion.

I take the proffered drink, the too-full glass of Harveys Bristol Cream, my hand shaking as I set it down on the table.

Now, and only now, do we dare to look at each other.

"Where do you want me to start?" she says, holding my gaze. It's me who looks away first.

I stare at my hands in my lap, the raised veins. "The beginning seems as good a place as any."

She nods. "But first, I need you to know that you and Alfie are the most important people in my life."

"More important than Liz?"

She looks as shocked as if I'd just marched over and slapped her. "How can you even ask that?"

"Maybe it's got something to do with the fact that she knows everything about you and I know nothing. You haven't been lying to her for thirty-four years. Maybe that's why."

She brings her hands to her face—a prayerlike gesture, her fingertips meeting at the top of her nose—and rocks gently in her chair like an injured child. I've wounded her with my words, I know I have, but I can't help it. Something cold and contained has lodged itself in my heart.

"Yes, Liz is the only one who knows the whole story. But that doesn't mean she's more important to me than you. You don't love Michael more than Alfie, do you? Of *course* you don't."

My fingers curl into fists. How dare she bring Michael and Alfie into this? How dare she make comparisons between her life and mine?

"Liz believed in me. She was barely an adult when she started working at Gray Willow. It was her first job after college. It must have been a baptism of fire, walking into that place for the first time."

She closes her eyes and leans back into her chair.

"Before I was released, Liz broke the rules and gave me a PO box address. She told me I could always get in touch with her if I needed her.

"And I *did* need her. I sent her letters. It was a risk, writing to her under my new name, giving her my address, but I trusted her. I've always been able to trust her. Liz was my touchstone. Still is."

She breathes in, and her face softens for a moment. "All through that scary time when I was on my own, out there in the world where everyone I met, everywhere I went, there was always the danger of being discovered, Liz was there. In her letters. They were the only thing that kept me going. Until I met your father, of course."

She leans forward and reaches for her drink. Takes a sip. "But I've jumped too far ahead. I was going to tell this story from the beginning. I need to go back. Back to where it started."

"No, tell me about Dad first. Did he know? Did he know who you were?"

She turns to the wall. "I wanted to tell him, just like I wanted to tell you, when you were old enough to understand, but I couldn't. I just couldn't. Every time I tried to find the words, I lost my courage. I didn't want to lose him, just like I didn't want to lose you. *Don't* want to lose you."

"But he found out in the end."

"Yes. And in the worst possible way. Hateful words painted on our front door. A rock through our window. All the neighbors standing outside screaming and shouting."

I think of that picture. It must have been taken the day after, when we'd all been spirited away. In the ambulance I now realize must have been an unmarked van.

"Is that why he left us? Because of who you were? The other woman, the new family—were those more of your lies?"

"No! Yes. But not lies exactly. We had to come up with something to explain things."

"We?"

"The small group of people who looked after me. Who look after me still. Keep me safe. Keep *you* safe. You and Alfie."

I recoil. Hearing his name on her lips sounds all wrong. I don't want him to be part of all this. It's too much. I picture him now, at Karen's. He's probably watching a DVD with Hayley, or maybe she's got him playacting a scene from *Frozen*. What I wouldn't give to be back at home with him. He's all I've got now. Him and Michael. The only two people in my life who are real. No, that's not true. My dad was real.

"Did he have a choice about seeing me again?"

"He stayed for a bit." She takes a breath. "There was this ex-cop I knew. Brian. He used to work for the feds as a handler for protected witnesses. He and Liz, they . . . they *arranged* things. We lived in a boarding house for a while, but it didn't work. Your dad couldn't deal with it. He said he still loved me, and of course he loved you, but things were never the same after that. How could they be? He did have the choice, though. He had the choice to stay with us and for all three of us to have new identities, or to leave and move away. Never to see us again."

She looks at the wall again. "He chose to move away. He went to England. He had family there."

My jaw aches from where I've been clenching it shut. Poor Dad. It must have been an impossible choice. Give up your whole identity—your job, all your relatives and friends—and stay with a woman you no longer know or trust, for the sake of your child; or move away and start again. Shove the whole sorry mess behind you. Part of me hates him for not staying, for not putting me first, but a bigger part understands. How could he love her after all those lies? How can *I*?

My phone buzzes in my bag. I pull it out. It's a text from Michael: *Are you ok? Do u want me to come in? Or go and get Alfie?*

I tap out a reply: *Can u get him? It's Apt. 2A, The Regal. Take him home. Will call u later.*

I glance at Mom. Her face is the color of putty and she's drained her glass already. It's going to be much, much later before I call. We've barely begun.

46

I SLIP THE PHONE BACK INTO MY BAG, WISHING MORE THAN anything that I could be with Michael now. Picking Alfie up. Going home together. A normal evening. Instead of which I'm here, listening to my mother systematically dismantle my life.

"So Dad left and you decided to turn *him* into the monster instead. Well, thanks for that. Thanks for making me think he was a total bastard, that he didn't love me enough to even keep in touch."

All those broken promises. All the times I cried myself to sleep because Daddy was gone. None of it was true, was it? He *couldn't* keep in touch. Once we had new identities, he wouldn't have known where to find me.

"It was hard for me, too," she says, her voice barely a whisper. "He was my husband, remember? I loved him. And how else could I have explained his absence? Would you rather I'd told you he was dead?"

"Maybe it would have been better, yes. For all I know, he *might* be dead now."

"He isn't."

I force myself to swallow. My throat feels thick and swollen. "How do you know?" I lean forward, staring at her. "Do you know where he is?"

I've never wanted to know before. Never wanted anything to do with him. She saw to that. But it's different now. This changes everything.

"No. But I've been told he's alive and well and living somewhere in London." She wrings her hands in her lap. "Not all of it was lies, Jo. He *does* have another family. Two daughters and a son."

"What made you do it? What made you kill a little boy?" The words are harsh and jarring in the stillness of this ordinary room. "A little boy not much younger than your own grandson."

She clutches her stomach as if she's been shot. For a second or two I almost feel sorry for her. Almost, but not quite. How do I know what's real anymore?

She stands and walks to the other side of the room. Rests her hands on the wall and hangs her head.

"When I talk about her," she says, "about Sally, you have to understand that I'm talking about another person."

She straightens up and returns to her chair. Folds herself back into it, her hands clasped around her knees.

"I suppose in some ways it's like that for everyone, isn't it? We change. Evolve. From one year to the next. One month. One week. Sometimes all it takes is a day. An hour. A minute." She inhales deeply. "A second."

All the time she's been speaking she's been staring into space. Now she squeezes her eyes shut, as if she's trying not to see something. When she opens them again, they slide toward me. A fleeting glance.

"She didn't have a childhood. Not in the same way you

did, or Alfie does. But then, you know something of her background already. You've researched it, haven't you?"

I don't respond.

"I saw your browsing history when you went to book club."

I stare at her.

"Oh, I wasn't being nosy. I was doing a crossword and I needed to look something up. Your iPad was on the sofa. I saw all the tabs at the top of the screen. All the windows you'd opened. Windows into her life. Sally's life."

"*Your* life," I say.

"No!" Her eyes flash, and for a second I'm scared. Scared of my own mother. Scared of the person she was, maybe still is, somewhere deep inside. Did she know about the tweets Liz posted? Were the two of them behind that horrible photo of Alfie, too? They *must* have been. How could she *do* that to me? To her own daughter.

"Not my life," she says. "*Her* life. I've told you. She's not me. I'm not her. I haven't been her for so long, I can't . . ." Her voice breaks.

I focus again on my hands. They're glued together so tightly the muscles in my forearms ache. I don't know who she is anymore. I don't know the first thing about this woman.

"You're so lucky, Jo. You don't know what it feels like to fear a man so much your blood freezes in your veins at the sound of his key in the door. You wet your pants as he comes up the stairs; every step nearer he gets, your time is running out. There's nowhere to hide and no point screaming, so you wait. You wait for it to happen all over again, and it does. It does. Every time, it does. It never stops. If he's not beating you with his belt, he's unzipping his pants. Planting his feet either side of you as you cower on the floor. Making you do things no child should even know about, let alone be forced to do.

"And when he wasn't terrorizing me, he was taking it out on my mother. Sometimes he used to grab her by the throat and lift her like that—*by her throat*—pin her up against the wall till her face went blue and her legs started flailing. I'd watch her slither down when he let her go. Crumple on the floor just like a rag doll. Sometimes he'd kick her for good measure."

She cringes into the back of her chair as if he's right there in front of her all over again.

"Oh, he was the devil, Jo!" she cries. "The devil."

I should comfort her. Scoop her into my arms and hold her tight. This is my mother. The woman I've loved and looked up to all my life, and here she is, reliving the horrors of her past, whimpering in her chair like the terrified child she once was. But I'm stuck to the sofa. Rigid and numb. It's horrendous, what she's telling me. Worse than anything I could have imagined, and I know there's more to come. I can see it in her eyes. I can scarcely breathe.

This can't be real. This *cannot* be happening. I am not sitting in my mother's living room, drinking sherry at seven o'clock in the evening, listening to this vile story. Watching her dredge up the memories, one by one, reliving them all in front of me. None of it is real.

"Are you telling me all this to make excuses for what you did? Because there aren't any excuses. You murdered a little boy."

"No," she says. "I didn't. It was a game. A game that went

horribly, horribly wrong. You have to believe me, Jo." Her hands grip the armrests of her chair. White claws digging into the fabric.

My phone rings in my bag. I fish it out and see that it's Michael. For fuck's sake. Why is he calling me? Surely he knows what this must be like.

"Hello?"

"Jo, there's no one there."

"What do you mean?"

"There's no one at the apartment. You did say 2A, didn't you?"

"Yes. It's on the ground floor. You have to press the buzzer on the door outside and . . ."

"Yes, I've done that. But there's no reply. Don't worry, I'll buzz one of the other apartments and see if I can get someone to let me into the building. Maybe her bell's not working."

The register of his voice changes. Becomes lower, more confidential. "How's it . . . how's it going there?"

I bite back a sob. "How do you think?"

"Shit. Stupid question. I'm sorry I've interrupted things. I was just worried I'd misheard the address. Don't worry. I'll take Alfie home and then I'll wait for you to call me."

47

I FOLD MY HANDS IN MY LAP, DO NOTHING TO KEEP THE BIT-
terness out of my voice. "So, where were we? I think you
were about to make more excuses for why you killed a child."

Mom winces. "They aren't excuses, Jo. I'm just trying to
tell you the whole story. Put it in some kind of context. I've
waited this long to tell you, you might as well hear everything."

"Waited this long to tell me?" I shake my head in disbelief. "You make it sound like it's *your* decision to come clean.
You wouldn't be telling me any of this if I hadn't found out."

"You're wrong. You're so wrong. I've been agonizing
over it for years. Long before I saw what you'd been looking
up on your iPad. Long before that poor woman in the gift
shop got targeted. I said as much to Liz. I told her I wanted
to tell my story and set the record straight. Show them how
a monster is made." She taps her chest with the forefingers
of both hands. "Is that what you think I am, Jo? A monster?"

I take a deep breath. "I don't know what I think anymore.
I just know I can't forgive you. Whatever you tell me, I can't
forgive you for lying to me all these years. For making me

believe my dad was a bastard, for ruining all those lovely memories I have of Nana and Granddad." Tears stream down my face. "Who were they, those people? Who *were* Lilian and Henry Brown?"

Now Mom's crying, too. "They *were* your grandparents. They might not have been your biological grandparents, but in every other respect they were. And they were the closest I ever got to a loving mom and dad.

"After your dad left, you and I started again. I began looking after guide dogs. Walking them, training them, taking care of them when they retired. It was part of my new identity and I loved it. It's how I first met them—Lilian and Henry. I took in Henry's dog, Lulu, when she got too old to work and Henry needed a younger dog. They were a lovely couple, so sweet and kind. They didn't have any children of their own and they doted on us, Jo. My new backstory was that my own parents had died in a car crash when I was fifteen. They were only too happy to be your stand-in grandparents. Lilian loved it when you started calling her Nana. You meant the world to her."

She pulls a hankie out of her pocket and blows her nose. "I wanted to tell you they weren't your real grandparents, but I couldn't. If I told you the backstory I was using, that your real grandparents had died in a car crash, I knew you'd be upset and you were already missing your dad. Besides, that was a lie, too, wasn't it? Because your real grandparents are . . . well, you know who they are."

That awful picture of Kenny and Jean McGowan materializes in my mind. I screw my eyes shut and try to replace it with one of Lilian and Henry Brown.

"Then Henry died, followed shortly afterward by Lilian. All the meaningful people in my life were gone," she says, twisting her hankie in her hands. "Your father. Lilian. Henry. You were all I had. You and Liz."

Liz. I'd wondered when we'd get around to her again.

"Liz kept me sane through the bad days. And there were plenty of those. Sylvia Harris was furious that I was released at all, and then when news broke that I'd been found again in Iowa but that I'd managed to escape unscathed, she went apeshit. She always said it wasn't fair that she and her family were bombarded by the press whenever an anniversary came around. You know, 'Ten years ago today, the monster Sally McGowan . . . Fifteen years ago today . . . Twenty . . . Twenty-five.' It never stops. Or whenever another child kills or hurts someone. It's never me they come to for an interview, because they can't. They don't know where I am. But Sylvia was fair game, and so were the rest of her family.

"When Sylvia passed away, I thought it would all die down. But then her daughter took up the baton. Robbie's older sister, Marie. She won't be happy till my face is in the papers all over again. Except this time it won't be my ten-year-old face, it'll be this one. And if that happens, my life will be over. I'll be harassed and vilified everywhere I go. And you and Alfie will be dragged into it, too. Your lives will be tainted, just like mine.

"I've been terrified ever since I saw what you'd been looking at online. It's why I've been so ill. I told Liz about it and she told me you'd mentioned it at book club, too. And then when Sonia Martins was targeted . . ."

"You and Liz concocted a little plan to scare me into keeping my mouth shut."

She stares at me as if I've taken leave of my senses. "If you think I'd do anything to scare my own daughter, you're insane. You're the most precious thing in my life, Jo. You and Alfie. I'd never do anything to hurt either of you. You *must* know that!"

"Must I? I don't know anything anymore."

And yet I do. Deep down in my bones, in the core of my being, I know what she's saying is true. She wouldn't hurt us. She couldn't.

She runs her hands through her hair, digs her fingers into her scalp. Then she freezes. Her head jerks up.

"Why did you say that? About us scaring you?"

I tell her about the tweets from Sally Mac and the Halloween photo.

"Liz wouldn't do that."

"Yes, she would. She's already admitted to sending the tweets."

Her mouth falls open. "But not the photo. She wouldn't have done that. I *know* she wouldn't." She looks straight at me, fear in her eyes. "Oh God, no! Maybe Marie's already found me. Do you understand what's at stake here, Jo? If Marie's gotten wind of where I am, God only knows what she'll do."

In one fluid movement, she's out of her chair and pulling open a drawer in the tall chest next to the sideboard. She pulls out a folder and shakes out the contents, starts leafing through them. At last, she finds what she's looking for and passes me a newspaper clipping, her hands trembling.

"Marie doesn't want justice for Robbie. She wants *revenge.*"

48

MOTHER OF CHILD KILLER
SALLY MCGOWAN'S VICTIM DIES
By Sam Adler

MONDAY, AUGUST 6, 2012
DAILY NEWS

Sylvia Harris, whose five-year-old son Robbie was the victim of child killer Sally McGowan, has died after a long illness, aged 75.

"My mother never got over Robbie's murder," said her daughter, Marie. "She tried her best to be a good mother to me, but her spirit was broken. I just hope and pray that she's at peace now. With Robbie."

Marie added: "Knowing McGowan's still out there somewhere while my mother and baby brother are dead is a thorn in my side. I'm convinced that Mom's illness was a direct result not just of what happened to Robbie, but of McGowan getting a second chance at life away from the glare of publicity, while we, her victims, never did. It sickens me to think that someone in my family might come into contact with her or her child and we'd never know.

"Mom always used to say, why should she get more rights than us? The right to a private life, the right not to be hounded by the press, the right to live in peace?

"She's not the victim in all this. McGowan's evil act has blighted our entire family. My parents' marriage collapsed. My mother suffered serious health problems and I lost my childhood. All because of what that monster did."

Marie Harris is reported to have said in the past that she will never stop searching for Sally McGowan in order to name and shame her. When questioned about this yesterday, Marie refused to either confirm or deny her comments, but said, "I will never give up fighting for justice for my little brother. Not until the day I die.

"Sally McGowan must pay for what she's done."

MY PHONE RINGS. MICHAEL AGAIN. I TAKE IT INTO THE KITCHEN, frustrated at yet another interruption, but relieved, too. The atmosphere in the living room is intense. I need to breathe.

"Listen, I managed to get through to one of Karen's neighbors and they've let me into the entrance hall, but we've knocked and knocked on the door and there's no one there. The apartment's completely empty and the lights are off."

It takes a while for his words to filter through the tangle in my brain.

"Hold on a sec. I'll try her cellphone and get back to you."

"What's happened?" Mom says. She's followed me into the kitchen and is standing in the doorway. I wish she'd go back into the living room. I can't deal with her hovering like this, asking me questions as if she has a right to know the answers.

"Alfie's babysitter isn't at home. It's fine. She probably just had to run out for something."

"What babysitter?"

I find Karen's name in my contacts and press CALL. Her phone rings but then switches to voicemail. I try again, but the same thing happens. An unspecified fear uncoils in my belly. They'll be back in a minute. Of course they will. This time, I leave a message.

"Karen? It's Jo. Michael's gone to your place to pick Alfie up, but you're not there. Can you call me?"

I turn my back on Mom's anxious face and call Michael. "I can't get through. I've left a message on her voicemail."

"I know. I heard it ringing."

"What?"

"She's left her phone in the apartment," he says. "Maybe she ran out of milk or something and had to go out."

Yes. It's something simple like that. Nothing to worry about. Milk. I'm always running out of milk. Although wouldn't she have left the kids with her mother if she was just running out to the store?

"I'll wait in the car till she gets here."

"What's going on?" Mom says, the second I finish the call. "Where's Alfie?"

"He's fine. Karen's looking after him."

"Who's Karen?"

"Hayley's mom. You met her at the playground. Her and her mother."

Mom looks worried. "How well do you know her?"

I almost laugh. "That's ironic, in the circumstances, isn't it?" I stare at my phone, check that the volume's on full. "She's fine. She belongs to the babysitting circle and I know her from book club, too. I've been to her apartment before. I told her I'd be late. Maybe she's taken the kids out to buy some candy or something."

"Bit late for candy, isn't it?"

I look at the clock in Mom's kitchen. It's half past seven. She's right. It is a bit late to be taking two six-year-olds to buy candy. But it's fine. Alfie will be fine. There's obviously some logical explanation.

Maybe something's happened and she's had to take her mother to the hospital. Forgotten her phone in the panic. Damn! I picture Alfie waiting in a crowded emergency room, bored and tired. Picking up all sorts of germs while he's there. There's no way for me to get ahold of Karen if she's forgotten her phone, and she's unlikely to have remembered my number. I just have to hope she knows one of the other mothers' numbers and can contact me that way.

But how likely is that? I don't even know Tash's number by heart, and she's my closest friend. I'd be lost without my phone. If Karen doesn't turn up soon, we'll have to call the hospital and see if she's there. Or drive there ourselves. Fuck. Fuck. Fuck!

I phone Michael again.

"Still no sign of them," he says.

He's trying not to sound anxious, but I can tell that he is. A dangerous thought starts to form somewhere deep in my mind. More a sensation than a thought, but I can't haul it into the light. It won't break free of its moorings. Won't reveal itself to me. I'm panicking over nothing. Wherever Alfie is, he's with Karen and Hayley, which means he'll be fine. And Karen's mother must be with them, too, or else she'd have answered the door. The more I think about this, the more convinced I am that Karen's had to drive her mother to the hospital.

"Can you ask the neighbor if she knows what the mother's name is?"

"What mother? What are you talking about?"

"Karen's mother. She's staying with her. She's not very well. I'm wondering whether she's had to take her to the emergency room. Can you find out what her name is and call the nearest hospital?"

"I'll find out and call you back."

Five minutes later, the phone rings.

"You're right. I've spoken to one of the other neighbors who said she saw Karen a little while ago. She's not sure about the mother's name. She thinks it might be Mary. Anyway, the thing is, Karen was definitely on her way to the hospital. I'm going to drive there now. Don't worry, Jo, I'll meet them there and bring Alfie home. You've got enough to think about right now. What's Karen's last name?"

"Fuck. I don't know."

Michael sighs. "Right. Well, it shouldn't be too difficult to find her if she's in the waiting room. I'll just look for Alfie. I'll phone you when I get there."

The call ends and my breath catches in my throat. That dangerous thought swims up through the depths. A powerful drug creeping through my veins.

Mom clutches my arm. "Joanna, your face! You're scaring me. What's going on?"

The surface is breached and here it is, thrashing about for oxygen. Michael's words play over in my mind. *She thinks it might be Mary.*

A cold hand clenches around my heart. Grips it with icy fingers.

Mom's screaming at me now. "What do you know that you aren't telling me?"

"The neighbor thinks Karen's mother is named Mary." My mouth's so dry I can barely form the words. "But what if she has it wrong? What if it's *Marie*?"

Mom blanches. I didn't think it was possible for her to look any paler, but she does. I hear her sharp intake of breath. See the horror in her eyes.

"And you think . . ." Her hands fly to her mouth. "You think Karen's mother is Marie? No. No, it can't be. That woman I saw at the playground was nothing like her. She was . . ."

She looks at me, her eyes blank with horror. "She was so thin. Her face . . . her hair. It . . . it couldn't have been her. It couldn't!"

Mom's landline makes us both jump.

We stare at each other, the tension and hostility of just a few minutes ago suspended by this new, frightening turn of events.

She turns on her heels and runs into the living room, snatches the phone from its cradle.

"Hello?"

I watch her face and know something's happened. Something bad. She presses the SPEAKER button and turns to me, a helpless expression in her eyes.

A woman's voice fills the room. An ugly, abrasive voice. "You have a lovely grandson, Sally." I crumple to my knees. I've heard that voice before.

Karen's mother is Marie. Robbie Harris's sister. The woman who has vowed never to stop searching for her brother's killer. The woman who wants Sally McGowan to pay for what she's done.

And right now, she's got Alfie.

49

HER VOICE SOURS THE AIR.

"You and I need to have a little talk, Sally. Somewhere quiet. Somewhere nobody will disturb us."

Mom's hands are trembling. "Where? Tell me where you are and I'll come. Just don't hurt him, Marie. Please, don't hurt him."

"Like you didn't hurt Robbie, you mean?"

Our eyes lock in silent horror.

"He's a lovely little boy, isn't he? So trusting. But then they all are at that age, aren't they?"

I can't speak. I can't breathe.

"Please, Marie," Mom says. "Leave Alfie out of this. If you've got something you want to say to me, I'll listen. But this isn't the way."

"Shut up! You don't get to tell me what to do. I'm in charge now, okay? So shut up and listen."

"Marie!" I scream. "Please, Marie. Tell me where he is."

"Ah, that sounds like your daughter. I met you the other day, didn't I, dear? Does she know yet, Sally? Does she know what you are? You did a good job keeping it from her all these years, didn't you? You always were the clever one."

"What do you want, Marie?"

"What do I want? I want justice, that's what I want. Justice for Robbie. And justice for my poor dead mother, and me and my dad. But let's not chat about it over the phone, eh? I'm sure you want to see your little grandson, don't you?"

Oh God, if anything's happened to Alfie . . .

"Remember where it happened, Sally? Remember that house in Dearborn? Of course you do."

"Where are you, Marie? Where have you taken him?"

She laughs. A horrible, mirthless cackle. "Believe me, if I could have taken him all the way back there, I would have. There'd be a nice kind of symmetry to that, wouldn't there? Only I don't think that old house is still standing. Don't think any of them are. I doubt we'd recognize the place now, to be honest. Probably just as well, all things considered.

"No. Your little Alfie's much nearer to home. It's much bigger than the house where you killed Robbie. Must have been quite something in its day."

"Where is he, Marie? What have you done with him?"

"Done with him? I haven't done anything with him yet. The little lamb. But I will. If you don't do what I say."

"Where is he?" I scream. "Where is he?"

"Ask your mother what happened, dear. Ask her where she stabbed my little brother. I bet, between the two of you, you can work out where I've taken him, but let me tell you this: I don't want the police involved. You bring any cops with you, or anyone else for that matter, and things could get nasty for your little boy. And I mean really nasty. See, I don't care what happens to me anymore. I don't care if they cart me off to prison and throw away the key. So don't get any ideas, will you? If I see any police sniffing around, I might have an *accident* with a kitchen knife. You know all about those, don't you, Sally?"

The phone goes dead.

"No!" Mom screams, her fingers stabbing the handset.

The phone is still on speaker and the words "the caller withheld their number" reverberate around the room.

Panic swells in my chest, surges up to my throat, almost drowning my words.

"Oh my God! I think I know the place she's talking about. That derelict house on the waterfront! It's just a few hundred yards from where Karen lives. She must have taken him there."

With trembling fingers I call Michael's number, but it just keeps ringing. Why isn't he answering? Of course, he's probably driving by now, with the radio on. He always puts it on full blast when he's on his own in the car.

"I can't get through to him. Let's just go. Where are your car keys?"

Mom stuffs her feet into her sneakers. "The garage door's acting up again. We'll be quicker if we run."

I race to the front door. Yank it open. Sol starts barking, but Mom shuts him in the kitchen.

"Come on!" I yell at her, and now we're outside, running down the driveway and out onto the street. Mom sprints ahead of me. I do my best to follow as fast as I can, but by the time we reach the end of the road, I'm breathless. Somehow, I find the strength to keep going. Chasing my mother down wet sidewalks, I'm powered by something more than fear. Adrenaline courses through me like fire, spurring me on. My son's life depends on us getting there. Nothing else matters. Nothing.

The rain's coming faster now. Sheets of it slicing into us sideways. My chest heaves with pain but we're almost there. I can hear the dull roar of the sea, can see the wall of darkness ahead where the cliff ends. Mom's already turning the corner. She knows the house, too. Must have passed it a thousand times, walking Sol.

My feet pound the sidewalks. My heart thuds in my chest, my neck. Blood booms in my ears. I have to be right. She has to be there. Where else could she have taken him?

At last I've caught up with Mom. She's outside the abandoned house, staring at its boarded-up windows, transfixed with terror. I push past her. The tiles on the path are jagged and broken, the ones still intact glassy with rain. My feet slip and slide. Mom's behind me now, her ragged breath in my ear.

Whoever's responsible for this place still hasn't secured it since it was broken into a while back. My hand closes around the doorknob, and the door moves.

Karen must be in on this, too. I've been played by her all along. She was only being friendly to gain my confidence. Why oh why didn't I ask Kay to pick Alfie up? Who cares if she's been lying about her daughter? There must be a reason for that. Kay's a kind, sweet lady.

We stumble through the doorway, Mom pressed up so close behind me it's like we're one person. We're inside a dark, cold hallway. It smells of damp and mold. It smells of decay. From somewhere inside the house comes the sound of rain falling on wood. But there's something else, too. Mom stiffens beside me. Cigarette smoke. It's unmistakable.

Shapes resolve in the darkness. Shadows loom. The

ghost of a family house stretches out in three directions: the corridor and stairs ahead, a room on each side. Both doors are open but there's no light coming from either of them. No sound, either, except for a faint rustling and scratching. It seems to be coming from the walls. I shudder. It must be mice. Or . . . a shiver of revulsion makes my shoulders tense and rise. Or rats.

Just the thought of them makes me cringe, but I have to keep going. If Marie and Karen have Alfie somewhere in this house, rats are the least of my problems.

I hold myself rigid, stomach muscles so tight they ache. Mom steps out from behind me and turns into the doorway of the room on the right. The floorboards creak under her step.

"Marie!" she calls out. Her voice startles me. Something scurries across the floor and I freeze.

"Marie!" she calls again. Louder this time. The name echoes in the shadows.

She pulls her phone out of her pocket and switches the flashlight on. I do the same on mine and follow her in. The room is empty apart from two old-fashioned chairs, the fabric torn and stained. Squashed beer cans and discarded roach ends litter the bare floorboards, and the charred remains of a fire fill the grate. The air is colder in here than outside. Thick and still.

The beam of white light snags on a tiny plastic figure and my heart stops. It's R2-D2. And though I know tons of kids have figures just like it and that any child in the past could have dropped this here, I know beyond a whisper of a doubt that this is his. This is Alfie's. It would have been just like him to smuggle it to school in his pocket.

My hand closes around it till the plastic digs into my palm. I stretch my hand out toward Mom and slowly uncurl my fingers. She gasps.

"Alfie!" My scream ricochets around the room. What has she done with him? Where is he?

Mom pulls me out of the room and into the one across the passageway. As she enters, the dusty threads of a cobweb snag on my chin and trail across my nose and mouth. I splutter and scrape them away, goosebumps surging down the backs of my arms.

This room must once have looked beautiful. An oval-shaped table with six hard-backed chairs takes center stage, and on the floor lies an ancient, dusty rug. Heavy velvet curtains still hang at the boarded-up windows, their ends pooling on the floor.

Apart from more trash there's nothing else here, so we ease our way along the hall toward the back of the house and the kitchen, my heart thumping painfully. My flashlight sweeps the torn linoleum floor and dated cabinets, the bare wooden counters ringed with ancient stains. We see it at the same time, both of us cringing in horror—a Perrydale Elementary School sweatshirt pinned to one of the counters by a knife, the blade warped and rusty. My knees buckle. Mom grips my arm so tight I feel her fingers pressing on the bone.

"No!" Her voice is barely audible.

I reach for the knife, hands trembling, and wrench it free of the fabric. It falls from my hand as I lift the sweatshirt up and check the back of the neckline, knowing what it's going to say before I see it. ALFIE CRITCHLEY in red cursive letters, my own clumsy stitching around the edges of the tag. I bury my nose in the fabric, inhaling his scent.

"Up here," comes a voice from somewhere above us. A now familiar, gravelly voice.

We freeze and look up to the ceiling. Mom darts toward the stairs, but I run after her and pull her back. Insist on going up first. I strain my ears for sounds of Alfie, but if he's here, he's staying silent. Dread twists in the pit of my stomach. An empty, griping pain. What if he *can't* make a noise? What if she's keeping him silent by . . . ?

I force the dreadful images from my mind and concentrate only on climbing the stairs. Rain spatters down on us from above. I crane my neck back and a drop of water lands straight in my left eye, making me flinch. There must be a hole in the roof somewhere. The treads creak and I motion to Mom to step on the outer edges in case the joists are rotten. Some of the spindles that support the handrail are missing, and the carpet is dangerously loose. It's soaked and it reeks.

With each step we climb, the smell of cigarette smoke gets stronger. The wallpaper—an old-fashioned print of sprigged flowers—is peeling away in damp scrolls. Chunks of plaster are coming loose, too. The darkness presses at our backs the higher we climb. Behind me, Mom's breaths come fast and shallow.

At the top, a strip of dull yellow light shows under one of the doors.

The door isn't fully closed. The wood must have swollen in the damp air, and the strike plate's out of alignment with the latch. Steeling myself for what I might find on the other side, I rest the flat of my hand on the door and push gently.

50

THE ROOM IS BARE EXCEPT FOR A NARROW BED AND A closet. The light is coming from a large candle in a saucer on the floor. Alfie's coat is hooked over the handle of the closet door. I'm across the room in a flash, tugging it off, clutching it to my chest along with his sweatshirt, hugging it tight as if, by some miracle, he's still inside it. Mom pulls at the closet door, but it's jammed shut.

"Alfie? Alfie, are you in there?"

At last the door judders open, and in that split second dread floors me. I sink to my knees, still clutching Alfie's sweatshirt and coat against my neck, and find myself staring at two empty hangers and some scrunched-up newspaper. He's not inside. Wherever else he is, he hasn't been shut up in this closet.

"Marie?" Mom's voice rings out in the stillness of the house. "Where are you?"

Nobody replies. Hurriedly, we check the other rooms. With boards covering the panes of glass, they're as black as windowless cellars. Without the flashlights on our phones, we'd be stumbling around half blind. We search each and every cupboard and closet, desperately checking even the smallest of spaces.

I can't bear to think that Alfie might be here somewhere, locked up in the dark, scared out of his wits. But except for an old suit hanging up in one of the closets and some ancient sling-back sandals, there's nothing here. The beds are still made and there are pictures on the walls. Ghost bedrooms—their previous inhabitants long since departed.

In the bathroom, I snatch the filthy shower curtain back and stare into the lime-scaled bath. The rank stench of damp and mold fills my nostrils.

"Up here." The disembodied voice seems to come from above the bathroom ceiling.

Ahead of us, at the end of the corridor, is a spiral staircase leading up to the top floor. A faint glow filters down from above. Rainwater trickles down the steps and drips through a hole in the floorboards.

Mom's already edging her way up, one hand on the wall, the other on the handrail, planting her feet carefully on either side of the sagging treads. The boards are rotten. This whole place is a deathtrap.

My knees tremble as I follow her up, aping her movements, the muscles in my chest clenched. If Marie has hurt Alfie in any way . . . God help me, I'll kill her. I'll tear her limb from limb. Panic rears up inside me. Panic and rage.

There's only one door in this tiniest of square landings at the very top of the house, and Marie is behind it. Mom reaches for the handle. I've never been so terrified in my entire life. This moment. This time. This place. It's all there is. It's all there ever will be.

The door swings open on a small attic room. Candles flicker from various vantage points, the light creeping on the walls. A slow, ghostly dance. An odor of mildew and dust mingled with cigarette smoke and damp cardboard assails my nostrils.

Marie is facing us. She's sitting on a wooden chair positioned in front of an old-fashioned dormer window, the glass gray with encrusted grime. A framed photograph of Robbie Harris is wedged on her lap so that his smiling, cherubic face is looking straight at us. At her feet is a small pile of cigarette butts.

My eyes scan each shadowy corner, but the images I've been holding at bay in my head aren't the ones that meet my gaze now. Alfie isn't here. I don't know whether to be relieved or horrified. Because if he isn't here, where the hell is he? What has she done with my son?

"Come on in, Sally," Marie says, her smile a deathly grimace, gesturing to an empty chair tucked under the steeply pitched eaves.

She's wearing a pale sweat suit that must once have fit snugly but now hangs off her in folds. Her skin is gray and waxy. In different circumstances, I'd find the sight of her pitiful. Now she inspires nothing but hatred and dread. And pure, unadulterated rage.

"Where is he?" I cry. "What have you done with him?"

"All in good time, my dear. All in good time. Your mom and I need to have a little chat first, don't we, Sally?"

I lunge toward her, grab her by her thin shoulders. I could wrestle her to the ground if I wanted to. I could kill her right now with my bare hands.

"Where's my son? What have you done with him? Is he here somewhere? In this house?"

Marie looks me right in the eye, daring me to let go of

her. "I know what you're thinking, Jo. I'm no match for you physically, not the state I'm in. But what good would that do, eh? I won't tell you where Alfie is until I've gotten what I want." She jabs a finger toward Mom. "From her. Anything happens to me, you might *never* find out where he is." A strange little smile twists her lips. "You'd better just hope I don't croak in the next few minutes."

A cry of anguish erupts from my lungs. We should have called the police. Whatever Marie said, we should have called them right away. Mom's not the only one I'll never forgive. I'll never forgive myself for being so stupid, for doing exactly what Marie said instead of phoning the police like any normal person would have. I've been an idiot. A stupid, fucking idiot. Running here at Marie's bidding. Straight into her trap.

"You'll never get away with this," Mom says. "You'll go to prison. For Christ's sake, Marie, where is he? What have you done with him?"

I wait with bated breath for her reply. All I want to do is hold my son in my arms. All this other stuff with Mom . . . the shock of the last few hours, it's nothing compared with the thought of losing Alfie. *Nothing.*

Marie inclines her head toward my phone. "Turn that off. Throw it on the floor where I can see it."

I stare at her.

"Do it," Mom whispers.

"You too, Sally. You too."

Mom lays her phone on the floor. Marie kicks it out of reach and points to the chair again.

"Go on, Sally, take a pew."

Mom does as she's told. I stand in the doorway, my feet rooted to the threshold.

"Whatever you want to say to my mother, it's got nothing to do with Alfie. He's an innocent little boy. *My* little boy. Not hers. Just tell me where he is, Marie. I need to see him. I need to know he's okay. You can't do this."

"My brother was an innocent little boy, too. Still got murdered, though, didn't he?"

Mom leaps to her feet. "But I didn't . . ."

"Shut up and sit down!" Marie snarls. "You want to see your grandson again, you shut the fuck up and listen! I mean it, Sally. You're not in charge here. I am. The sooner you accept that, the better it will be for everyone. Especially Alfie."

My stomach churns with dread and nausea as I turn my phone off and set it on the floor.

Mom lowers herself stiffly into the chair. "What do you want from me?" she asks Marie.

"A full confession, that's what I want. A full confession on video for the world to see." Marie glares at her. "This has destroyed our family for long enough. It ruined my mother's life. It's ruined mine, too. And my father's. It's consumed us.

"But first things first, eh, Sally? Tell your daughter what happened that day. Tell her why the jury got it wrong. Tell her why you should have gone down for murder, not manslaughter." She fiddles with her phone, holds it up in front of her.

"Speak nice and clearly now, won't you? And don't leave anything out."

A small germ of hope flutters somewhere deep inside me. "Does Karen know you're doing this? Has she got Alfie somewhere?"

Marie laughs. "Karen doesn't have a clue. Oh, she knows about her uncle Robbie, of course. She's always known that.

But as far as she's concerned, I've given up on all that now. All that anger, all that hate." She strokes what's left of her hair. "The cancer, you know? Puts things in perspective."

Her eyes seem to flash in the candlelight. "Except it doesn't. When I saw her at the playground that time, I recognized her right away. I'll never forget your face, Sally. Not in a million years." She shakes her head. "You've forgotten mine, though, haven't you? Guess that's what cancer and a lifetime of smoking does to you."

"So where's Karen now?" My voice comes out thin and strangled. "I don't understand. Where's Alfie?"

"She's on her way to the hospital with Hayley. The silly girl banged her head on the sink. Karen left Alfie with me because you were on your way to pick him up, she said. Forgot her phone, too, in the panic."

She sighs and shakes her head. "Too bad my mother couldn't have found her earlier, when you were just a kid. Too bad my mother went to her grave knowing she was still out there somewhere, living the life she's never deserved to live. I'm doing it for her. For my poor dead mother. Your mother took little Robbie away from us and ruined our lives. And unless she tells the truth for once in her diabolical life, I'm going to ruin hers, and yours." She narrows her eyes. "And Alfie's. What did you think of that photo, by the way? Karen did it as a joke—she didn't notice my little addition. Bet you did, though."

My blood freezes.

"Now do as you're told, Joanna. Sit down and listen to your mother's confession. Then maybe, just maybe, you'll see your boy again."

Mom looks ready to pounce. She grips the sides of her

chair and leans forward. "You'll never get away with this, Marie," she hisses. "You're insane if you think you will."

Marie laughs. "I don't care. By the time this comes to court I'll probably be dead. I've got stage four metastatic breast cancer, in case you hadn't noticed. Now come on, Sally. Camera's rolling. We're all ears, aren't we, Jo?"

51

MOM HOLDS MY GAZE AS SHE SPEAKS. HER FACE IS BLEAK. Her voice bleaker.

"We were playing," she says. "A whole bunch of us." Her eyes slide toward Marie. "Marie was there, too. And Robbie. I was the one in charge. I was always the one in charge. Mainly because I thought up the games."

My chest feels like it's going to explode with fear. I have to make myself breathe in and out, will my lungs to expand and contract. It's no longer something that just happens automatically. All I can think of is Alfie, frightened and alone. Where has she taken him? Is he here in this house, shut up in one of the rooms? Did we miss somewhere? What if there's a cellar and he's all alone down there in the dark? Why didn't we *think* of that?

But all I can do is listen while my mother speaks.

"Scary games, they were. There was always something threatening us, something we had to escape from. A fiend of some sort, swooping at us through the rubble in the streets. An escaped convict, with chains on his feet. A gunslinging cowboy intent on revenge. And only I knew how to outwit him."

She rocks as she speaks.

"All the others did what I said. I think they were a little bit scared of me. I'd had a good role model, you see. I knew how scary people acted. I knew the sorts of things they said. The way they looked at you and turned your insides to liquid. I was acting out the only thing I knew. What happened at home. What I'd seen. What I'd heard.

"We didn't want Robbie joining us. He was too small and he couldn't run fast enough, but Marie had to look after him so we didn't have a choice. He kept whining and spoiling our game. Then I found an old knife in one of the houses we used to play in. I picked it up and started waving it around. All the other kids ran away, screaming. They knew it was just a game and they loved it, pretending to be scared. They knew I wouldn't really hurt them.

"But little Robbie didn't run away. He wanted a turn at being the bad guy. He wanted the knife and he tried to grab it out of my hands. I snatched it away and it sliced right into his fingers."

She closes her eyes. "It was just an accident. I didn't mean to do it. But then he started screaming and crying and saying he was going to tell his mom and dad and they'd send me to jail, and I just wanted him to shut up before all the others came back and saw what had happened. I just wanted to scare him a bit, to tell him to shut up because it was an accident.

"I pinned him against the wall, my hand on his collarbone."

My hand flies instinctively to my neck.

"I'd seen my dad do this a million times to Mom and it always shut her up." She takes a ragged breath. "I had the knife in my other hand, but I'd never have hurt him with it on purpose." She looks straight at me, beseeching me with her eyes. "Never. But it's hard holding a little kid still, and Robbie suddenly lunged forward. I didn't know a little boy could be that strong, but he was so angry it was like he suddenly had the strength of a much older kid. The knife went right into him. Then Marie was standing next to me, screaming her head off, and then they all were."

Marie shakes her head in disgust and stops filming.

Mom bows her head and starts to cry. "If I hadn't been holding that knife, if I hadn't been so determined to be the bad guy at all costs, it would never have happened. If I'd just let him be the villain for a little while, let him have his fun . . . He was only a little boy."

"Nice story, but it's not true, is it?" Marie jeers, her voice scornful. Anger has ground her features into sharp blades. She stabs a finger at Mom's face. "Tell the truth, you murdering bitch!"

Mom ignores her and looks directly at me. Marie might as well not be in the room, for all the attention Mom's giving her. Everything she's just said has been to me.

"So why didn't they believe you," I ask, "when you told them what happened?"

"Because Marie told the police I'd been horrible to Robbie all day, as if it was just me. But we'd *all* been picking on him. She said I'd done it on purpose, that she'd come into the room and seen me lunge at him with the knife. I don't know, maybe it was her guilt that made her say that. She was supposed to be looking after him and she hadn't. She'd run off laughing and squealing with all the others. She'd left him on his own. Maybe she wanted someone to blame so she wouldn't be in trouble."

"Your mother's always been a liar," Marie says, a low, growling menace in her voice. "A liar and a bully and a manipulator. Oh, she can turn the charm on when she wants to. Do the old 'poor little abused child' act. But it's all crap. So what you're going to do now, Sally, is tell her the truth. Tell her what really happened. I'd hate for something bad to happen to Alfie, I really would. He's such a lovely little boy."

My chest heaves with sobs. I can barely speak for crying. "Where is he? What have you done with him?"

"You'll find out where he is when your mother finally tells the truth."

Mom stares at the floor and doesn't speak. She's holding her breath. I hold mine, too. At last, she releases it. She raises her head and looks at the phone in Marie's hand. Tears flow unchecked down her face, and, even though a part of me hates her for keeping this secret for so many years, for lying to me day in, day out, for being the one who's put us in this position in the first place simply by being who she is, I feel her pain almost as if it's my own and I'm crying, too.

"There isn't a day goes by that I don't think of Robbie. He haunts me. Every year that passes I try to picture what he'd look like now, what he might be doing if he was still alive. The life he might have led. Sometimes I see a little boy that looks like him and I can't breathe." Her voice falters. "I can't breathe . . ."

"*Remorse* isn't a big enough word to describe what I feel. It doesn't come close." Her breath judders as she speaks. "Sometimes I think about how things might have turned out differently. If I hadn't gone out to play that day. If I hadn't thought up the monster game. If that house had been flattened like all the others in the row. If it hadn't somehow missed the wrecking ball. If I hadn't been nosy enough to open that drawer and find the knife, bold enough to pick it up. A whole list of ifs. All the significant moments in our life hinge on choices made in the blink of an eye. Choices that define us forever."

She hangs her head over her knees. When she finally straightens, she looks right into Marie's eyes for perhaps the first time.

"I know you want some kind of closure, Marie, and I'm sorry how your life turned out. I really am. I think of your mother every day, too. The grief that destroyed her, that stole away your childhood. You have to believe me."

Her hands are still, in her lap. Her spine is straight. "I know you think I've had a life I didn't deserve to have. A beautiful daughter. A grandson. I know you think I should have been punished for what happened, but I swear to you, Marie, it was an *accident*. I should never have pinned him against the wall. He was a little boy and I was being a bully and that was wrong. Whatever happened to me at home, it was wrong of me to do that. I knew it then just as I know it now.

"But if you think I haven't been punished, you're wrong." She taps her temple. "What goes on in here is my punishment. This is my life sentence and it never stops, Marie. It never stops. I was responsible for killing a little boy. Your beautiful brother. The uncle Karen never met. But I didn't mean to do it. I didn't. If you want me to say it's my fault Robbie died, then I'll say it. Because it's true. It's my fault your brother died. I was holding him by his neck against a wall and I had a knife in my hand. But I didn't stab him on purpose, Marie. I wouldn't. I didn't. You have to believe me."

A hard lump gathers at the back of my throat. My cheeks are wet with tears. This is my mother. The veil she's been wearing all her life has slipped—the one I didn't even know *was* a veil—and here she is, raw and exposed. An open wound. She looks at me, eyes imploring me to understand, to forgive, and I want to, but I'm wounded, too. I can't respond. My muscles won't work. My voice is gone.

"I always knew you'd never stop looking." She turns her head to one side, addresses the wall. "I hated you for that. For never giving up the fight. But part of me admired you, too. Admired your tenacity. I often think that, if our roles had been reversed, I might have done the same thing. I didn't have any brothers or sisters, so I don't know what it feels like to lose one. But I know what it's like to have a daughter and a grandchild."

She turns to me now, her eyes brimming with tears. "And I'd willingly give up my freedom—give up my life—to save theirs."

She inhales slowly through her nose and exhales through her mouth, her lips rounded so it looks like she's blowing the air out.

"So if you want me to confess to something I didn't do, so you can post your video on YouTube, or whatever it is you're planning, then I'll do it. I'll do it willingly. If that's what it takes for this to end now and for your family to move on, I'll do it."

"This isn't right, Marie," I say. "Whatever happens to my mother, it doesn't change anything. Robbie's dead. Nothing's going to bring him back."

Marie sits in her chair, her face ashen in the half-light. "I promised my mother I'd make it my business to get justice for Robbie, to make her pay for what she did."

Mom turns to face the camera. Part of me wants to stop her, to shake her by the shoulders and tell her not to be so stupid. This lie she's about to tell will be her undoing. Her face will be all over the internet in a matter of minutes and there'll be nowhere for her to hide. She's throwing her life away. But she's doing it for me. And for Alfie. Telling lies to protect us. It's what she's always done, and I know I can't stop her. Because the only thing that matters right now is Alfie, and getting him back. I know it and she knows it and this is the only way.

Her voice, when it comes, is devoid of emotion. Flat. Empty. It reminds me of something I saw on the news as a child, a group of traumatized hostages telling their loved ones they were being well looked after when anyone could see they were in fear for their lives.

"I, Sally Catherine McGowan, hereby confess to the intentional murder of Robbie Harris. It wasn't an accident. I lied in court. I *am* the monster you all think I am."

She closes her eyes. "Now please, for the love of God, tell us where Alfie is."

52

A NOISE FROM DOWNSTAIRS—A LOUD BANG—MAKES US ALL flinch. It's the front door being flung against the wall.

"Mom? Are you in here?"

Karen's voice echoes through the house and my knees give way. I grab on to the wall for support. Thank God! Karen will talk her mother around. She'll make her tell us what she's done with Alfie. She has to.

Marie drags her chair nearer the window and tries to scrabble up onto the windowsill. But as she does, she drops the phone. It skitters across the floor. Mom and I both make a grab for it at the same time, but Mom gets there first.

"You wouldn't dare!" Marie screams, knocking the chair over in her haste to get the phone back. "You wouldn't dare."

"Don't delete it, Mom! Not until she tells us where he is."

Mom holds the phone high so Marie can't snatch it back. The three of us just stand there glaring at one another. A tableau of figures, frozen in shocked anticipation.

Then Marie rights the chair, clambers back onto it, and somehow manages to maneuver herself onto the sill. For one terrible moment I think she's going to reel backward into the filthy glass and fall to her death before she's told me where Alfie is.

"No!" I scream. "Don't do it!"

Feet pound up the first staircase below. "Mom! Mommy! What are you doing?"

"We're up here!" I shout. "I think she's going to jump!"

The stairs up to the attic room groan under the weight of feet. Is someone else with her?

When I see not just Karen appear in the doorway but Michael, too, their faces etched with dread, it takes everything I have not to break down and weep.

"She's got Alfie. She won't tell us where he is!" The words spill out of me. An alien twang that reverberates in the frigid air of the room.

Michael edges in, his eyes trained on Marie.

"It's okay," he says. "Alfie's safe."

Mom's eyes meet mine. Did we hear right? Did he say Alfie's safe?

Tears are streaming down Karen's face. Her eyes dart from Marie to Mom and then to me. "He's with Kay," she says. "I took him to Kay's before I drove to the hospital."

Instinctively, I fall into Mom's arms and we cling to each other, sobbing in relief. Alfie is safe. He was never in danger. Marie tricked us. Then I hear Mom gasp, feel the change in her body. I turn to see Marie forcing the window open. The steady grumble of the ocean enters the room and, with it, a blast of icy, wet air.

Michael rushes toward her.

"Stay back or I'll jump," she says, her hands gripping the rotten window frame.

"No!" Karen shrieks. "Mom, please!"

"Marie, don't do this." Michael's voice is soft and calm. "Come down from there and let's talk."

"Talk? What's there to talk about? I've ruined my last chance of getting justice for Robbie. There's nothing left for me. I'm dying anyway."

"But your daughter!" cries Mom. "Your granddaughter. They *need* you, Marie. Don't do this to them." Mom's face is stained with tears, her voice tight with emotion.

Karen is sobbing now. "Oh, Mom! I thought you'd finally come to terms with what happened, that you wanted to spend what time you've got left with me and Hayley. We were going to do nice things together, remember? Lay down some memories for her. *Good* memories. Why spoil all that for the sake of this . . . this *obsession* with McGowan. Vengeance solves nothing. It won't bring Robbie back."

Marie's face twists in disgust. "You've never understood. Always going on about coming to terms with the past. You haven't a clue—"

"Marie, please!" Mom cries. She clasps her hands together and sways in silent pain. "It was an accident. A terrible, tragic accident. What do I have to do to make you believe me?"

Marie shuffles on the sill. Her eyes are wild. The wind catches her wispy hair. Michael moves closer.

"No!" Karen screams. "Don't you see what she'll do? She's going to tip herself backward if you go anywhere near her."

"Come on, Marie," Michael says. "You don't have to do this. Is this the last thing you want your daughter to see you doing?"

Marie turns to Karen. "She confessed. I recorded it." She glares at Mom. "You might have gotten away with it again, but I heard you confess. And so did your daughter. You murdered my little brother."

"A forced confession," Mom says. "It would never stand up in court. You *know* it wouldn't."

Tears roll slowly down Marie's cheeks. "That wouldn't have mattered. Your life would have been over once it was on the internet and people knew your face."

Suddenly her features change. Oh God! She's really going to do it.

"Don't do this, Marie," I plead. "I know you've suffered, but this isn't the way."

But Marie isn't listening. She's staring at Mom, her knuckles white as they grip the windowsill. Her eyes narrow. Her teeth bite down on her lower lip. I sense the tension in her upper body, watch her rock slowly backward and forward, an almost imperceptible movement, her right foot flexing in midair. And in that split second I know what she's going to do. She's not going to tip herself backward. She's going to use every last ounce of her strength to launch herself forward. She's going to jump off the windowsill and hurl herself at my mother, shove her into the void of the staircase.

I think of the broken floorboards at the foot of the stairs, see them splinter and collapse under the weight of my mother, her body plummeting like a stone through the rotting plaster of the ceiling below and landing on the concrete floor of the kitchen.

No one could survive a fall like that.

I try to warn her, to scream at her to get away from the doorway, but it's as if I've been paralyzed, my tongue welded to the roof of my mouth. Can't any of them see what's going to happen?

As Marie pushes herself clear of the windowsill, I know

what I have to do. Whatever lies Mom told, whatever secrets she withheld, my life with her was real, wasn't it? The things we did together, the things she taught me. The love that's enveloped me all my life like a blanket, keeping me warm and safe. Wherever she came from, whatever happened in her past, she's still my mother and she doesn't deserve to die like this because of one terrible mistake she made as a child.

Marie is a ball of compressed rage, just like her little brother must have been when he charged at Mom all those years ago, incensed at being held against the wall, overcome by a surge of adrenaline and white-hot fury at the injustice of it. Unless I can cross the room and push Mom out of the way, it'll be too late.

Marie's feet touch the floor and time, which has stretched like elastic, snaps back into place and I'm throwing myself across the room at a right angle to her moving body, hitting Mom side-on and pushing her clear of the doorway. She staggers under my weight and the two of us stumble headlong into the eaves and crash onto the floor in a tangled heap of arms and legs. Something clicks at the front of my shoulder and a splinter of pain shoots up my arm and across my chest. Then I hear another crack, but this time it's the sound of wood splitting.

The pain in my shoulder intensifies. My fingers land on something sharp and wet. My collarbone has not only fractured, it's protruding through the flesh. My chest heaves and pain skewers me to the floor. My vision narrows to a pinprick, then fades to black.

The last thing I hear is a piercing scream and a sickening thud.

53

Michael's voice is soft in my ear. He's holding my hand. "The doc says you'll be good as new in a couple of months, although it might take a little longer to regain full strength in your shoulder. They had to pin it."

I open my eyes and blink in the bright light.

"Where is he? Where's Alfie?"

"Alfie's fine. Kay's just taken him to buy a comic book in the gift shop. They'll be back any minute." He strokes my cheek. "He slept in her spare room last night. I stopped in to see him while you were in surgery and he was fast asleep, clutching a soft giraffe called—wait for it—Long-Neckie Boy."

Relief floods my veins like a drug. It's better than any painkiller they could have given me.

"And Marie?"

He shakes his head. "Once you pushed your mother out of the way, there was nothing to break her forward momentum." He winces at the memory. "She went headlong down that staircase and straight through the floorboards. They were completely rotten—they couldn't take her weight as she landed." He pauses. "You saved your mother's life, Joey."

I close my eyes, but all I can see behind them is Marie's body sprawled on the floor like a broken doll, her limbs sticking out at weird angles, dark crimson blood seeping out of her ears and into her wispy hair. In saving Mom's life, I made Karen's mother lose hers.

"Your mother and I had a hell of a job, what with making sure you were all right and trying to stop Karen charging downstairs to get to Marie. That place is a deathtrap—she could have fallen through, too. She only stopped trying when the paramedics arrived and told her there was nothing any-one could do to help Marie. She must have died on impact." He sighs. "I suppose that's some consolation for poor Karen.

"As soon as I got to the hospital and realized Alfie wasn't there, I started to panic. Then Karen said it was okay because she'd left him with Kay. She thought that would be better than leaving him with her sick mother, so when I told her I'd been to her apartment and couldn't get any answer she started to worry that something bad had happened to Marie. Karen had left her phone behind in the rush to take Hayley to the ER, so she tried calling her mother on mine but there was no reply. Then I tried you, and when I couldn't get ahold of you on your cell I tried your mother's landline and couldn't get an answer there, either.

"Something twigged in my brain then and I knew some-thing was wrong. I asked Karen what her mother's name was, and when she told me it was Marie my blood ran cold. I asked her a few questions and my worst suspicions were confirmed. I knew she was Robbie's sister."

He runs his hands through his hair. "I didn't want to endanger you both by telling Karen who you were, but when

I said I thought you and your mother might be in danger, she guessed. She guessed right away, Joey. It was Karen who first told her mother about the rumor. It's why Marie asked to come and stay with her in the first place, to see if it was true."

I close my eyes and let that sink in. So it was me telling them about it at book club that started this whole thing.

Michael takes hold of my hand again and massages my palm with his thumb. "Karen thought her mother was done with all that fighting-for-justice stuff and that she'd finally turned a corner. She thought Marie just wanted to come and stay with her because she had cancer and needed looking after. But of course Marie would go with her sometimes to pick Hayley up from school. That's when she must have recognized your mother."

"But how did you and Karen know where to find us?"

"We were wracking our brains trying to work that out. Then Karen mentioned how her mother always seemed drawn to that derelict house on the beachfront. Every time they walked past she told Karen it stirred up bad memories. It all just clicked into place. How it was a derelict house where Robbie got killed. We drove there as fast as we could."

"Where was Hayley in all this?"

"Karen's husband came to the hospital to take over. Karen had already phoned him before she left and asked him to meet them there when he finished at work. Karen didn't tell him much, just said her mother was ill and she needed to get back."

"She'll have told him now, though, won't she? It'll be all over Flinstead in a few days." My eyes are wet with tears. "Seems like Marie got her way after all. We'll all have to move now. Mom won't be safe. None of us will."

Michael bites on his lower lip and looks down.

"The thing is," he says, meeting my eyes at last, "your mom's already gone."

"What? What do you mean, gone?"

"Liz and some old guy named Brian have taken her somewhere safe while they decide what to do."

"Brian. Yeah, she told me about him. He's the ex-cop who's been helping her all these years. But where have they taken her?"

He shakes his head sadly. "I don't know, Joey. I honestly don't know."

"Will I be able to see her?"

He looks down again. "Brian said they'll try to find a way, but I don't know how long it will take."

Before I have a chance to fully register the implications of what Michael has just told me, I hear a familiar little voice chattering away in the corridor.

"If she's not awake yet, Long-Neckie Boy's going to tickle her ear with his nose until she is."

"Poor Mommy might not want to be tickled." It's Kay. Lovely, kind Kay, who's been looking after him all this time.

And here he is. My beautiful little boy. My darling Alfie. If only I could sit up and take him in my arms.

He runs toward the bed, but Michael catches him just in time, before he clambers on top of me. He holds him up so he can give me a kiss without hurting me. Not that that would matter. A kiss from Alfie is worth all the pain in the world.

"Why are you crying, Mommy? Does it hurt?"

"I'm crying because I'm so happy to see you, darling, but yes, it does hurt a bit."

"Long-Neckie Boy wants to kiss you better, too," he says,

and he lifts the soft giraffe and touches its head gently on my bandages.

"Where did this come from?" I ask him.

Kay clears her throat. "It was supposed to be a present for my grandson, but . . . but Gillian sent it back. It's a long story, Jo. We had a terrible argument once. I said things about Gillian's life I shouldn't have. I've begged her to forgive me but, so far . . ." She shakes her head sadly. "I shouldn't have lied about the Skyping, but I was ashamed to tell you the truth. I didn't want you to think I was some horrible woman who'd alienated her own daughter."

"Oh, Kay, I would *never* have thought that."

"I know. It was just my silly pride."

She squeezes my hand and leans in to kiss me on the cheek. "But what about you! Promise me you won't take up jogging ever again. I couldn't believe it when Michael told me what happened. The sidewalks around here are treacherous even when it's *not* raining. If you want to keep fit, you should try the Zumba class I go to. Much safer, and a whole lot more fun than jogging."

Michael winks at me from over her shoulder.

I smile. "You're on. But give me a while to get better first, okay?"

54

Two weeks later

IT'S A TYPICAL FAMILY SCENE ON A COLD NOVEMBER SATUR-
day. Alfie playing with his Legos on the living room floor,
lost in an imaginative world of his own. Michael on one end
of the sofa and me on the other, my arm in a sling and supported by cushions. We're watching back-to-back episodes of
NCIS.

The warmth of the radiators is making me sleepy.

Michael hooks his ankle around mine absentmindedly
and I allow myself to close my eyes and drift off briefly. I
haven't been sleeping well for the last two weeks—hardly
surprising in the circumstances—so lazy afternoons like
this allow me to catch up.

We said goodbye to her yesterday. Michael, Alfie, and
me. It was all very clandestine. We drove to a garage on the
outskirts of Cambridge where we met Brian (probably not
his real name—he looked more like a James or an Anthony
to me), and then we were driven to a state park where Mom
was waiting for us at a picnic bench. My heart lurched when
I saw her, sitting there all alone. She looked old all of a sud-

den. Old and sad and defeated. But then, when she turned to face us, all I could see was a frightened little girl. The one who used to cower in her room waiting for her dad to come upstairs and torment her.

Alfie sobbed when she told him she was moving away but, actually, I think he's taken it pretty well. She knew exactly what to say to him. She told him that someone had been very mean to her so she was moving somewhere else to make new friends. He understood that, just as she knew he would. He could relate to it because that's sort of what happened to him, too. She also told him that, one day, when she was settled in her new house, he could come and see her.

We all could, she said, switching her gaze from Alfie to me and lowering her voice. If we wanted to. Tears well up as I think of her face. The sadness in her eyes.

I know that, in time, Alfie will adjust to not having his grandma around the corner. Having Michael move in full-time has helped, of course. Michael *and* Sol, who's snoring near the radiator at the moment.

Whether I will adjust is another matter.

"I still don't see why they had to move her," I say when Alfie runs upstairs to fetch his action figures. "There's no video and Marie is dead. Surely she could have stayed in Flinstead. She loved it here."

Michael sighs. We've been over this so many times he must be fed up with it by now, but somehow he still has the patience to go through it all again.

"It's too big a risk. We don't know who else Marie might have told. Just because she didn't tell Karen doesn't mean she didn't mention it to someone else. And Karen knows *now*, doesn't she? I know she's sworn never to go public, but how do we know she won't change her mind at some point in the future? And can you honestly believe she won't tell her own husband? I know she's promised she won't, but he's her *husband*. Why *wouldn't* she confide in him?"

He gives me a sidelong glance. "Maybe she already has."

I know what he's thinking—that if word gets out, maybe we'll have to move, too. Either that or ride out the storm. Put up with people whispering behind our backs, reporters at our home. What a story that would be: Devastated daughter discovers her mother is notorious child killer Sally McGowan.

I pick up the letter Karen has sent me, the one that arrived a few days after I came home from the hospital, the one I've been reading and rereading ever since. This time I just stare at the envelope.

"Karen's spent her whole life in the shadow of her uncle's murder. She's seen firsthand what it did to her grandmother and her mother, and she wants it to end. She doesn't want Hayley to grow up knowing what her grandmother did, using an innocent child as a pawn to get revenge. She says if she'd known Marie had recognized Mom, she might have been able to talk her out of it, but Marie knew Karen's feelings on the matter so she kept it to herself. You've read this letter. You *know* all this. She's not like her mother. She understands that Mom was as much a victim in all this as poor Robbie was."

"The trouble is, some people will *never* be persuaded of that," Michael says. "It doesn't matter to them that Robbie ran into the blade. That it was an accident. In their eyes, your mother was a bully with a knife in her hands and that makes her guilty."

"Is that what you think, too?"

He shakes his head. "No. She was a bully because that's all she'd ever known. She might have hated what her dad did to her and her mother but, somewhere deep down, she must have loved him, too. Because he was her dad and he won't have been vicious every single minute of every day. He'd have been nice to her, too, sometimes. And to her mother. That's how abusers get away with it for so long."

He shuffles nearer and kisses me. I don't know what I would have done without Michael looking after me and Alfie these last couple of weeks. There are so many emotions swirling around in my head. Most of the time, I just sit on the sofa and stare at the TV. The worst part is how I keep reliving it, over and over again. Not just the shock of finding out about Mom and who she is—who she *was*—but the horror of what came next, how terrified I was that Alfie was in danger.

We spoke on the phone yesterday, Karen and I.

"Your secret's safe with me, Jo," she promised. "This has gone on long enough. It needs to end now. With us. My mother and grandmother destroyed their lives seeking revenge. I'm not going to let the same thing happen to me and Hayley."

I told her how sorry I was for what happened to her mother, how I felt responsible, but Karen told me I shouldn't. She said it was better than the kind of death Marie might have had. Being in pain for months on end as the cancer destroyed her.

The awful thing is, I feel like I've lost my mother, too, for although we'll be able to write and speak on the phone, Skype or FaceTime each other maybe, it won't be the same. And as for seeing her again, Liz has hinted that there's a strong possibility she'll have to go abroad this time. It's not going to be easy.

The phone rings and Michael leaps up and takes it in the other room. He's so fiercely protective of me at the moment I feel like I'm in a bubble, sealed off from the real world and its intrusions. It won't last forever. Sooner or later I'm going to have to pick up the pieces and get back to some semblance of normality. We all are. Our new normal.

Five minutes later, he's back. "That was Dave. He and Carol send their love and hope the pain is easing off. He said to take as long as you need."

He sits back down on the sofa. "He also said to tell you that Susan Marchant has changed her mind about selling her house. Apparently, her neighbor's husband is an accountant, and when they found out she was donating the proceeds to charity he had a chat with her and, basically, she's found out she can just donate the house without having to go through the rigmarole of selling it, save herself the agency fees, and gain a large tax credit to boot. Dave sounded truly pissed off."

Oops. So Maddie must have picked up on what I said about Susan not wanting the money and talked to her about it. Oh well, the poor woman deserves all the luck she can get, after what she went through as a child. And if Maddie's right and Anne Wilson really *did* post those pictures on Sonia Martins's shop window, there's a kind of justice there, too.

I snuggle up to Michael. Well, as much as I *can* snuggle with this damn sling on. "Michael, there's one thing I haven't asked you yet."

"I know, and it's about time."

"What are you talking about?"

"Oh, sorry." He grins. "I assumed you were going to pro-
pose."

"No, you idiot! I was going to say, I don't suppose you'll
be writing that book now."

He laughs. "Probably not, all things considered." He
kisses me on the lips. "Some stories are best left untold,
don't you think?"

A different ocean this time. A warmer ocean. The waves are larger here, large enough to ride on a surfboard. I watch them sometimes, the surfing crowd, waiting to catch the waves at just the right point, riding on top of the breaking curl, knees bent, arms outstretched for balance.

Such grace and beauty.

Such courage and strength.

Sometimes I walk to one of the quieter bays to sit and read, to swim when I need to cool down. The sand is white and soft and hot on the soles of my feet. My size-six feet with their long, slender toes and their neatly filed nails—which, just recently, I've taken to painting in pastel colors. Pinks and mauves and baby blues.

There is safety in numbers here. The transient crowd of tourists. The surfing dudes and dudettes. The ever-changing bar workers and waitstaff. Nobody takes much notice of the pale-skinned older woman with pretty toes, the one with the large floppy sun hat and shades, her nose in a book.

I like to choose my spot with care. Not too near the water's edge but far enough away from the cafés that line the beach so that I'm not bothered by the noise or the smell of barbecued meat. I like to sit near young families if I can, ones with little boys who look a bit like Alfie. Near enough to watch them dig holes in the sand. Near enough to catch their beach balls if the breeze blows them my way and to toss them back in return for one of their shy little-boy smiles.

She says they'll come and visit soon, she and Alfie, and though I crave the sight and sound and touch of them, sometimes I wonder whether it might be too much. Too much for all of us. I wonder whether it might be better to leave things as they are and just communicate by email. Nice and anonymous. Nice and safe. Because if I see them again, if I hold them, I'll never want to let them go, and I must. I must. There's no way they'll move here and I can't go back. I can never go back. Not now.

I'm the hunted. I'll always be the hunted. This is the price I pay for my past. That one fateful, fatal second I'd undo in a heartbeat if I could.

I close my eyes against the sun and I'm back there all over again. That cold, dark kitchen. The spores of mold on the wall. The filthy rag rug on the floor. Just me and Robbie Harris. All the others had gone. All the others had run away like they were supposed to, run away screaming. They were waiting for me to come after them. Expecting me to.

But Robbie kept on whining. "Let me be the bad guy. Let me have the knife." And then he grabbed at it and cut his fingers and started screaming. I just wanted him to stop. I just wanted him to shut up and stand still for a minute so I could see how deep the cut was. I knew what to do when someone was bleeding. I knew you had to wrap the wound up tight. I was going to take my sweater off and use that. But he wouldn't shut up. He wouldn't stand still.

The rage engulfed me like a fire. A fire blazing in my brain. So I let him have it. The knife. I let him have it.

ACKNOWLEDGMENTS

THERE ARE MANY PEOPLE WHO HAVE HELPED ME ON MY journey to publication and I want to thank them all.

My husband, Rashid Kara, for understanding my need to write and always believing in me and supporting me; my writing group (Deborah Klée, Paula Guyver, Anita Belli, Gerald Hornsby, Catherine Rendall, and Janine Swann) for their razor-sharp critiquing skills and supportive friendship; my Faber Academy tutors, Maggie Gee and Richard Skinner, and my fellow students (especially Peter Howard, Susan de Villiers, Hannah Cox, Richard O'Halloran, Brandon Cheevers, and Hanife Melbourne) for their encouragement and feedback on "*the novels that came before*"; my agent, Amanda Preston at LBA Books, for her wisdom, energy, and creative insight; my British editors, Sarah Adams and Natasha Barsby, and the rest of the hugely talented Transworld team for their enthusiasm and championing of *The Rumor;* and last, but by no means least, the wonderful Kate Miciak and her team at Ballantine Books, New York, for helping me "translate" *The Rumor* for an American readership.

PHOTO: CHRISTIAN DAVIES PHOTOGRAPHY

ABOUT THE AUTHOR

Lesley Kara is an alumna of the Faber Academy Writing a Novel course. She completed an English degree and PGCE at Greenwich University in London, and has worked as a lecturer and manager in further education. She has now relocated to the small town of Frinton-on-Sea on the North Essex coast. *The Rumor* is her first novel.

lesleykara.com
Twitter: @LesleyKara